THE HOT LINE

CATHRYN FOX

HEAT

Heat
Published by New American Library, a division of
Penguin Group (USA) Inc., 375 Hudson Street,
New York, New York 10014, USA
Penguin Group (Canada), 90 Eglinton Avenue East, Suite 700, Toronto,
Ontario M4P 2Y3, Canada (a division of Pearson Penguin Canada Inc.)
Penguin Books Ltd., 80 Strand, London WC2R 0RL, England
Penguin Ireland, 25 St. Stephen's Green, Dublin 2,
Ireland (a division of Penguin Books Ltd.)
Penguin Group (Australia), 250 Camberwell Road, Camberwell, Victoria 3124,
Australia (a division of Pearson Australia Group Pty. Ltd.)
Penguin Books India Pvt. Ltd., 11 Community Centre, Panchsheel Park,
New Delhi - 110 017, India
Penguin Group (NZ), 67 Apollo Drive, Rosedale, North Shore 0632,
New Zealand (a division of Pearson New Zealand Ltd.)
Penguin Books (South Africa) (Pty.) Ltd., 24 Sturdee Avenue,
Rosebank, Johannesburg 2196, South Africa

Penguin Books Ltd., Registered Offices:
80 Strand, London WC2R 0RL, England

First published by Heat, an imprint of New American Library,
a division of Penguin Group (USA) Inc.

First Printing, March 2008
10 9 8 7 6 5 4 3 2 1

HEAT is a trademark of Penguin Group (USA) Inc.

LIBRARY OF CONGRESS CATALOGING-IN-PUBLICATION DATA:
Fox, Cathryn.
    The hot line/Cathryn Fox.
      p. cm.
    ISBN: 978-0-451-22305-0
    I. Title.
    PR9199.4.F69H67 2008
    813'.6—dc22   2007032553

Set in Centaur MT
Designed by Ginger Legato

Printed in the United States of America

This book is dedicated to all the heroic firefighters
who bravely serve and protect.

And to my husband,
who continues to light my fire.

ACKNOWLEDGMENTS

Thank you to my wonderful editor, Kerry Donovan, for her fabulous editorial and for making writing these stories so much fun.

Thank you to Paula, for her continued support; to Shelly, for the brotherhood; to Mary Lou, for her honesty and friendship; and to Heather (her husband is a volunteer firefighter), who answered all my endless questions, but still refuses to tell me how she knows some fire trucks are flat on top!

Thank you to the Allure Authors for your friendship and support. This journey wouldn't be half as fun without all of you.

And, as always, to my agent, Bob Diforio, who is always in my corner.

THE HOT LINE

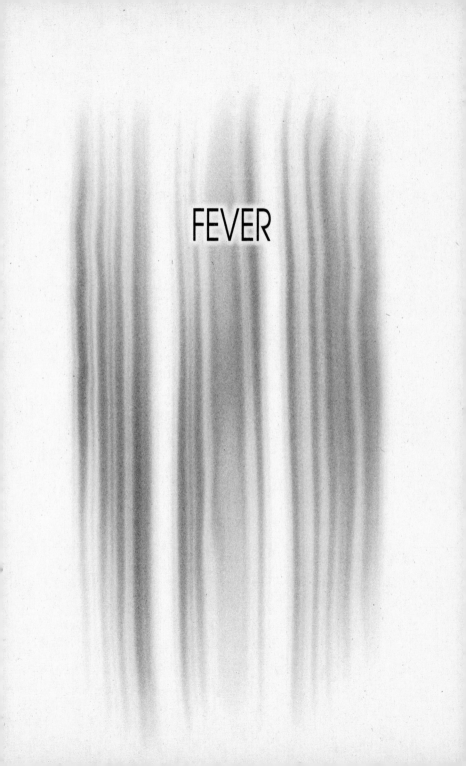

FEVER

ONE

trawberry daiquiri in hand, Sara Jack blew a wispy auburn curl off her forehead and glanced around the Hose, her reporter's eye stopping to examine the men crowded around the pool table. She studied them for a long moment, as though the sight of their scrumptious backsides was actually newsworthy. Of course, back in Trenton, Iowa, aka, Butthole Nowhere, such a sight really *was* newsworthy. But here in Chicago, tight firefighter buns were a dime a dozen, she supposed. And damned if she didn't want to grab herself the *baker's* special, to go. Thirteen fresh, warm honey buns.

Mmmmm . . . yummy.

She sipped her fruity drink and considered the name of the establishment again. The Hose, she mused. What a perfectly delicious name to describe the local watering hole where the firefighters from Station 419 gathered nightly for a game of eight ball.

As Sara blocked out the din of the crowd, and completely ignored the bridal party members lounging around the table beside her, her lascivious gaze panned the hotties in the room a second time. Her investigative eyes zeroed in on one very sexy, very "well-equipped" Mitch Adams as he turned in her direction. The man had been warming her blood and getting under her skin during their rehearsals without even trying.

As she devoured his broad shoulders, his firm stomach, and his even firmer thighs, a slow heat gravitated south and burned her body from the inside out. She licked her suddenly parched lips, her mind wandering, conjuring up all the wicked ways Mitch, with his lethally honed physique and panty-soaking smile, could help extinguish those slow-burning embers.

The Hose, she mused again, her glance settling a few inches below Mitch's leather belt. What a great name for the firefighters' bar—a name, she suspected, or at least hoped, had nothing to do with their profession.

Beer in one hand, pool cue in the other, Mitch lazily crossed his legs at the ankles and leaned against the pool table. Dark hair cut short gave him a charming boy-next-door look, but Sara suspected he was anything but.

Unlike the "nice boys" she'd dated back home, pleasant, spineless boys who bored her to death—inside the bedroom and out—Mitch had a raw sexuality about him that screamed of sex, sin and . . . *danger*. Sara shivered. Almost violently. Surprised at just how much his carnal edginess aroused her.

Her gaze brushed over him again, taking pleasure in his square jaw, perfect white teeth, long athletic body, and bad-boy attitude. Sexual awareness prowled through her, warming her blood. Her glance traveled onward and upward until she met with a set of bedroom blues that shimmered with dark desire when they locked on hers. Mitch shot her a look that held all kinds of suggestions, all kinds of wicked possibilities.

Sara drew a sharp breath, her pulse pounding in her throat. She wiped her hands on her snug jeans, letting the denim drink in her moisture.

As he watched her watching him, his nostrils flared and his body tensed, tension lines bracketing his sensuous mouth. In that brief moment when their gazes collided, they shared a heated exchange, one that could undoubtedly set the crowded establishment ablaze.

It occurred to Sara that she wasn't the only woman in the bar taken by his edgy sexuality. She twisted sideways, noting the way the other women in the room watched him, their body language indicating they'd like a tour of his station, with up close and personal instructions on how he handled his hose.

Just then, Cassie Williams, the beautiful bride-to-be, the same woman who was responsible for Sara's unexpected trip to Chicago, stepped up to the table. Sara welcomed the distraction and shifted in the chair to face her.

Sara had been best friends with Cassie since kindergarten, which was why she, along with her other best friends, Jenna Powers and Megan Wagner, had dropped everything and hopped on the first plane to Chicago. Nothing short of a category-five catastrophe would keep them all from attending Cassie's nuptial exchange with sexy firefighter Nick Cameron.

With Sara's body still feeling the effects of Mitch's lusty gaze, she focused fully on Cassie.

"Pretty cute, isn't he?" Cassie asked with a knowing look on her face as she gestured toward Mitch with a nod.

"What? Who?" Sara asked, feigning innocence.

Ignoring her question, Cassie sat down and shimmied closer. She tapped Sara's nose. "Watch out for him, Sara. He's not like the nice boys you know from back home." Cassie remained quiet for a moment, while Sara mulled over that warning. A moment later, Cassie pitched her voice lower and added, "Mitch Adams is . . . dangerous."

"Dangerous?" Sara asked, her pulse racing a little faster, her internal temperature rising a little higher.

"Yeah, dangerous. A guy like that can capture your heart without even trying. And since I know you're a girl who wants commitment and doesn't want her heart broken, I suggest if you start anything with him, you go into it with your eyes wide-open."

Eyes wide-open . . . legs wide-open. Oh, the possibilities.

"I've known Mitch long enough to know he's a no-strings playboy, a woman's fantasy. It's the way he likes it."

Playboy. Fantasy. No strings. Sara wasn't seeing a downside here.

Cassie angled her head. "When you meet the right guy, you'll know it."

Sara shrugged one shoulder. "Maybe I'm not looking for the right guy." Honestly, she'd love to find Mr. Right and settle down. Not that she expected to find her "knight in shining armor" in a bad ass like Mitch. What she expected to find with him was a bad boy who was also so very, very good.

"He's a great guy to have fun with, but don't expect more," Cassie said. "I just don't want to see you hurt."

Sara worked to tamp down her desire and keep her voice even. Trying for casual she toyed with her straw and said, "How could he possibly hurt me? I'm here on a two-week vacation." She dragged her finger around the perimeter of her glass and continued. "From work and from reality." It suddenly occurred to her that a break from reality, along with a red-hot fling with a "dangerous," drop-dead-gorgeous firefighter, was just the thing she needed. What was that old vacation motto? What happened in Vegas stayed in Vegas. Surely that could apply to Chicago, too. Why couldn't she have a wild, no-strings-attached affair and live out a few firefighter fantasies of her own? At least then she'd have something to warm her thoughts when she returned home to Iowa, to her mundane fluff job as reporter for Trenton's small-time gazette.

The thoughts of going back to that office only to write another cow-tipping story made her shiver. Her dream job was to write sexy features for *Entice*, a young, hip, Chicago-based magazine for today's strong, sexually empowered women. The trick was to come up with a great, hot-topic story, one that would impress the *Entice* editors. Unfortunately, hot-topic stories were few and far between in her small town.

Cassie's voice brought Sara's attention back around. "To him, women are just sperm banks."

Sara twisted her lips. "Sperm bank, huh?" It really had been far too long since she'd taken a deposit.

Sara looked over Cassie's shoulder and spotted Mitch watching their exchange with interest, giving her the impression he knew exactly what they were talking about. He scraped his hands over his chin, dragging her gaze to his fingertips.

Her heart beat in a mad rush as she thought about how those fingers would feel tracing the pattern of her body, and touching her most private areas. She pictured his mouth ravishing hers, his hands on her breasts, his thick cock ramming her pussy, fucking her like she'd never been fucked before.

Just then their eyes connected, and in that instant, Sara knew she'd like nothing better than to take a few deposits from the bad-ass firefighter.

Someone from across the room called out to Mitch. He twisted sideways and followed the sound, vanishing from her line of sight.

Sara pulled in a fortifying breath and focused all her attention back on the girls, playing catch-up on their conversation, which, from the sounds of things, was just beginning to heat up.

Never one to be subtle, Megan got right to the point. "So tell me, Cassie. Is Nick any good in bed?"

Cassie kept a telltale grin from her face, but the fire in her eyes spoke volumes. "You know I don't kiss and tell."

"I'm not asking about his kissing abilities. I'm asking about his fu—"

"Jesus, Megan," Jenna piped in, "what kind of question is that?"

Megan shrugged. "I'm just asking, is all."

"What you really should be asking is, does he know his way around a vagina? Because the last guy I dated couldn't find my G-spot without a compass and detailed directions from MapQuest."

A round of laughter erupted from the table and gained the attention of those around the four friends.

Still chuckling, Sara planted her elbow on the table and dropped her voice. "You think you've had it bad," she whispered, resting her chin on her palms. "My last date thought a G-spot was the crisp five-dollar bill he handed the waitress every morning in exchange for his coffee and paper."

"Okay, since we're having a whose-boyfriend-thinks-a-vulva-is-something-they-drive-to-work-every-morning contest, I want in," Megan added, laying her palms flat on the table, a wry grin curling her lips. "My ex-husband thought fellatio was something you ordered off the dessert menu at Applebee's." She smacked one hand to her forehead. "And to think I married him! What the fuck was I thinking?" A round of groans followed Megan's confession.

"Okay, you win," Sara piped in, going back to her drink. Maybe alcohol would lessen the painful truth that *all* the men back home were as boring in the bedroom as they were out of it.

Cassie leaned forward. She slipped something under her hand and slid it to the middle of the table. "Actually, there is a way you can all win. Except this time winning means *no* MapQuest, *no* detailed directions, and *no* Applebee's."

Before Cassie continued, her gaze darted around the room. Her voice dropped an octave as though all four women gathered around the table were masterminding some secret plan to take over the world. "This is just good, old-fashioned fun where those involved know what a G-spot is and how to work it."

The other women all huddled forward, mimicking Cassie's actions.

Megan lowered her voice to match Cassie's. "What are you talking about?"

Cassie lifted her hand from the table to reveal a small white business card. A hush fell over the group as all sets of eyes focused on the rectangular piece of cardboard.

After a long moment, Jenna broke the silence. "The Hot Line?" She crinkled her nose, her glance going from the card to Cassie, then back to the card again. "What the hell is the Hot Line?"

With a fairly good idea of what Cassie was suggesting, Sara scooped the card up for a better look. It simply read, *The Hot Line*, with a phone number, *555-HEAT*.

Sara shot Cassie a look, her mind racing with indecent ideas. She furrowed her brow, the reporter in her needing clarification, the woman in her blazing to life. "Yeah, what the hell is the Hot Line, Cassie?" she asked, examining the card.

"It's a way for you all to have a little fun, with men who know their way around a woman's body."

"Oh yeah?" Megan rushed out, eyes bright with excitement. "Enlighten me, chicky."

Cassie tapped the card, which Sara continued to clutch like her life depended on it. Okay, so maybe her *life* didn't depend on it, but her libido sure as hell did.

Cassie got right to the point. "If you call the Hot Line and mention that you need assistance, it will bring a sexy firefighter—a sexy, 'fully equipped' firefighter, that is—to your door, ready and willing to tamp down your fires."

"Damn girl, give me that card!" Megan flashed a wide smile. Mischief danced in her eyes as she whipped the card out of Sara's hands.

Pussy clenching in anticipation, Sara snatched the card back, the investigative side of her demanding proof. "Is this for real?"

Cassie's hand closed over hers and squeezed. "Absolutely. How do you think I met Nick?" There was honesty in her eyes when she spoke, and nothing in her voice to suggest otherwise. "It's also a very well-kept secret." She grew quiet for a moment and then said, "I trust you know what to do with it."

Suddenly Sara's entire body went on high alert. She knew Mitch was standing behind her, felt him long before she saw him. His heat reached out to her, his scent closing around her like a warm blanket. She inhaled, pulling his spicy aroma into her lungs, noting the way her body stirred to life whenever he was near. Lust burned through her, and her mind sifted through all the ways Mitch could help stoke that fire.

Mitch leaned over her shoulder and grabbed a handful of nuts. Sara drew a shaky breath, cream pooling between her legs. She closed her hand over the card, and angled her body to face him. The sight of him up close and personal had her libido reacting with urgent demands, clamoring for his undivided attention. His bad-boy smile did delicious things to her insides. Her body flushed, immediately. The man made her feel so edgy, so out of control, so fucking hot.

In a hushed tone, he spoke to her, and her alone. "I have to take off. I'll be at the firehouse." His voice was low, deeply intimate. His sexy tenor curled around her, her nipples tightening in response. As sexual tension whipped between them, basic elemental need took hold. Her mouth salivated, and her pussy ached to slide down his pole and ride him with wild abandonment.

A round of "G'nights" followed a path around the table as he prepared to leave.

Before Mitch stepped away, he cast Sara a suggestive look and touched her shoulder, his knuckles brushing her cheek in a gentle caress that stimulated all her nerve endings. Something compelled her to touch him in return. When her fingers closed over his, it brought passion to his blue eyes. His dark, seductive gaze told her that not only could he fuck her, and fuck her good, but he could also make all her fantasies come true. His glance went to her other hand, the one covering the card.

Did he know what she had hidden under there?

He paused for a moment, as though weighing his words carefully. Then, with his expression tender and hot, he whispered to her in the deepest, sexiest tone, *"Later,"* and disappeared into the crowd.

Holy. Shit. That one word, combined with everything in his voice and everything in his manner, spoke volumes and had her aching to discover the truth behind the Hot Line.

Did these firefighters risk their lives daily to put out dangerous fires, save little kittens from trees, and rescue libidinous women? She took a moment to entertain the idea. If she dialed the number, would a very sexy, very "well-equipped" Mitch Adams show up at her door and help tamp down the flames of desire engulfing her?

She swallowed. Hard.

Her mind raced, the reporter in her perking up. With casual aplomb, she scooped up the card and slipped it into her pocket, realizing that if the Hot Line really did exist, she'd just been presented with the perfect opportunity to write a hot-topic story. And if she gave it her own sexy spin, it could be just the article she needed to launch her career at *Entice.*

She looked up in time to see Mitch slip out the door. The scrumptious sight of his tight backside made her shiver with longing. She drew a centering breath and worked to push back the rising lust.

As her fingers toyed with the edge of the card, her mind filled with wild and wicked ideas. Naturally, like any good reporter, she'd have to do a little investigative research of her own before she wrote the article. And in the process, she planned on exploring a few firefighter fantasies along the way.

"I'm out." With a disgruntled huff, Mitch tossed his cards onto the table and pressed his palms to his eyes. Jesus, he'd never felt so antsy or so on edge before. Here it was, hours since he'd last set eyes on Sara Jack, yet he still couldn't shake his goddamn arousal.

His mind wandered, envisioning what it would be like to lose himself in those gorgeous mocha eyes of hers. To run his fingers through her silken auburn curls and caress her curvy body until she gave herself over to him, completely, his to do with as he pleased.

There was a wholesomeness about her, a fresh girl-next-door look that really got under his skin and warmed his blood faster than a quick shot of Scotch. It surprised him, really. With her good-girl features and curvaceous body, Sara was the antithesis of the hip, polished urban women he normally dated.

But, with just one smoldering look, Sara could set a fire to his libido—a fire that if left unattended, would likely rage out of control and reach dangerous proportions.

Naturally he had no intention of leaving said fire unattended. As a firefighter, it was his duty to tamp down every blaze, even if it meant taking matters into his own hands. Nostrils flaring, he clenched and unclenched his fingers at the mere thought of doing so.

Although he'd been duly warned to stay away from Sara, she'd been invading his dreams as well as his every waking thought for the last few days. Christ, he'd never met a sexier woman. And the way she looked at him with dark, passionate desire smoldering in her eyes had his cock swelling to the point of pain.

"What's the matter? Can't take the heat?" Dean Beckman taunted, laying his cards out to reveal three jacks. "Or is Shelly at it again?" He nodded toward the private phone kept near their sleeping quarters.

"She called here earlier," Brady Wade piped in before he, too, tossed his cards down. He then bent to pat Jag, his chocolate Labrador retriever. Since Brady had a love of Labs, Station 419 was the only one around without the requisite dalmatian.

Mitch cursed under his breath and rocked his chair back on two legs. Shelly, his ex-girlfriend of over a year now, never failed to call on the heels of a bad breakup. The woman went through men faster than their trucks went through water.

"She sounded upset, like she'd been crying. I guess she's looking for a strong shoulder to latch on to," Dean said.

"That's one way to put it," Mitch replied. They all knew it wasn't his shoulder she was looking to latch on to, and he certainly had no intention of being her bedmate between guys.

A while back, he'd thought that he loved her and that she actually cared about him. But he quickly learned that like every other woman he'd been with, she merely wanted the fantasy. It was his dangerous, heroic job that attracted women, not the man beneath the uniform—a man who worked long hours and was away from home frequently. Since his last breakup, he'd finally learned to shut down emotionally, giving himself physically while keeping a cool, hardened exterior.

At the sudden thought of giving himself physically, his mind raced to Sara. She wanted the fantasy with him, he could tell. One night of hot lust while on vacation. He'd seen it in her eyes, read it in her every gesture.

Although Mitch was more than willing and capable of fulfilling Sara's wild firefighter fantasy, he'd been duly warned by Nick Cameron to keep his distance. Since Mitch had a reputation as a one-night kind of guy, Nick had cautioned him that Sara was a small-town girl who didn't delve into brief affairs. According to Nick's fiancée, Cassie, Sara didn't take sex lightly; therefore Nick asked Mitch to keep his distance because the last thing he wanted was to see one of Cassie's best friends hurt while in Chicago for the wedding.

Not only was Nick Mitch's coworker—he was also his friend. A friend who'd saved his ass a time or two in the line of duty. Mitch held Nick in high regard and owed it to him to abide by his wishes.

Which meant that tonight, and every night hereafter, until Sara returned to Iowa and he managed to work her out of his system, he'd be taking matters into his own hands.

Literally.

Still he could lie in bed and fantasize about her, couldn't he? Imagining what it would be like to taste her mouth and her breasts or to open her soft pink lips with his tongue and taste her sweet femininity. To have her climb over him, impale herself on his hard cock, and ride him feverishly until her juices poured down his shaft.

Mitch gritted his teeth and shifted uncomfortably in his chair, deciding it was well past time to call it a night and answer the ache in his groin.

The shrill of their special phone pulled him from his musings and helped marshal his thoughts. "I got it." Welcoming the distraction, he jumped to his feet and pushed away from the card table. Without haste, he made his way across the room.

Fuck. Maybe tonight he'd take the call. Although it had been a long time since he'd participated in the Hot Line, perhaps a soft bed and an even softer woman would help take the edge off and get his mind off Sara.

When he glanced at the caller ID, his heart raced, his blood pressure soared. Jesus H. Christ. Everything in him reacted to the name displayed in the small glass window. Tension rose in him as his cock urged him to answer the phone, along with the sexual demands of his body.

What the fuck was he supposed to do now?

Despite his rock-hard cock screaming at him to pick up that phone and give Sara exactly what she wanted, he took a measured step back, but not far enough that he still couldn't reach it. If he wanted to. But he didn't want to. Okay, he wanted to, but he wasn't *going* to.

He was not going to pick it up.

No way.

No how.

Walk away, Mitch. Just walk away.

Before he could stop himself, his fingers closed over the receiver and squeezed until his knuckles turned white.

Just then Dean poked his head around the corner. Grinning like the crazy, intuitive son of a bitch he was, he asked, "You want me to get that?"

"I got it," Mitch growled and ripped the phone from the cradle. He pressed it to his ear and said gruffly, "Hello."

Sara's soft, sexy voice sounded on the other end. "Mitch?"

"Yeah?"

Forgoing pleasantries and getting right to the point, she said, "My kitty stopped purring. I think it needs to be resuscitated."

Sweet Mother of God! Mitch slapped his hand to his forehead and drew a steadying breath, working overtime to tamp down his roaring libido. He failed.

Lust ripped through him like a raging forest fire, making him tremble with pent-up need. He growled low in his throat, unable to tame the primal animal rising up inside him, crumbling his resolve to keep his distance. Despite knowing better, he had every intention of breathing life back into her kitty, over and over again, using every means possible, if he had to.

If she expected anything less, she'd called the wrong guy on the wrong night.

TWO

Heart racing in a mad cadence, Sara snapped her cell phone closed and dropped it onto the kitchen table. She swallowed, loving how Mitch reacted to her naughty, suggestive words.

She wasn't normally so sexually aggressive, but the second she'd heard Mitch's voice on the other end of the line, the inner vixen in her had stirred to life, demanding she play out her fantasies to the fullest.

As her gaze darted to the front door, a quick flash of nervousness stole through her, because she'd never indulged in a wild affair before. Nor had she ever slipped between the sheets with a rugged, untamed guy like Mitch.

It was utterly scandalous.

And so damn exciting!

The vanilla sex she'd had in the past had left her wondering if she'd ever reach an earth-shattering orgasm. Something told her that not only would Mitch bring her to the moon and back—he'd rock her world and alter it forever.

Sara tiptoed through Cassie and Nick's cozy bungalow in the sub-urbs, taking care not to wake Nick, Cassie, or her friends, Jenna and Megan. She noted that Cassie's place wasn't all that different from the homes in Trenton. But here on the outskirts of Chicago, she was fortunate enough to have big-city living at her fingertips—a city where Sara could get lots of hot-topic ideas for *Entice* magazine, no doubt. And soon, if her article garnered the attention she hoped it would, she'd be packing her bags back home and permanently taking up residence near Cassie.

Sara pulled back the white lace curtain and stared up at the star-studded sky. A summer breeze rushed over her face and chilled her flesh, but did little to help cool the heat blazing inside her. She dropped the curtain, tightened the belt on her housecoat, and padded barefoot to the front door to peek out.

Until Mitch arrived, she wouldn't know for certain whether the Hot Line truly existed. She had to wait for him to show up to know if he'd come to rescue her kitty, or if he'd come to . . . "rescue her kitty."

Time slipped by much too slowly for her liking as she paced restlessly. She'd practically worn a hole in the carpet by the time headlights appeared in the quiet cul-de-sac. She noted that Mitch had parked on the street—to keep their indiscretion private, she assumed.

Stomach swaying more than a trapeze artist's, Sara made her way to the door, but before she opened it, she smoothed down her hair and then wiped her damp hands on her housecoat. Her entire body heated in excited anticipation as her fingers closed around the brass knob. She drew a quick breath to pull herself together.

Without giving him time to knock, she swung the door wide-open. The second she set eyes on him, her heart lurched and lust sang through her veins. His primal essence completely overwhelmed her. Light-headedness overcame her as she took in the erotic vision standing before her. Grin reckless, stance casual, Mitch leaned against the doorjamb, looking like a knight in shining armor or, rather, a knight in firefighter gear. When she met his smoldering baby blues, she knew all she needed to know.

Mitch Adams was there to . . . "rescue her kitty."

Hot damn!

As she stole a glance at his attire, her knees liquefied, and her breath hitched. She clenched her jaw to stop it from dropping. Dressed in his work wear, Mitch was the epitome of sex, sin, and seduction. A real live walking fantasy. Her pussy creamed, gearing up for the ride of her life.

She nearly faltered backward when his richly seductive gaze raked over her body. She gripped the knob tighter in an effort to balance herself.

His helmet was tucked under his arm, and his dark hair looked mussed, as though he'd been running his fingers through it. The air around them sizzled as she clenched and unclenched her fingers, itching to do the same.

He didn't speak. He just stood there, looking at her, his hungry gaze appraising her. The fire in his eyes licked over her skin and burned hotter than molten lava. His jaw tightened and his nostrils flared. With two measured steps, he invaded her personal space. He looked edgy, dangerous, carnal. And so damn sexy. Sara bit back a heated moan and rolled her tongue around her dry mouth.

As silence stretched between them, his eyes fixated on her robe, on her knotted belt to be precise. Setting his helmet down, he gripped her hips and backed her up, matching her step for step. With his mouth parted slightly, his tongue made a slow pass over his lips, as though preparing them for a kiss.

Head spinning, she became delirious with pleasure and began to tremble when his rich, spicy scent singed her senses. The feverish attraction between them was undisputable.

With single-minded determination, he nailed her to the wall and pressed his body to hers, his arms going on either side of her head, pinning her in place. He gave her a look that conveyed his hunger, his need for her.

Warm wetness dripped down her thighs when she felt his huge cock through his suit. Arousal flamed inside her stomach. Heat spread like wildfire through her body.

Eyes burning, he stared at her for another endless moment. She could feel the passion, the desire, and the untamed lust rising in him.

Her skin grew tight, her libido restless. She parted her mouth in invitation. When his kisses didn't come, she started to speak, to protest, but his lips crashed down on hers, silencing her objection. The soft blade of his tongue pushed inside her mouth in a mad frenzy, claiming her, branding her with his heat. Raw desire seared her insides. Her hands went to his coat, attempting to rip it from his shoulders so she could touch his gorgeous, athletic body all over.

Mitch gave a lusty groan. His breath washed over her face, causing her flesh to quiver in erotic delight. Without warning he was all over her, his hands pulling, pushing, taking, and giving. Desire slammed through her. Her heart raced like she'd just conquered Everest.

Large palms kneaded her aching breasts through her cotton housecoat, lifting them high as his thumbs circled her pebbled nipples with precision. His pelvis thrust forward, pressing his arousal harder against her pussy, letting her know in no uncertain terms he was more than capable of fulfilling her every fantasy. Her fingers moved onward and upward, to tangle in his thick midnight hair.

Mitch's mouth moved to her neck for a long, thorough taste of her skin. The sexual tension between them was so palpable, surely even the neighbors could feel the electricity crackling in the air.

He pressed his lips to her ear and spoke in whispered words. "Where is everyone?" She heard the raging lust in his voice and sensed the effort it took for him to leash his control.

Still shaken from that incredible, mind-numbing kiss, she could barely breathe, let alone speak. With effort, she found her voice, but the two simple words came out broken, fractured. "In . . . bed."

He slipped his big hands around her waist so that his large fingers splayed over the small of her back, one finger slipping lower to caress the crest of her buttocks. He put his mouth close to her ear. "Come with me."

Sara obliged without hesitation and followed him outside. She glanced around, curious yet excited, her mind racing a hundred miles an hour, wondering where he was taking her. Truth be told, as long as it was somewhere they could be alone, quickly, it didn't matter.

A few minutes later, after padding barefoot across the cool, damp grass, she found herself standing outside the pool house at the edge of the property. While Mitch lifted the mat in search of the key, her gaze went to the kidney-shaped pool. With her body burning from the inside out, the water looked damn refreshing, but she suspected jumping in wouldn't even begin to extinguish the fire inside her. She suspected there was only one way and only one man capable of putting out those flames.

When she stole a sideways glance at Mitch, her heart raced, and her lips tingled. Eyes locked in concentration, he stood to his full six feet, key in hand. She couldn't believe how much she wanted him. In fact, she couldn't recall ever wanting anyone as badly. It amazed her how much his rough edges and bad-boy attitude affected her.

Considering his rugged good looks and raw sexuality, she knew she wasn't alone in that attraction. No doubt other women had fought for his attention or had called the Hot Line in search of his services. She felt a weird pang of jealousy in her gut. Good Lord, she might be a small-town girl who didn't delve into wild affairs, but surely she could handle this. She wasn't going to go all mushy inside thinking tonight was about more than research and fantasies. Because it wasn't.

When he caught her watching him, she turned back to the pool, not wanting to appear too anxious, too needy.

Too emotional.

Honestly, she was shocked at how easily she could fall for him. But this was just about sex, she reminded herself. Sex and seduction and nothing more. Except maybe a little resuscitation, she hoped.

"Do you want to swim?" He stepped up behind her, his chest pressed to her back, his voice at her ear, his mouth barely making contact.

Not only did his nearness make her breathless, but his deep, sensual tone did the most weird and wonderful things to her insides. "I don't have a suit."

He breathed the words over her neck as his hot, silky lips lightly brushed her flesh. "You don't need one, babe." Slipping strong hands around her waist, he loosened the belt on her robe.

The way his rough voice played down her spine filled her with need. Her gaze darted around the quiet neighborhood. "You don't think?" she asked, shocked that she had actually managed to form a coherent sentence.

He murmured in her ear. "Look around, Sara. The world is asleep."

She felt him ease away. Her tortured body shivered, immediately missing his warmth. She turned on the ball of her foot to face him, to watch him. He slipped the key into the lock and opened the door. With a wave of his hand, he shifted his stance sideways and gestured for her to enter. Before she had a chance to slip past him, he blocked the path for a moment, hooked her elbow, and drew her to him. "We'll swim, Sara, but not just yet. There's something I need to do first."

Her skin came alive at his suggestive words. Please let that "something" have everything to do with putting the purr back into her kitty.

Anxious to see what he had in mind, she stepped farther into the small room and clicked on a corner lamp. The soft light bathed the room in a seductive glow and created an instant intimacy. She took a moment to survey her surroundings, taking note of the hose, pool toys, and small changing area, but what really caught her eye was the blow-up lounge chair, a cushiony flotation device specially designed for two.

The sound of the lock clicking in place gained her attention. Sara listened to his footsteps as Mitch advanced purposefully toward her. A second later she felt his hands on her waist. He spun her around to face him. When their bodies collided, passion consumed them both. Mitch pulled her closer, the bulge in his pants indicating his needs, his desires. She tipped her head and nearly burst into flames when she met with deep blue eyes that glimmered with dark sensuality.

Mitch cocked his head and ran the pad of his thumb over her lips. He pitched his voice low. "You mentioned something about needing resuscitation?"

Her cunt quivered as she mentally visualized him breathing life into her kitty and easing the tension inside her. Her knees buckled and she forced them to straighten. Unable to find her voice she gave a quick, tight nod.

He flashed her a bad-boy grin, and in a low, barely controlled voice, he said, "I believe a little mouth to mouth is in order." Mitch's hand slipped between their bodies and cupped her passion-drenched sex. Pleasure engulfed her and she nearly orgasmed right there, on the spot, all over his hand. She clamped her thighs together and leaned into him, her nipples crushed into his chest and tightening to the point of pain. She made a sexy noise and shifted.

He sank to his knees, and shot her a glance, all traces of humor gone from his eyes. "Or, rather, a little mouth to kitty."

THREE

The wild, wanton look in Sara's dark eyes took Mitch's breath away and made him ache with the need to fuck her. Her wholesome pink cheeks had taken on a ruddy hue when he reached around and cradled her lush ass in his hands. The lethal combination of sweet and sexy nearly shut down his brain and had his cock swishing out of control like a loose fire truck hose.

After he'd spent a long moment just holding her, lips pressed to her navel, breathing in her delectable scent, his hands came back around to the front, to her belt. He untied the knot and peeled open her white cotton housecoat.

Gorgeous.

Needing to touch her, he slid his hands over smooth silken skin. As he reveled in the texture, some inner voice reminded him that she was a small-town girl who didn't delve into brief affairs. But the fact that she made that call to the Hot Line and had asked for him told him how much she wanted this, how much she wanted *him*.

Suddenly, giving this sweet, sexy girl a fantasy night to remember became more important to him than his next breath.

He curled his fingers around the thin elastic band on her lacy white panties and tugged. Her gorgeous body trembled in response to his touch. Knowing he had that kind of effect on her brought a smile to his face and urged him on.

Slowly, he began to ease the silky scrap of material lower and lower, until he glimpsed a few soft, silky sprigs of auburn hair. She arched her back, moving her pussy closer to his mouth, demanding he answer the pull in her body. Of course he'd be more than happy to accommodate those demands. All in good time, of course.

Mitch glanced up at her, his gaze moving over her passion-imbued face. The sight of her dark eyes flashing with desire had his blood pressure skyrocketing and did the strangest things to his insides. He gulped air, fought back the raging lust, and worked overtime to level his voice. He needed to gain some measure of control over himself if he wanted to make this fantasy great.

For her.

Kneeling before her, he transferred his thoughts back to the apex between her legs and tugged her panties down lower. As he exposed her pussy, a burst of heat bombarded his whole body. Taking a moment of reprieve, he drew in air and swiped away the moisture pebbling his forehead.

Inclining his head once again, he lifted one of her ankles and slipped her panties off. Sara adjusted her footing and kicked the flimsy scrap of material away.

He slid his hands up her long, creamy thighs until his fingers were merely a hairbreadth away from her moist opening. "Open your legs, babe."

She did as he instructed, which pleased him immensely. His gaze surfed over her, taking a moment to pan the gorgeous specimen before him. Body quivering, Sara stood there in nothing but a housecoat, a bra, and a come-hither smile. Body language telltale, her dark, sensuous eyes dimmed with desire, begging him to take her. As his gaze skated over her, it occurred to him that even though she was half naked, she was still completely overdressed.

"Take off your housecoat, and spread your legs wider," he demanded, positioning his mouth directly in front of her gorgeous pussy.

When she widened her legs, the soft lamplight fell over her twin lips, catching the light. He swallowed at the way they glistened with damp arousal. He couldn't believe how much his body ached to join with hers, how much he wanted to slide into her cunt and lose himself in the heat between her legs.

The tangy, intoxicating scent of her heady aroma saturated the small room. He inhaled, deeply, letting it curl through his blood, letting it awaken all his senses. As her sweet scent seeped under his skin, he gave a low, primal growl, his groin aching with a primitive need to ravage her. Until sunup. The day after tomorrow.

"Mitch . . ." The lust in her voice fragmented his thoughts and made his whole body shake. The intensity of his hunger for her really threw him off guard.

Using his thumb and index finger, he pulled open her drenched pink lips for a better look. His knuckle purposely brushed her clit, hoping to make her as crazy as she was making him. Her nub swelled and poked out from its fleshy hood. Mitch closed his eyes against the flood of heat gravitating south and drew a rejuvenating breath.

He pitched his voice low and breathed the words over her pussy, knowing the heat from his mouth would stir her juices. When his hot breath bristled her damp hairs, her body responded in kind. He put his lips near her belly button, his mouth absorbing her tremor.

"Tell me, Sara. How long has it been since your kitty has purred?"

Her fingers raced through his hair, and it shocked him how her touch went right through him. Her head lolled to the side, her lids fluttered.

"What?" she asked, and he could tell it took effort for her to speak.

"I need to assess the situation and devise my treatment plan accordingly. If your kitty hasn't purred in a very long time, then I believe extreme measures might need to be taken. And I, of course, want to use the right tool for the right job."

He could tell his words excited her by her quick intake of air and disjointed response. "Oh, yes, yes, extreme measures, right tool."

This time Mitch blew a cool breath over her clit, and using slow, sinuous circles that seemed to drive her wild, he stroked her delicate flesh with the rough pad of his thumb.

"Oh God," Sara cried out. He felt her legs buckle. With a slight nudge, he urged her backward, and propped her against the wall for support.

Turning his attention back to the juncture of her legs, to her beautiful, perfect pussy, he made a *tsk*ing sound and shook his head.

"What is it?" Sara whimpered, her hands tangling in his hair, guiding his mouth to her sex, conveying without words what she needed.

"It's not looking good." His nose nudged her clit and she gasped, her hips jutting forward, her pink lips colliding with his mouth, seeking more. Her boldness thrilled him. His groin screamed, demanding attention, demanding he strip off his gear and fuck her, like she wanted. Like he wanted. But he was so goddamned revved up, he knew he wouldn't last five fucking minutes, and he wanted to last. He wanted to take his time. He wanted to play with her and give her the wild fantasy she craved. All night long.

"Please, Mitch," she begged, her voice as shaky as her body. Her fingers left his hair and moved to her pussy. She spread her wet lips wide, offering her sex up to him so nicely.

His body hummed with passion, need, and sexual frustration. "Jesus Christ," he cursed under his breath as she stood there, her plump pussy lips spread wide-open, his for the taking.

Lust rushed through his bloodstream and made him mad with the need to devour her. His flame-resistant coat did little to keep the fire at bay. He stood, inched back, and tore it off, never once taking his eyes off her glistening cunt and the way she'd offered it up like a dessert tray at a buffet.

He sank to his knees once again. The urgent need to delve into her sweetness and savor all her offerings took hold of him. Unable to control himself any longer, he leaned in for a deep, thorough taste. "Mmmmm . . ." he moaned, inhaling her aroused aroma. His tongue made a slow pass over her clit and then dipped inside to lap at her sweet feminine syrup. He stroked from front to back, slowly at first, and then harder with each pass. A low hiss came from Sara's lips. She moved restlessly beneath him.

"God, you taste exquisite," he whispered from between her thighs.

His passion reached new heights as he dusted kisses over her creamy pussy. Fuck, he'd never tasted anything finer.

He spent a long time between her legs, devouring her delectable softness. He nibbled, licked, and sucked greedily on her lush clit, until her moans of pleasure merged with his. He loved how her entire body quivered beneath his ministrations. His hands climbed higher to touch full breasts through her lace bra. She closed her fingers over his, kneading her hard nipples right along with him, fueling his lust and sparking his imagination. There was nothing like a woman who took her pleasure into her own hands.

After his mouth had had its fill, he inched back. The sound of her sexually frustrated groan reached his ears and pleased the hell out of him. He loved how she responded to him, he loved how crazy his tongue made her, and he especially loved this sexy, little resuscitation game they were playing.

In a low, hushed tone, he said, "Sara, after a closer examination, I realize extreme measures must be taken. Your kitty is in dire need. It's much worse than I'd originally thought."

Her lids sprang open. "It is?" she asked, feigning surprise.

"Yes, it is. I think you should see for yourself." He took one of her fingers and guided it to her gorgeous, kiss-swollen opening.

Her lashes fluttered and she moaned deep in her throat, seemingly understanding his intentions immediately. It surprised him how easily she slipped into her role, how easily she read his desires.

She shot him a smoldering look and eased one of her fingers inside. In a low, sultry tone, she said, "Ah, yes, I see, Mitch. No worries though. I believe I know just what to do."

Exhaling quickly, Mitch went back on his heels, watching in mute fascination as Sara pushed her finger all the way up inside her passion-soaked cleft. Her lids drifted shut as her other hand went to her clit, for a deep, therapeutic massage.

Mitch's body broke out in a sweat, but he didn't dare move, didn't dare breathe as he watched her masturbate for his pleasure.

She began moving her finger in and out, in and out, touching herself without inhibition, taking control of her own needs, the same way one would when alone in bed, the same way he had for the last week while visions of Sara danced in his head.

As she took great pleasure in riding her finger, his muscles bunched, and without thinking, he slipped his hand inside his pants to grip his cock. He was ready to explode just from watching her. He groaned low in his throat as he stroked himself. The sound gained Sara's attention. Her lids inched open, and the two of them exchanged a long, heated look. When their eyes connected and locked, something inside Mitch softened. Before he had time to examine it further, Sara's gaze dropped to his crotch, where she could see the outline of his hands working overtime inside his pants. She gave him a slow smile to let him know that she was enjoying his sexy show.

She spread her legs impossibly wider, affording him a better view of her sex as her finger dipped in and out of her liquid silk.

She was so goddamned wet, her cream was dripping down her legs. Mitch swiped his hand over her soaked thigh, coating his finger with her juice. When he brought his finger to his mouth and licked it clean, she threw her head back and pinched her clit. Her bold behavior excited him more than he would have expected. He couldn't believe how sexy, how wild she was with him.

He knew she was performing this sexy little solo act—for him. Despite everything warning him to keep the night about sex and fantasies, her actions touched him on another level. A rush of tenderness overcame him and he fought valiantly to suppress his emotions.

Sara might be a sweet, small-town girl, but he loved that she was comfortable enough with him, and her own sexuality, to masturbate for his pleasure.

No woman had ever done that for him before. It was always about their pleasure, their fantasy, never his. He watched for several more minutes, until the need to touch and taste her propelled him into action.

"Let me give you a hand, babe." His index finger breached her opening and together they moved their fingers in and out of her slick entrance. Sara's eyes glazed; her head wobbled to the side.

Mitch nudged her chin with his. "We're getting there, but I'm afraid it might take me all night long to breathe life back into your kitty and get it purring again."

"Yes, yes, all night," she murmured, her voice raspy.

He pushed his finger in deeper, her walls closing around him like a silken glove. "Are you up for that, Sara?"

She drew her finger out, granting him deeper access, and gripped his shoulders for support. "Oh yes, I'm up for that." She began rocking her hips, riding his thick finger feverishly. With his free hand, Mitch snaked his arm around her waist, following the sensuous sway of her body.

Watching her gyrate on his finger pushed him to the edge of oblivion. What he really wanted was to watch her gyrate on his cock, but she wasn't quite ready for that.

Face flushed, her hands gripping his shoulders, she picked up the tempo. Her movements became quicker and faster as she chased an orgasm. He slipped another finger inside her for a deliciously snug fit.

"That's a girl, Sara. Keep riding. It's going to take effort on both our parts to get your kitty up to par."

He could feel soft quakes begin at her core and knew she was close, so very, very close to release, but he wasn't quite ready to bring her over just yet. He wanted to give her so much more than a quick, hurried orgasm. Nostrils flaring, he eased his fingers out, giving her no reprieve from the tension building inside her.

She looked alarmed. "No, don't stop."

Mitch chuckled. He had no intention of stopping. He was far from done with the little vixen. In fact he'd only just begun to discover all her fantasies. "I don't think that's working, Sara. I believe I'm going to have to amp up my efforts and switch tools."

Gone was her alarm. Intrigue moved in to take its place. Dark eyes came alive with curiosity. Her breathing was heavy, labored. The soft blade of her tongue darted out to moisten her lips. "Yes, Mitch, of course. You're a professional firefighter, so I trust you to choose the right tool for the right job." Her voice deepened with undeniable excitement.

He loved how she played along. He smiled as everything in him reached out to her. Damn, she really was something else. Unlike all the other women he'd been with, Sara was interested in this being a fantasy for him, too.

Mitch climbed to his feet and gathered her into his arms. Her hair fell over her face and he brushed it back, taking great care in tucking it behind her ear. Desire clouded her eyes and her breath caught. She shivered, her body reacting to his touch.

Wanting to keep the intimate contact at all times, he pulled her closer. Her small hands raced around his neck, her fingers linked together.

Seeking an even deeper intimacy, Mitch put his lips close to hers and ravished her mouth. Warm and firm, she pressed against him. Aching to feel his cock inside her hot heat, he pulled her bottom lip between his teeth and sucked until her mouth was raw and swollen. His tongue sank inside, an urgent exploration. With deep, hungry thrusts he lashed against the side of her mouth, and then tangled his tongue with hers, swiping her teeth, her lips. As they traded kisses for a long time, her arms tightened, holding him to her, offering herself up to him completely. Her body melted against him as he pillaged her with his tongue. When she gave a needy whimper, an unexpected rush of emotions and sensations ripped through him and caught him off balance. Mitch broke the kiss and inched back.

Sara sucked in air, her eyes smoldering. She touched his cheek and whispered in a soft tone, "Wow." A flurry of emotions passed over her face and he wondered what she was thinking.

His body thrummed, and blood pulsed through his veins. His grin was slow and easy, even though that kiss had shaken him to his core. He worked to compose himself before he dropped to his knees, dragged her down along with him, and fucked her until sunup.

Reining in his lust, he said, "Wow yourself."

Fuck . . . he cursed under his breath, berating himself for feeling so emotional. He tried to keep his feelings under wraps—he really did—but with just one kiss, the little vixen had broken through his defenses without even trying.

Her seductive voice pulled him from his musings. "Maybe seeing you naked will help with the resuscitation." She gripped his shirt and tugged.

Mitch stepped back, tore off his shirt in one swift movement, and discarded it.

"Keep going," she whispered, her voice low and hoarse.

His pants and everything under them followed until he stood

before her stark naked, his arousal throbbing, clamoring for her undivided attention.

"Oh my," he heard her murmur as dark eyes latched on to his cock. "I believe we've just found the necessary *tool*." She wiggled her finger, motioning him closer.

When he stepped into her personal space, her soft hand closed around his shaft and stroked gently. She moaned, low in her throat. Her fingers felt like fire on his flesh. Her other hand slipped between his legs and cupped his balls. As she cradled them with the utmost care, her thumb caressed his sac.

Sweet fuck!

His cock clenched and tightened; his sperm put on their running shoes and lined up at the starting gate. Dammit, the last thing he wanted was to explode on impact. He was a firefighter, not a crash-test dummy for Christ's sake. He eased back, his cock throbbing and begging for release as it slipped from her hand. Her groans of protest morphed into moans of pleasure when he gathered her in his arms and laid her out on the cushiony chair. Heat and desire colored her skin from head to toe, making her look so damn sexy.

He needed to fuck her. Good God, did he ever need to fuck her. But first he wanted to help cool her body down. By any means possible.

Reaching behind him, he pulled his ice-cold water bottle from his jacket. Sara watched his every movement. "I think the first thing we need to do is gain control over that fever. You're burning up."

He snapped open the lid on the bottle and offered her a drink. When she finished, she handed it back.

"Thanks," she whispered. "That's much better."

If she thought that was all he had in mind for the ice water, she was sadly mistaken.

Mitch inched her legs open and nestled himself in between them. He leaned over her. "You're still dangerously hot, Sara. Let me check your temperature." Pressing his arms to the chair on either side of her, he bent forward, swiped her nipple with his tongue and then drew it into his mouth for a thorough taste. He released a low moan as her bud tightened in heavenly bliss.

"Oh God," she cried, quivering beneath him.

Mitch scraped his teeth over her tender flesh. "You're burning up, babe. Extreme measures definitely need to be taken."

He went back on his heels and without warning poured a generous amount of cold water over her breasts. The water practically sizzled when it reached her hot flesh.

Her eyes sprung open. Her body trembled. "That's cold," she whimpered.

In his most serious, professional voice he said, "It's the only way to take down the fever, Sara."

Mitch dipped his head and watched the droplets slide off her nipples and pool in the valley between her mounds. He gulped air as his throbbing cock jutted forward and brushed against her drenched pussy.

She gyrated until the tip of his shaft breached her opening. Mitch inched back, spread her pussy wide, and poured cold water over her hot center.

"Oooh, that feels so good," she murmured.

His thumb went to her clit. He circled her hard bud slowly and bent forward to lap at the water pooling on her chest.

She began panting, her breath coming in labored bursts. Long fingers tunneled through his hair and he could feel her heart pound inside her chest. Mitch eased a finger inside her pussy, offering her only a little at a time. She was so goddamn tight he wondered how she'd handle his cock.

"More," she cried out, writhing beneath him.

Deciding it was well past time to alleviate the pull in her body, he changed the tempo, giving her exactly what she needed to bring her to climax. Increasing the pressure on her clit, he tongued her tight nipples, nipping, nibbling, and sucking until the soft quakes at her core became stronger and stronger.

"Mitch . . ."

"I know, babe, I know." He took a quick drink of water, and held it in his mouth. Sliding down her body, he slipped another finger inside her. His mouth moved to her pussy, where he released the water. The second the cold liquid hit her hot clit, she tumbled into an orgasm.

"Yes," she cried out, fisting his hair, her sex muscles spasming and clenching. Her face lit in euphoria. Mitch worked his tongue over her throbbing clit, lavishing her cunt with his undivided attention, prolonging the pleasure as she rode out every last delicious quake.

He held her for a long time, until she stopped quivering. After a comfortable moment Mitch slid up her body, leaned over her, and said, "I believe your kitty is purring again, Sara."

Her hand slid over his chest, slowly, seductively. "Really? I don't hear a thing," she said, eyes wide and innocent as her hand traveled lower, until she gripped his cock. "I believe there really is only one *tool* that will do the trick."

He grinned. "You're a wild woman, Sara Jack."

"Wild and *wanton* woman," she corrected, stroking his shaft until he just about exploded. "I think it's time to plug that *tool* in, Mitch."

"Keep that up and my *tool* will run out of power before I get started. And I don't think your kitty wants to wait while I have to recharge."

Sara laughed out loud and gave him a light and easy kiss on the mouth. It rocked his world.

He pushed one finger inside her heat. Her eyes lit with pleasure and she shifted beneath him. "It's pretty hot in there, Sara. I guess I'd better gear up properly." He reached behind him, grabbed a condom from his jacket, and quickly sheathed himself.

When he turned back to face her, her eyes were wide and anticipatory, her smile was soft and perfect, and her gorgeous body was wide-open and welcoming. When she reached her hand out to him, myriad emotions rushed through him.

"Come here, baby," she said, in the sweetest, nicest, girl-next-door voice.

The sudden need to lose himself in her became so intense, it was almost painful. He began trembling from head to toe.

"My pleasure," he whispered, his voice barely recognizable to himself. He pressed his lips to her quivering flesh and kissed a path to her mouth, taking time to indulge in her belly button, her breasts, and the deep hollow of her throat before his lips climbed higher to close over hers.

"Mmmm . . ." she moaned and drew his tongue into her mouth, tasting and savoring him like she couldn't get enough. He knew that feeling all too well.

His cock probed her opening and no longer could he play their seductive little game or fight down his carnal cravings. He needed her. Now. Hard and fast.

When her hips bucked forward, his composure completely vanished. His voice came out rough, edgy. "I need to fuck you, Sara."

"Yes, fuck me, Mitch. I want your cock inside me," she murmured, making him forget all rational thought.

Her tight pussy lips closed around his engorged tip and prompted him into action. He balanced his arms beside her head and in one swift movement slammed into her, hard and fast. With that first sweet contact, an intoxicating mix of heat and fire curled around him.

He threw his head back and growled. "Jesus," he cried out as her sheath scorched him. Sara began rocking and her legs slipped around his back, tightening over his ass, taking every inch of his girth inside her.

He matched her movements, driving harder and harder, going deeper and deeper yet never getting deep enough. Her hands clawed at his back, her teeth biting into his flesh. Mitch drew a quick, sharp breath but was unable to fill his lungs. As he pumped harder and deeper, his skin grew tight, his balls constricted and he could feel pressure brewing deep inside him.

"I'm not going to last, babe," he said on a moan.

He inched back and glanced into her eyes to gauge her reactions. The desire reflecting there became his undoing. His cock began to pulse and throb, and he knew release was only a push away.

Her legs tightened around him, her fingers burrowed through his hair. "I'm . . ." she said, her words falling off as her muscles bunched and her liquid desire seared his shaft.

He felt her muscles tighten around his cock. Flames surged through him and his senses exploded. He bucked forward, driving his cock impossibly deeper. As her juices dripped over him, fire pitched through his blood.

When she came apart in his arms, Mitch gave himself over to his own orgasm. He threw his head back and came on a growl, enjoying and savoring every delicious pulse. A moment later he collapsed into a heap beside her and angled his body to pull her in close. She turned to face him, her hand going to his cheek, a contented sigh cutting through the silence.

After their breathing regulated and their tremors subsided, she whispered into his mouth, "I believe *now* my kitty is purring." The satisfaction written all over her face filled him with male pride.

He chuckled, slipped his hand between their bodies, and dipped a finger inside her. "I believe it might actually be singing a show tune."

Sara laughed out loud and swatted him.

"Hey," he said, loving her playful side, "play nice or I just might have to tie you up and spank you."

Her eyes went wide with anticipation, with excitement. "Really? Is that something you'd like to do, Mitch? One of your own fantasies perhaps?"

Before he had time to answer, a noise outside the pool house gained their attention.

Body tense, Mitch pressed his fingers to his lips. Sara nodded in understanding. A moment later he heard Nick's and Cassie's whispered words, then a splash in the pool.

Mitch quickly removed his condom and went in search of a tissue.

"In my housecoat," Sara whispered. Mitch pulled out a couple of tissues and, after wetting them with his ice water, washed himself.

"Christ, that's cold," he whispered.

Sara grinned. "No kidding."

"Don't worry. You're next," he said. After he washed himself, he slipped between her legs and wiped her down. She shivered but he suspected it wasn't from the icy water.

Once that was completed, he climbed back in beside her. Sara pitched her voice low. "Looks like we're going to be stuck here for a while." She touched her finger to his lips, her eyes dark, seductive. "What should we do now?" she asked, arching into him, her body giving a little shiver.

Noticing that the temperature around them had dropped a few degrees, Mitch wrapped his arms around her body, offering his warmth. "I guess we wait," he said.

Sara got quiet for a moment, as though deep in thought. A moment later she crinkled her brow and asked, "Don't you have somewhere else to be?"

She didn't come right out and say it, but her words implied that he might have other calls to take, other women to satisfy.

He shrugged easily and lowered his voice to match hers. "I'm covered at the station and I have my phone for emergencies. I don't have anywhere to go if you don't," he assured her, knowing that if he spent any more time in her arms, it'd be emotional suicide at best.

Sara was merely in it for the fantasy, and he wasn't naive enough to believe otherwise.

She curled her body against him and marched her fingers over his chest. He grinned, his cock stirring to life as her body molded to his. "Well, since my *tool* needs time to recharge, maybe we can sleep . . . or talk," he added as an afterthought, eager to learn more about Sara, who she was and what made her tick.

"Okay," she agreed readily, bright eyed and bursting with questions. "Tell me, have you always wanted to be a firefighter?"

He nodded. "I think all boys want to grow up to be a fireman."

"But not all do. What kept you on that path?"

"My dad. He's a firefighter, retired now, though. I spent more time at the station than I did at home."

"And your mom?" Sara trailed her fingers over his chest and abdomen.

"She worked part-time as a baker and was more than happy for me to hang out at the station." He rolled his eyes. "Apparently I was a bit of a handful. Always getting into trouble. The guys at the station put me to work, keeping my hands busy and out of mischief."

Sara's soft chuckle morphed into a moan when his fingers went to her nipples. He stroked her there, slowly and sinuously, as though it was the most natural thing in the world for him to do.

She cleared her throat. "Ah, yeah, I can see how those hands of yours have gotten you into trouble a time or two."

Mitch gave her a wicked grin and continued right on with his slow seduction.

"So you grew up in Chicago then?"

"Born and bred." He inched closer, still unable to get close enough. "What about you? Born and bred in Iowa?"

She let out a sigh. "Yeah."

"What? You don't like it there?"

"Not always. My mom, dad, sister, and two brothers are still there, but sometimes the small town feels suffocating."

He nodded in understanding and then asked, "Do you like writing for the *Trenton Gazette*?"

She raised a curious brow. "How do you know I write for the *Gazette*?"

He smiled. "If I told you, then I'd have to kill you."

Sara chuckled. "That might be a blessing, because if I have to write another cow-tipping story, I'm going to hang myself."

Mitch threw his head back and, forgetting himself, laughed out loud.

"Shh . . ." Sara warned, stifling her own laugh. "Cassie and Nick will hear us."

"Right," Mitch said, remembering that Nick had warned him to stay away from Sara because she was a small-town girl who could get hurt.

She turned the conversation back around to him. "Was there anything else you ever wanted to do?"

He grinned, humor edging his voice. "Why would I?" He gestured with a nod. "When I put on that suit, I'm a chick magnet. Who wouldn't want that?"

She whacked him again. Hard.

Smiling with her, he continued. "Honestly, I never really gave it much thought. It was just natural for me to follow in my dad's footsteps. My two brothers did, too."

They grew quiet for a moment, both lost in their own thoughts. A short time later, Sara's voice broke the comfortable quiet.

"Why don't you tell me a secret?"

He chuckled and pulled her in tighter. "If I tell you, then it won't be a secret anymore, now, will it?"

Sara's warm finger touched his chin and gently traced the tiny scar near his earlobe. Her intimate caress went right through him. He shivered, his cock stretching after its short nap, poking its head out in search of a little mischief.

"Tell me how you got this."

"If you guess, I'll give you a surprise."

Sara leaned in for a closer inspection, her breasts sliding over his chest with innocent sensuality. *Jesus.*

She narrowed her eyes. "So you said you had brothers."

He nodded, his fingers going to her hair, smoothing it from her flushed cheeks.

She arched a brow. "Older?"

He nodded again, unable to contain his smile as he watched her. Her dark eyes were narrowed, deep in concentration. Her sensuous lips puckered as she pieced the clues together.

She threw one hand up in the air, palm out. "That explains everything then."

He furrowed his brow and shot her a glance. "You want to enlighten me?"

She rolled her eyes, like it was so obvious. "Well, I have two older brothers, both Packers fans, both with similar scars. Let me guess." She tapped her finger to her chin. "Chicago Bears fan. Roughhousing on the lawn with the big boys. Going for the winning touchdown."

Dammit, she was right. But what really surprised him was that she didn't go for the obvious: that he'd been injured in the line of duty.

Was it possible that she saw the man beneath the uniform?

He brushed her hair from her face, unable to stop touching her, needing the intimate contact to continue. "Now it's your turn to tell me a secret."

She tossed him a mischievous look. "Maybe later. Right now I want my surprise."

With his cock up, fully showered, and raring to go, he bumped groins with her, feeling very playful. "Are you sure you're ready for it?"

Her lips thinned provocatively. "Oh yeah."

He took her hand and placed it over his rock-hard erection. "I'm fully recharged."

With a haughty huff, she glared at him, but she couldn't keep the humor from her voice. "What's up with this? I was right about the scar and now you're trying to pass off some consolation prize. Sheesh."

Mitch rolled on top of her, his cock slipping between her legs. A strange sense of belonging rolled over him as her body molded to his. "Why, you little . . ."

Sara chuckled, but he quickly muffled the sound with a kiss.

FOUR

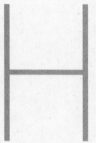ours later, Sara and Mitch crept from the pool
house and made their way up the dimly lit path
to the back door. The night had slipped away in
a haze of lust, and now, much to Sara's dismay,
morning was upon them. Bursts of orange and
red hues colored the horizon as the sun began
its ritual ascent. Sara stifled a yawn. She felt
tired, yet at the same time, she felt a little weird, wonderful, and alive
inside.

Fingers linked and bodies pressed together, they halted outside
the door. Jaw clenching, Mitch glanced quickly at his watch, then furrowed his brow and his gorgeous blue eyes turned serious. "I guess I'd
better get going." He pulled her against him once more, his actions
contradicting his words.

"Yes, and I guess I'd better get some sleep. I have a busy day
tomorrow. After our dress fittings, we're all getting together to plan
Cassie's bachelorette party." She was babbling, she knew, but couldn't
seem to help herself. "And I have to help Megan book the stripper."

She waved her hand in front of her. "Naturally I would have suggested you, but since Cassie's got a firefighter of her own, maybe we'll hire a police officer. Now there's a fantasy man in a uniform."

Mitch chuckled. "Go get some sleep, Sara."

Sara nodded, her stomach tightening, her heart sinking. She hated that the night had come to an end. She felt like a giddy teenager back in high school, playing the "No, you hang up first" phone game.

Mitch leaned in and pressed his mouth to hers, giving her a warm, tender kiss. A kiss so intimate and so full of emotions it took two locked knees to keep herself upright.

Tonight she'd glimpsed a whole new side of Mitch. His dark and dangerous side drew her in, but it was his soft and tender side that kept her there.

"Good night, Sara."

Sara smiled and worked to find her voice. "Good morning, Mitch."

His warm chuckle curled around her and momentarily chased away the chill of his departure.

He squeezed her fingers. "Go get some sleep," he whispered, but added before he left, "Oh, and for the record, I only perform in private."

Sara watched him go. When he disappeared from her line of vision, she snuck inside and tiptoed to her bedroom. As she climbed into her bed and yawned, Megan spoke in whispered words and startled her. "Just getting in?"

"Sorry to wake you. I couldn't sleep," she replied, holding the blankets to her chest, but holding the memories of the evening even closer.

"No problem. I was awake anyway. What have you been doing?"

Misty, Cassie's midnight black cat, was tucked in beside Megan. Sara smiled. With Megan's love for animals, it hadn't taken long for her to bond with the cat.

"Working." It was a half-truth. Sara had called the Hot Line in search of a hot story and a hot guy, but what she found instead had rocked her world.

"What were you working on?" Megan stroked the purring cat.

"An article for *Entice* magazine."

"Yeah?" Megan perked up. "Did you come up with a great story idea?"

"I'm still toying with it," Sara said, not wanting to share the details of her phone call to the Hot Line or her night with Mitch. She wanted to keep the memories close, savor them, and nurture them so she could call on them during her lonely nights back home. By blabbing the details to her friend, she felt it would somehow sully the experience and reduce it to a frivolous affair. And although it might have been a frivolous affair for Mitch, seeing as he was a participant in the Hot Line and all, deep in Sara's soul it felt anything but trivial.

Dammit!

She thought she could handle this. One night, hot sex on vacation, no strings attached. So much for her vacation from reality.

She closed her eyes and willed herself to sleep but her mind was too busy racing, her body too wound up to relax. Flustered, she kicked the covers off. Maybe she should get up and work on her article. Fantasy men in uniforms, she mused. What a great title. So very delicious, and oh so very scandalous. She knew firsthand.

Megan sat up and stretched. The springs on the old twin bed groaned in protest. "Coffee?"

Sara smiled. "Love some. I'd also love some of those yummy

breakfast frittatas you make." Since Sara hated to cook, having a sous chef for a best friend was like the icing on the cake or, rather, a yummy frittata on her plate.

With Misty curling around Megan's feet, they padded to the kitchen, taking care not to wake the others. Megan went to work on the coffee while Sara grabbed her pen and notebook. Her mind raced to create the perfect catchy opening. She scribbled a few things down, but her mind kept wandering to the amazing fantasy night she'd just had and to the amazing man beneath the uniform.

Just then Jenna appeared. "Doesn't anyone sleep in Chicago?"

"It doesn't appear that way," Sara said, using her toes to push a chair away from the table in offering. "What's keeping you up?"

Jenna combed her fingers through her long hair. Even after a night of no sleep, she was the epitome of perfection. Jenna designed her own clothes and owned a chain of lingerie boutiques, and with her long chestnut hair, green eyes, beautiful face, and perfect figure—a perfect figure that she kept hidden beneath baggy clothes—she could easily be a top lingerie model herself.

"I've been up all night thinking about my business and the fashion show Cassie asked me to put on for her friends and colleagues. It really is great exposure for the new Siren line, especially now that I'm thinking of expanding into new territories." She bit her lip and glanced around as though gauging her friends' reactions.

Megan's blue eyes lit up. "Really? That's wonderful, Jenna. I knew one day you'd grow your business and venture into new territories. You certainly have the brains and drive for it."

"I've just been waiting for the right time and the right opportunity to expand. I think this might be it. Cassie and I were talking last night and she has some great ideas. As a public-relations liaison for one of Chicago's largest marketing firms, she has lots of contacts in the industry."

"So you're thinking of opening a shop here, in Chicago?" Sara asked. She tossed Megan a grateful smile as she brought her a steaming mug of coffee.

Jenna nodded. "Yes. With Cassie's help, I know I can do this."

Sara leaned in for a hug. "How exciting for you, Jenna!"

Megan offered Jenna a cup of coffee and handed Sara utensils, along with a bottle of raspberry jam. "Can you open this for me?" Megan asked.

Sara laughed and twisted off the lid. "How do you ever manage to cook when you can never open anything?"

"I manage because I have you to help me. And when you're not around, I skip the jam or anything else with a screw cap, for that matter." She wagged her finger. "Tight caps are not my friends."

As Megan went to work on breakfast, Sara said, "Since we're all gathered here, we should talk about the bachelorette party. We need to get cracking on that. Any ideas?"

For the next hour, the three girls tossed around ideas until Cassie and Nick surfaced. After an exchange of pleasantries, they all went their separate ways, agreeing to meet up again for the formal dinner that Cassie and Nick had planned for the bridal party.

As Sara made her way back to the bedroom to work on her article, she thought about the dinner party—a party that Mitch would attend. Her stomach tightened, and her heart raced in anticipation. She couldn't believe how eager she was to see him again. Damn him for being so irresistible.

How in the hell could she possibly act like a normal human being and make it through a meal with him sitting next to her? Especially after all the intimacies they shared last night. And how in the hell could she be expected to keep her hands to herself, knowing how amazing that toned body felt beneath her fingertips . . . between her legs?

Her thighs quivered in erotic delight as she indulged in the provocative slide show.

Even though last evening was just supposed to be one hot night of fantasy sex, she knew she wanted to be with him again. She also knew this wasn't the time to be worrying about getting in too deep. She'd deal with that later because right now was time for fun and fantasies and dammit she planned on spending the rest of her vacation indulging in as many as she could.

She took a moment to recall the way Mitch lavished her with so much attention. Indulging her wayward thoughts, she envisioned his tender lips on hers again, his cock inside her cunt, stroking deeply as they both reached earth-shattering orgasms. Suddenly, her mind raced with indecent thoughts—thoughts like getting him in the pool house again and fulfilling a few of his fantasies, the same way he'd fulfilled hers.

A smile touched her lips. What was that he said about tying her up and spanking her? Oh yeah, she mused, her mind plotting and tweaking the details of her own sexy seduction. Maybe it was time to give the fantasy man his own private fantasy. One he wouldn't soon forget.

Dressed in a hot red barely there dress that dipped into her cleavage, Sara drew a sharp breath as she, along with her friends, entered Chez Frontenac, the finest French restaurant in Chicago.

She turned to Cassie and spoke in a whisper. "You must have booked this months ago. I hear this place is harder to get into than Fort Knox."

Cassie smiled and gave her a wink. "Not when you have connections."

Sara adjusted her black evening bag under her arm, stepped farther into the foyer, and soaked in the elegant ambience. "You have connections?" she asked, brow arched. "Do tell."

Before Cassie had time to answer, Megan stepped up beside her, eyes opened wide and glowing like a child's on Christmas morning. A hand over her chest, she gasped and said, "This is Lucien Beaufort's restaurant."

Cassie nodded. "Yes. Do you know him?"

"Yes, I know him. Well, I don't really know him, not really—" She stopped midsentence to wring her hands together. Seemingly flustered and excited at the same time, Megan babbled on. "Not personally, anyway. But his reputation precedes him."

Following Megan's lead, Sara glanced around the cozy restaurant. Soft light and rich decor set the mood for elegance and seduction. Strategically placed candles and minilights created warmth and comfort while rich orange and pink hues played off the plush velvet upholstery.

Megan turned to face Sara. "Ohmigod, Sara, I'd give a kidney to meet Lucien."

Cassie chuckled and touched her arm to draw her attention. "I don't think you need to go to such extremes, Megan. I'll try to introduce you to Lucien a little later on if he's not too busy."

Megan's jaw practically hit the floor. Face animated, she rushed on. "You will? Really? Cassie, you have got to be kidding me. And if you are, you really shouldn't kid about such things."

Sara chuckled and hugged Megan to calm her down. "Relax, honey." She turned to Cassie. "Imagine how she'd act if she ever had the chance to work under him?"

Megan shot her a frown. "Don't even joke about such a thing, Sara."

"So how do you know him, Cassie?" Sara asked. Just then the maître d' came up and gestured with a wave that their table was ready.

"Lucien had a fire in his kitchen a few months back. Nick was the first firefighter on the scene. He saved the restaurant. The guys make a lot of connections that way." When Cassie cast a glance toward Nick, a look of love came over her face and warmed Sara's heart. Would the day ever come when someone looked at her like that?

As they walked to the table, Sara listened to Megan mumble something about Lucien Beaufort under her breath, then grinning from ear to ear, she turned to Cassie. "Have I told you how much I love you?"

Cassie arched one brow, her mouth turning up at the corners. "I think you're about to love me even more."

"That's not possible," Megan said, arms folded, face adamant.

"Lucien will be a guest at the wedding. It should give you plenty of time to chat with him."

Megan practically shrieked and threw her arms around Cassie. "Okay, you win. I do love you more."

As they approached the table, Sara spotted Dean Beckman and Brady Wade already seated, looking so darn handsome and proper in their tailored suits. Her pulse leapt and her stomach tightened as her mind conjured the image of Mitch all decked out in his finest attire.

Sara moved around the table, searching for her place card. After seating herself, she peeked at the card beside her. Her body fairly vibrated when she read Mitch's name. She quickly panned the restaurant, but he was nowhere to be found. Impatience mingled with nervousness as she mentally indulged in all the sexy things she had planned for him later that night.

She glanced around the table, taking stock. Dean was seated beside Jenna, and Brady was placed next to Megan. By the looks on her friends' faces she'd say both seemed rather happy with the arrangement.

Who could blame them? Really, the guys were gorgeous. Every woman's fantasy. But they were no Mitch Adams.

Trying for casual, she asked, "Where's Mitch?"

Cassie piped up, but before she could answer, she heard Mitch's deep, sensuous voice. His seductive cadence bombarded her body with rich, evocative sensations. She shuddered and warmed all over as his intoxicating, familiar scent teased and tormented her libido.

With casual confidence, he pulled his chair out and sat beside her. Heat and strength radiated off him and seeped under her skin.

Desire thrummed through her veins when she took a moment to peruse him. He looked like sin and seduction all rolled into one. Seeing him all heroic and sexy in his firefighter suit was one thing, but seeing him in formal wear made her breath catch and her heart turn over.

"Hey, I heard my name. Is someone talking about me?" He glanced at Sara and his simmering blue eyes flitted across her body with intimate recognition. Sara acknowledged the flare of desire inside her, and for a moment, she wondered if Mitch could see the telltale hardening of her nipples.

Mitch gifted her with a sexy wink, his eyes full of teasing warmth. "Don't believe a thing these guys tell you, Sara," he said, grinning like the devil himself. "I was not responsible for losing that twenty-pound trout on our last fishing trip, no matter what they say. It was Dean's fault. He couldn't keep the damn boat steady. He was lurching all over the place like a drunken sailor."

The guys all laughed and threw around words like "baby," "boat," "lurched," "my ass," and "slippery fingers." Sara grinned, loving the camaraderie among the men. It occurred to her that the firefighters from Station 419 formed a brotherhood. Men who worked together, played together, and trusted one another with their lives. She was in awe of them, really.

After goading them on, Mitch chuckled and told them all where they could go, giving specific directions and offering a map should they need it. Sara laughed with him, marveling at his playful side and the way his deep, sensuous laughter warmed her blood and curled her toes.

When the laughing settled down, and pleasantries had been exchanged, all eyes turned to the menu and a few people began to talk among themselves.

Sara felt Mitch's hand close over hers under the linen tablecloth. He gave a tender squeeze—a small affectionate gesture that touched her down deep and created an instant air of warmth and familiarity around them. She angled her head to see him. His eyes flared when they met hers. His smile looked warm, inviting, and intimate.

"Hi," he whispered.

The silky warmth of his voice drew her into a cocoon of need and desire. Longing swamped her.

She drew in air, taking a moment to compose herself. "Hi, yourself."

He pitched his voice low, his eyes glimmering with dark sensuality. "You look beautiful."

When she smiled at the endorsement, something tender and powerful passed between them. Something, she knew, that there might be no coming back from. It took effort for her to keep her voice light. "You're not so bad yourself."

"I guess I clean up okay," he teased, his lips twitching with amusement.

They shared a private chuckle, and then Sara admitted honestly, "Better than okay, Mitch." His nearness was playing havoc with her libido, and she suspected it was the same for him. Heat gathered in her body as she worked to keep her passion at bay.

Scrubbing a hand over his jaw, he leaned in and whispered, "It's no firefighter suit, though, right?" When he mentioned the suit, the mental image of him stripping it from his lethally honed body while she watched in heated anticipation had her hormones jumping to attention like an obedient fire cadet.

"It's better," she assured him. Then, in a low sultry voice meant to entice, she added, "And probably a lot easier for me to rip off."

She watched his expression change. Light humor segued to dark desire. His fingers tightened over hers. Sexually frustrated curses rumbled in his throat. Desire and need burned in his blue eyes.

Under his breath he whispered, "Jesus, Sara, you're going to pay for that."

She matched his low tone. "I thought you might say that. Good thing I have the rope and paddle all ready."

Picking his jaw up off the table, Mitch cleared his throat and practically leapt to his feet. "If you'll all excuse me for a minute . . ."

Sara sipped her wine. Eyes wide and innocent, she tipped her head up and asked, "Are you okay, Mitch? You look flushed."

As though flustered, his words came out all jumbled and broken. "I'm. Fine. Running late. Wash up. Busy."

Sara kept a smile from her face although she was loving the way she affected him. Loved how she could reduce him to speechlessness so easily.

After Mitch returned, the waiter took their orders. With Mitch barely able to form a coherent sentence, Sara turned her attention to Cassie as she and Jenna discussed the details of the lingerie party. Sara took note of the look in Dean's eyes as he listened to the exchange with heated interest.

A short while later, after eating dessert, they all made plans to head over to the Hose for after-dinner drinks. Sara excused herself. When the group gave her a questioning look, she explained she had work to do.

After everyone agreed that Sara would take the car home and the others would share a cab, since they all planned on having a drink or two, she stepped out into the night, Mitch tight on her heels.

Sara stood back and watched her friends pile into a cab. Mitch moved in beside her. Draped in darkness, she whispered into his ear. "Follow me home."

Gaze dark, scalding, he looked at her, his eyes serious. His hand closed over hers, warm and strong. He put his mouth close to her ear, his breath hot on her neck. A moan caught in her throat.

"I don't have my firefighter suit with me."

Sara grinned, and in her most sultry voice, she said, "You don't need it." She fingered his lapels. "Like I said, this is probably easier for me to rip off."

His nostrils flared. "Jesus, Sara, do you enjoy torturing me?" he asked, curiosity and excitement in his tone. He shifted his stance as though in agony.

She cocked her head playfully, her eyes full of promise. "Torture?

Oh no. What I have planned for you tonight isn't going to hurt one little bit." Before she stepped away, leaving Mitch in the shadows to tame his arousal, she said, "Oh, and meet me out back."

Heart racing with excitement, Sara made her way to the car. Just seeing the look on Mitch's face and knowing how eager he was to follow her home fired her libido and moistened her panties.

Fortunately, traffic was light, and she arrived back at the house in record time. Wasting no time getting ready, she grabbed two towels from the house and rushed around back to the pool. Shrouded in darkness, she quickly stripped off her sexy red dress and dove in. She was right, not even the cool water could help smother the flames of desire engulfing her. Only Mitch was capable of that feat.

Sara waded into the deep end while waiting for Mitch, her mind swimming with all the delicious things she wanted to do with him— and to him. She thought about how she wanted to kiss him all over, to feel his warm flesh beneath her lips. How she wanted to take his cock into her mouth and lap at him until their moans of pleasure merged. Her breasts swelled with heated blood, as she imagined it now. She ached to stroke, suck, and nibble his magnificent shaft. Ached to feel his sex muscles spasm as his tangy juices erupted in her throat.

Footsteps on the walkway pulled her from her reverie. As soon as Mitch rounded the corner and she set eyes on him, her heart leapt, her body pulsed, desire singed her blood. Out of nowhere a wave of passion and possessiveness rushed through her and caught her by surprise.

In that instant it occurred to her just how bad she had it for him. Just how much she wanted to lose herself in him, and how much she ached for something far more intimate.

He came closer and knelt down at the edge of the pool. He narrowed his gaze and a muscle in his jaw clenched. One hand went to her cheek, his thumb tracing the pattern of her lips. She liquefied under his touch. His low, sensuous voice covered her body like a blanket of warmth. "Hey."

That one simple word did such amazing things to her insides. "Hey, yourself." She pushed off the edge, allowing him to see her naked body below the surface, letting him know exactly what she wanted.

Mitch's dark, hungry gaze slid over her flesh, generating deep desire. He took a long moment just to look at her. She watched his eyes fill with lust. Her body began humming with excitement. His breath came in a low rush, his gaze shifted to her face. "Are you coming out or am I coming in?"

With two easy strokes, she made her way back to him, needing to touch him, to feel connected on some deeper level. As her hand closed over his, unrelenting pressure brewed in the depths of her womb. "I believe you promised me a swim last night," she said.

He stood, pulled off his jacket, and began loosening his tie. "I believe I did." His voice came out rusty, labored. "And I never break my promises."

He tore off his shirt and tossed it aside. Nipples tingling in awareness, Sara watched him undress. The pleasure was most exquisite. When she caught the intent look on his face, an erotic whimper bubbled in the depths of her throat. Chaos erupted inside her. Her body grew tight and needy while her breathing grew shallow.

This was way better than any fantasy she'd ever had.

His eyes locked on hers. "Only one problem."

Sara didn't miss the mischief dancing in his eyes. "Oh yeah?" she asked as flames surged through her. "What's that?"

Mitch made short work of his clothes. Sara gulped air as she took in his wide chest, corded abdominal muscles, and rock-hard cock. Hot pleasure shot through her, and at that moment, she was sure, no matter how many times he fucked her, nothing would ever satiate her cravings for him.

"I can't swim."

She shook her head as her cunt throbbed for him. "That's not good, Mitch."

"Nope, not good at all."

She lifted herself from the water, just far enough to entice him with her rosy red nipples. "I guess you'd better stay out of the deep end, then."

His glance went to her breasts. His sensual eyes studied her. He swiped his tongue over his lips. "But you're in the deep end, Sara, and there are things I need to do to you."

And there were things she needed to do to *him*.

Playing along, she tapped her chin, as though mulling things over. "Well . . ."

"Well, what?"

"You could try swimming, and if you take in water, I could always *resuscitate* you."

As soon as the words left her mouth, Mitch dove in. He came up right in front of her. Strong arms circled her waist and pulled her under with him. Her legs wrapped around his waist; her mouth went to his. They stayed down for a long time, touching, stroking, and trading deep, heated kisses.

A moment later they both resurfaced, breathless. Sara brushed her hair from her face and then splashed him with water. "Hey, I thought you said you couldn't swim."

His killer smile curled her toes. "I lied," he admitted. "I just wanted a little mouth to mouth."

Her hand sheathed his magnificent cock. "I have a better idea, Mitch."

His eyes lit, intrigued. "Yeah?"

"How about a little mouth to cock?"

He growled, low in his throat. With that, she pushed away and swam to the shallow end, Mitch following right behind her.

She took a seat on the stairs and gestured with a nod for him to sit beside her. As soon as he did, she went down on her knees and positioned herself in front of him. Her fingers closing around his engorged cock, she took great pleasure in his length and girth. She stroked him, reveling in his warm texture and masculine scent.

With her whole body quivering in delight, she leaned forward. Her tongue snaked out, and with a light, barely there touch, she caressed his wet tip.

Mitch growled and touched her cheek. His legs tightened around her hips and prevented her from moving. She tipped her head and met with eyes so dark and so full of desire, her pussy swelled, begging to be filled. "I want you to fuck my mouth."

"Jesus, Sara," he murmured.

Emotions ambushed her at the sound of his deep, sexy tenor. She really hadn't anticipated that she'd fall so hard for him, but Mitch had taken her beyond her wildest fantasies.

She turned her attention back to his arousal and let out a slow breath. When her breath fanned his cock, it pulsed in response. He brushed the pad of his thumb over her mouth and drew in air, as though centering himself. His eyes clouded. "I want you so much, babe, I'm aching," he said.

Sara could feel the passion and raw hunger rising in him, and there was nothing she wanted more than to answer the demands pulling at his body. She pressed her lips to his for a deep kiss. A moment later she abandoned his mouth and moved her lips to his neck and his chest and then down lower. Pleasure raced through her when she felt the way his body reacted.

She sank lower into the water and glanced at his gorgeous cock. "Actually, you're throbbing."

His edgy chuckle curled around her as she inclined her head and fed his cock into her mouth.

"Sweet Mother of God," he whispered under his breath, the pleasure in his voice exciting her. His fingers raked through her hair, his hands following the motion of her head, up and down, up and down.

Sara moaned and slipped her hand lower to cup and massage his balls. She inhaled his heady scent, noting the way it aroused all her senses. She stroked her tongue down the length of him and kissed him deeply. His whole body trembled in response to her seduction.

He threw his head back and groaned. "That feels so fucking good." His hips pitched forward, driving his cock deeper down her throat.

She arched into him, her body beckoning his touch. As though in tune with her every emotion, her every desire, Mitch reached down and closed his hands over her breasts, kneading them, pinching her nipples until she gasped in heavenly bliss.

With much greed she laved the soft folds underneath his bulbous head and lapped at the juices pearling on his tip. She teased and caressed his erection, taking time to savor every delectable inch.

Moaning and purring with pent-up need, she began moving restlessly, her internal temperature igniting to a boil.

She spent a long time between his legs, working her tongue over his cock, raining kisses over his length, licking, sucking, and nibbling until she could feel his veins fill with heated blood. He brushed her hair from her face, watching the way she took him into her mouth.

Mitch's muscles bunched and his cock tightened with the tension of an approaching orgasm. Every nerve in Sara's body came alive, heat flamed through her, her cunt lubricated in preparation.

"Mmmmm . . ." Sara moaned, working her hands and tongue over his cock at the same time, urging him on.

His breath came in a ragged burst. "I'm going to come, babe," he growled. He gripped her head, and tried to ease her back.

She refused to budge, needing to taste his juice. "I want to taste you," she murmured from deep between his legs. "Come in my mouth."

She heard him groan low in his throat and knew the pressure brewing deep in his groin had come to a peak. Sara flicked her tongue over his slit while her hands stroked over his cock, drawing out his orgasm.

Hands fisting her hair, he began rocking, pressing against her, and she knew his explosion was only a stroke away.

"Come for me, Mitch." As soon as the words left her mouth, she felt a tremor rip through him. He came, fast and hard, sending his liquid heat down her throat. She swallowed every delicious drop. Once he stopped trembling, Sara eased back on her heels to look up at him.

Gorgeous blue eyes met hers. A deep, contented sigh curved his handsome face. He reached out and cupped her chin, stroking her with the utmost care. His hand slid lower to grip her elbow. "Come here, babe." His voice was so tender and soft it filled her with longing and stirred all her emotions.

Sara slid up his body until her mouth hovered near his. When he drew her close and cradled her in his arms, her heart twisted.

"That was amazing, Sara."

She grinned. "My pleasure." He held her tighter, their slick bodies melding together. After a long moment of just holding each other, Sara inched back. "Mitch?"

"Hmmm . . ."

"I still owe you a secret."

"What?" he asked, his voice deep, drowsy.

"Last night I promised you a secret. I'm ready to tell you now."

His eyes perked up. "I'm listening."

When Sara stood, water dripped from her body, gaining Mitch's attention. She reached a hand out to him. "Why don't you come with me, and I'll show you instead?"

He nodded and was on his feet in seconds. He grabbed their pile of clothes and came up beside her. When the cool night air brushed against her skin, Mitch scooped up their towels, wrapping one tight around her body. Shielding her from the cold, he pulled her in closer, using his body to warm hers. That small gesture had her feeling all warm and wonderful inside.

Relinquishing his hand, Sara unlocked the pool house door and entered. Mitch followed her. Once inside she turned to him. Strong arms snaked around her waist, gripping her hips, positioning her pelvis next to his. "Tell me your secret," he commanded in a soft voice, his fingers going to the knot in her towel.

She met his gaze, her mind racing with wild and wicked ideas.

Her body trembled with the urgent need to answer the incessant ache between her legs. "It's more of a confession than a secret."

His brow arched. "Go on," he urged.

She shivered as the towel slid down her body and fell to the floor. The shiver had more to do with the man standing in front of her than it did with being cold.

Mitch pulled her tighter; she melted against him as her flesh absorbed the heat radiating off his body. She gestured with a nod toward the sexy toys she'd purchased at a boutique earlier that day. "Well, I've never been tied up and spanked. And I'd really like to try it." She touched his chest with her index finger. "With you."

His eyes darkened; his throat worked as he swallowed. His whole body broke into a sweat. "That's some confession, Sara."

She trailed her fingers over his chest. His skin burned beneath her fingertips. "Last night you fulfilled my fantasy. Tonight I'd like to fulfill yours."

He drew in air, then slipped his hand down her back to cradle her ass. "And you think my fantasy is to tie you up and spank you?"

She nodded eagerly. "You mentioned something about that last night."

His chest heaved. He inclined his head, his expression tender and perplexed. "And you'd do that for me, Sara?" He pulled her impossibly closer. As his cock brushed against her inner thighs, her pussy flooded with heat.

She bit down on her lower lip and could feel her body grow hot beneath his touch. "Yes, but I have to admit, I'd probably really like it, too."

Something in his face softened. Sara saw warmth fill his eyes. His hands went to her cheeks, where he caressed her with the backs of his fingers. She became pliable in his arms.

Mitch cleared his throat before speaking. "Sara, maybe we'll fulfill that fantasy later. Right now this is what I want." His hands circled her waist and splayed over the small of her back. His mouth closed over hers for a deep, soul-stirring kiss. So deep and soul-stirring in fact, it nearly brought her to her knees.

Their bodies pressed together, his hands began moving, tracing the pattern of her curves gently, lovingly. His mouth went to her neck.

"I want you, babe." Urgent need colored his voice.

"I want you, too, Mitch." She coiled her arms around his shoulders and held on, never wanting to let him go.

One long finger slipped between her thighs. She widened her legs in invitation. His finger rubbed her inflamed clit, then parted her damp pink lips. She began panting, her hips rocking forward. Mitch pressed his finger inside her cunt, priming her for his thickness.

His breath rushed over her face, and she sensed he was hovering near the edge right along with her. "I don't have any condoms on me, Sara, and I need to be inside you." She felt a tremor race through his body. He hastily raked his fingers through his hair. "I really, really need to be inside you." His strangled voice shook as he spoke.

She gyrated against him, needing to assuage the deep ache in her core. She put her mouth close to his and framed his face with her hands. "I stashed some in here earlier today."

Perspiration dotting his forehead, Mitch scooped her body in his arms and deposited her on the fully inflated pool lounger.

"Where are they?"

The intensity in his eyes was almost frightening to her. Sara reached behind the chair and pulled one out. Mitch took it, ripped the package open, and quickly sheathed himself. Once complete, he climbed over her, his cock centered between her closed legs.

Unbridled desire burned in his eyes. "Open for me, Sara." His voice was rough with emotion.

She widened her legs as he requested, granting him better access. Her skin came alive. Their breath mingling, his mouth came down on hers. Soft lips played over hers, and tongues joined in a mating dance.

Sara whimpered and moved restlessly beneath him, aching and hungering for him in ways that shocked her. Without his lips ever leaving hers, Mitch's hand dipped between their bodies, circled her clit and prepared her for his entrance.

He inched back, blue eyes smoldering with need when they met hers. Heat flamed through her and boiled her blood. Gentle fingers brushed her hair from her forehead. She loved the way he touched her in such a familiar way. Her heart slammed in her chest; she was amazed at how easily she'd lost herself in his touch.

His breath was coming in ragged bursts, and his voice thinned to a whisper. "I love how wet you get for me." The tip of his cock breached her opening. She moaned and wrapped her legs around his back, forcing him in deeper. His earthy scent closed over her and she thought she'd go mad with desire.

"Please, Mitch," she begged, threading her fingers through his hair.

There was such tenderness in his gaze when his eyes locked on hers. "Please what?"

Desperation to feel him inside her fueled her on. She touched his cheek. "I need you to fuck me."

With that, he offered her his entire length. She let out a little gasp as his girth pushed open the tight walls of her pussy. Her heart increased its tempo and a shudder raced through her.

They were joined as one, and Mitch began moving, rocking his hips slowly. The sweet friction took her places she'd never been before, filling her with need, with longing.

Together they established a rhythm, meeting and welcoming every push, each giving and taking at the same time.

She pressed her breasts against his chest and moved beneath him. Heat poured from his body to hers, back to his again. Moaning deep in his throat, Mitch cradled her in his arms, his cock stroking the spot that needed it most, bringing her to the edge in record time. The man certainly had a talent for knowing just how she liked it, just what she needed.

Even though their lovemaking was softer, slower, deeper, and far more tender than last time, it didn't mean it was any less powerful. In fact, it was so raw, so powerful, and so intimate it sent a riot of emotions coursing through her.

Eyes full of want, he shot her a tender look of intimacy. Her throat clogged, her insides turned to mush.

"You feel so good," he whispered.

Her thoughts scattered. All she knew was she never wanted this to end. She wanted to keep him inside her forever, but the pressure building in her body became too much to bear. Her tongue found the warmth of his mouth again. He kissed her with such passion, it left her gulping for her very next breath.

Her pussy muscles quaked and gripped him hard. A growl crawled out of his throat as her tension mounted. Concentrating on the tiny points of pleasure, she gripped his backside, following his motion with her hands, urging him on.

The world around her went fuzzy; her entire body burned from the inside out. "Harder, Mitch," she cried out as a powerful orgasm rolled through her.

Mitch began panting, picking up the tempo, driving her to the moon and back over and over, giving her body what it needed to bring her to the peak and keep her there. As her muscles quaked and quivered in erotic delight, she felt his cock clench and throb, and knew his orgasm was fast approaching.

He tangled his fingers through her hair. Moisture sealed their bodies together. *"Sara . . ."* He called out her name and stilled as his own orgasm tore through him. Balancing his weight on his arms, Mitch lay on top of her with his chest rising and falling in an erratic pattern. His lips closed over hers for a soft, tender kiss. Everything in her reached out to him. He stayed inside her for a long time, until his cock grew flaccid and slipped out.

Mitch inched back and discarded his condom. He rolled to his side and tugged her along with him. When their eyes met, it triggered a craving she couldn't sate.

He angled his head, his gaze going to the sexy toys she'd purchased. "So I take it you had this seduction planned all along." She could hear the pleasure in his voice.

"I think we already established that I'm a wild, *wanton* woman, Mitch."

"Who wants to be tied up and spanked," he added, humor edging his voice.

Chuckling softly, she asked, "Are you making fun of me?"

"Hell, no. I just never met a woman as open and uninhibited as you. And it's not every day a woman asks me to tie her up and spank her." He dropped a kiss onto her mouth.

"Not every day?" she asked.

A slow lazy grin tugged at his lips. "Nope. More like every second day."

Sara laughed and swatted him, loving the easy, playful intimacy between them.

"There you go again, hitting me. Keep it up and I'll just have to punish you," he said, humor in his voice.

She batted her lashes, playing along. "That's what I'm counting on." When he chuckled, Sara snuggled tighter into his arms. Mitch laced his fingers through hers. It felt so good to be held by him.

Eyes heavy, and feeling drained, she was overtaken by fatigue. She rested her head against his chest and listened to his heart beat. They remained quiet for a long time, both lost in their thoughts.

Mitch broke the silence. "When do you go back?"

"A week and a half."

"Back to writing cow-tipping stories."

She shrugged. "I guess."

"Have you ever thought about staying in Chicago and finding a job here?"

"About a million times an hour." She tipped her head to look at him.

His eyes were wide, filled with intrigue and delight. "Really?" he asked.

"Yeah. It's my dream to write for *Entice* magazine."

He tossed her his trademark panty-soaking smile. "Hmmm."

"What?"

He crushed her body to his, his fingers marching over her arm. "If you move here, it will give us a chance to explore all our fantasies."

She scoffed and rolled her eyes, teasing him. "Like that's an incentive."

"You didn't happen to pick up a little French maid outfit to go
with that paddle and satin rope, did you?"

"You are so bad." She whacked him. Hard.

He grasped her hands and pinned them to her sides. "Now you're
really asking to be tied and spanked," he said, his lips hovering over hers.

Sara freed one hand, slid it down his body, and sheathed his cock.
"I think we'll have to postpone that until you recharge." When she
chuckled, Mitch smothered the sound with his mouth. After they
shared a long, lingering kiss, Mitch packaged her against his body, her
head resting on his chest. Silence reigned once again as they both went
back to their own thoughts. Sara stifled a yawn, exhaustion easing
itself into her bones.

Mitch grabbed their beach towels and covered them. A short
while later, she listened to his breathing level out and deepen. She
glanced up at his handsome face and smiled, waiting patiently while
he slept and recharged. Soon enough she'd wake him, because, as far
as she was concerned, this night was far from over. There were many
more fantasies to fulfill, a few toys to be used, and one spankable ass
in need of a firm firefighter palm.

"Mitch."

He inched open his eyes, still half asleep. "Hmmm?"

"It's time."

"Time for what, babe?" he murmured, automatically reaching out
beside him. Disappointment settled in his stomach when his hand
came up empty.

"Time for you to get up."

He rolled toward her voice, and his cock brushed against the pool lounger. He glanced down at his erection. "I already am up."

"Precisely." Her sultry tone snapped him to attention.

His head shot up. "Sweet fuck," he whispered, his body rocketing to life. Mouth gaping open, he took in the erotic vision before him. Dressed only in a pair of firefighter pants, with the suspenders covering her nipples, Sara held a rope out to him. He spotted a paddle and a few other sex toys on the shelf beside her. Holy hell. She really did have a night of fantasy sex planned for him. And dammit, who was he to disappoint her? When he looked at the toys again, his mind raced with delicious ideas, and he knew he had every intention of playing his fantasies out to the fullest.

Mitch blinked and pinched the bridge of his nose. "Either I'm dreaming or you just tapped into my fantasies."

Sara offered him a sultry smile, her glance roaming over his naked body. "You're still dreaming, Mitch. It's your erotic dream, and it's yours to play out any way you like."

He could barely formulate a response. Climbing to his feet, he approached her slowly. "So this is all just a dream?"

She nodded and licked her lips.

"Which means I can do whatever I want to you?" He touched her flesh and felt her quiver. Keeping close, he circled her body, his cock brushing against her pants. He positioned his mouth close to her ear. "I like your costume."

"It's no French maid outfit—"

"It's better." Oh yeah, so much better. The way the suspenders pressed against her nipples made his mouth salivate, and those loose-fitting pants covering all her sexy curves played havoc with his imagination and shook him to the core.

He took the rope out of her hand and stepped behind her. "In my dreams, I have you tied up." He held her hands and tied them together behind her back. Her sharp intake of air thrilled him. Once she was secure, he rubbed his palm over her fine, spankable ass and squeezed. "Very nice," he whispered.

He came back around to stand in front of her. "In my dreams, your legs are always spread." She quickly widened her legs. "Yeah, just like that."

He met her smoldering eyes. Her chest rose and fell as her breathing deepened. "And you're always wet when I come to you." He slid his palms under the suspenders and ran his hands from her shoulders to her pants, his knuckles brushing against her hard nipples. "Are you wet, Sara?"

She grinned. "I'm always wet when you come to me."

That brought a smile to his face. He slipped a hand down her pants and brushed her pussy. "Mmmm, very creamy. Just the way I like it." He nudged her clit and watched the storm brew in her eyes. He loved the way she wanted him.

He could smell her arousal. He pushed his finger inside her pussy, stirring her heat.

"What . . . what else happens in your dreams?" she asked him as she pitched her hips forward.

"Well, first we kiss because I can never get enough of your mouth." He pressed his lips to hers, reveling in her sweet taste. She drew his tongue into her mouth and sucked it. His cock throbbed, aching to move in and take its place. He raked his thumb over her clit and felt her shudder. "Sometimes I let you come right away. Other times I like to tease it out of you."

She was so goddamn close to coming right now, it amazed him. He pulled one suspender and then let go. It snapped against her nipple. Heat flooded her cheeks and her eyes widened, erotic delight apparent in her expression.

Aching to claim her, to taste her—every fucking inch of her— just like he did in his fantasies, he covered his finger in her cream and walked behind her. Slipping his hand down the back of her pants, he pulled open her ass cheeks and coated her puckered opening. She tightened.

"Mitch—"

"Shhh . . ." he whispered. "You never protest in my dreams."

"But—"

"I *know* how to take care of you, Sara." Her words fell off when he unhooked her suspenders and let her pants fall to her ankles. He grabbed the paddle and smacked her ass.

"Oh. My. God." Her whole body quaked.

He pitched his voice low. "See, baby, I know what you like." Brushing his lips over the back of her neck, he lowered himself to his knees, inhaling the scent of her skin. Heat exploded inside him when she shook beneath his touch. It took all his effort not to back her up against the wall and sink into her. He whacked her ass again, leaving a bright red mark.

"That stings," she cried out, clearly enjoying it. Her head rolled to the side. "Tell me more about your dreams," she coaxed, her words coming out breathlessly.

He hit her a third time, then dropped the paddle. "You always like my tongue, no matter where I put it."

With the soft blade of his tongue, he caressed her ass cheeks, working his way to the center, giving her time to get used to the new feeling. He reached between her legs to get more cream and knew she was damn close to erupting.

"Sometimes you come when I do this." After generously slathering her cream on her puckered opening, he ran his tongue between her cheeks. As he pillaged her with his mouth, he reached around and pinched her clit. Her aroused scent curled around him and his body grew needy. Desperate to sink into her heat, his cock pulsed, his balls constricted.

She fisted her fingers and moved restlessly against him. He continued with his gentle assault, stabbing her sweet hole with his tongue. "That's it," he whispered, encouraging her to let go. He worked his tongue over her rim harder, making her delirious with pleasure. A moan caught in her throat. Her breath came in a rush. When she pushed her ass into his face, he felt her give herself over to him.

"That . . . that . . . feels . . ." Her body convulsed with pleasure. Her hot juice dripped down her legs.

Not quite done with her ass, he slid up her back and came around to face her. He reached for one of her sex toys. A small silver bullet with a remote control meant for ass fucking.

"In my dreams you like it when I fuck your hot little ass and cunt at the same time."

She began panting. "Mitch, I bought that for you."

He gave her a lopsided grin. "I kind of thought so."

"The clerk suggested it," she rushed out. "She said her man loves it. I thought it might have been one of your fantasies, too."

He circled her and rubbed her cream all over her puckered back passage. His lips caressed her neck. He murmured into her ear. "But this is my dream, and you are mine to do with as I please. So I'm using it on you."

After pulling her cheeks wide open he pressed the silver bullet to her opening and gently eased it in. "You're so tight, baby. Spread for me." Once he pushed pass the ringed opening, she took the toy in easily. He groaned low and deep as it disappeared inside her.

With the little bullet in place he turned it on to vibrate and captured Sara by the waist. He backed her up against the wall.

She swallowed hard, drew a labored breath, and shot him a smoldering look. "I've never felt anything like that before, Mitch."

The sudden urgent need to fuck her overtook him. Lust, need, and desire churned inside him. He grabbed a condom and rolled it on. Without releasing the rope binding her hands, he lowered himself to the floor and pulled her on top of him.

"Fuck me, Sara." He could hear the urgency and emotion in his voice. He widened her pussy lips as she impaled herself on him. Jesus, she was tight. When he grabbed her hips, she began riding him, hard and fast, her head whipping from side to side, her wet cunt massaging his shaft. The position allowed him to watch her full breasts bounce up and down.

This was better than any dreams he'd ever enjoyed.

As he drove his cock into her, he could feel the buzzing little bullet in her ass. He'd never quite felt anything like that, either. It damn near drove him to the brink in record time. Blood pounded through his veins, and his hunger for her made him quake. He drove into her, seeking more than just her heat.

His hands bit into her flesh as they indulged in each other's body, her ripples of pleasure urging him on. "That's it, Sara. Come all over my cock."

She threw her head back and bit down on her bottom lip. "Mitch," she cried out. The second her hot cream covered his shaft, a growl ripped through him and he released deep inside her. She collapsed on top of him, their wet bodies melting together, both of them gasping for air.

After a long moment he turned off the vibrator and eased it out of her. Sated from the best sex he'd ever had, he untied her hands, carried her to the inflated lounger, and curled in beside her.

"Mitch."

She sounded so drowsy. He brushed her hair back. "Yeah, babe? What is it?"

"It's not time to wake up, is it?" Her breathing leveled off and he could tell she needed rest before they fucked again.

"No, it's not time to wake up, Sara. Not even close."

"Good."

As he tightened his arms around her, emotions overtook him. Their sex was perfect, she was perfect, everything was perfect—and by God, if he had anything to do with it, they'd never wake up from this incredible fantasy.

FIVE

ara looked so beautiful and peaceful that Mitch hated to disturb her, but he didn't want her to open her eyes and think he'd run out on her either. Last night, after she'd fulfilled his fantasy, they had both fallen into an exhausted slumber, and he hadn't roused until his cell phone rang and work beckoned.

As he drifted off last evening, with her tucked securely in his arms, he'd reflected on the emotions she brought out in him. Mitch had had every intention of grabbing a short nap and then telling her exactly how he felt, praying she reciprocated his feelings. For the first time in his life, he felt that a woman had fallen for the man beneath the uniform. Now he was ready to lay it on the line to find out for sure.

"Sara, I have to go."

She blinked up at him. When her eyes focused, a wide smile split her mouth and it brought warmth to his darkest corners. She glanced at his body, then down at her own. Her hand snaked out and cradled his cheek. "Hey, you're overdressed."

He closed his hand over hers and said around the lump forming in his throat, "Hey, babe, I have to go. I'm needed at the station."

She propped herself up and glanced around. "What time is it?"

"It's early. Why don't you go back to sleep and I'll come find you after my shift?"

"Now that sounds like a great plan to me."

Mitch dropped a kiss on her cheek and crept from the pool house. With morning fast approaching, he had to check in, which gave him little time to get home, shower, and get to work.

Over an hour later, Mitch made his way to the firehouse. All was quiet, which suited him just fine. Not only did he need time to sort through his thoughts, but he needed to figure out a way to talk to Nick, especially after Nick had warned him to stay away from Sara.

Sara . . .

He couldn't get her out of his head. She'd taken up residency in his heart and unearthed things in him he thought he'd buried. No woman had ever considered his needs and desires before. The fact that she wanted to fulfill his fantasy, and had gone and purchased all the sexy props to do it, filled his heart with love.

And if Mitch got his way, which he had every intention of doing, the two of them would have many more nights in each other's arms fulfilling fantasies.

Right now he needed to compose himself and get his mind on the job. But first he allowed himself one more minute to think about Sara. Reveling in the heated memories of the way she felt in his arms, and the way she opened her body to him. He licked his lips, recalling the taste of her mouth, her breasts, and the valley between her legs. His whole body quaked with the need to sink into her again and again. His cock tightened in anticipation; pleasure resonated through him. He couldn't wait to hold her again, to reacquaint his lips with her body.

He glanced at the clock. Damn, it was going to be a hell of a long day.

Hours later, after a grueling afternoon, Mitch had finally finished for the day and set out in search of Sara. Without preamble, he made his way to Nick's house and hurried up the walkway. His heart leapt when Sara opened the door before he had a chance to knock, as though she'd been waiting for him.

Dressed in a gray jogging suit, a notepad in hand, she looked absolutely gorgeous. Of course it didn't matter what she wore—she'd always be beautiful to him.

Her eyes brightened when they locked on his. Her hand went to her hair to tame a few wayward curls. "Hi."

Mitch stepped in and closed the door behind him. He crushed her body to his and anchored them hip to hip. Sara shivered in his arms. His heart skipped. Damn he loved the way she reacted to his touch. "Where is everyone?"

"Running errands."

"Are we alone?"

She nodded.

"Good, we need to talk." Without giving her time to speak, he grabbed her hand and guided her to the kitchen table. While his heart raced, he gestured for her to sit, but before she had a chance, the sound of a ringing phone in the other room gained their attention.

She crinkled her nose. "That's my cell. I'd better grab it. It could be a wedding emergency."

Mitch blew out a patient breath and nodded in understanding. Sara dropped her notepad on the table and disappeared around the corner. Mitch sat, planted his elbows on the table, and propped his chin on his palms. His gaze went to Sara's notepad.

When he saw the title—Fantasy Men in Uniforms—he furrowed his brow. A wave of unease curled around him.

He picked it up, narrowed his eyes, and scanned the paper. He read it once and then a second time. As he took in the words "*Entice,*" "*magazine,*" "*Mitch,*" "*research,*" "*no strings,*" and "*fantasy-inspired nights,*" his stomach plummeted, his mouth went dry, and his bliss disappeared.

What the hell was going on?

As he scanned the words a third time, reality hit hard. His blood ran cold, penetrating his bones.

Jesus H. Christ. He was an idiot. A total fucking idiot.

How could he have allowed himself to believe there was more to their relationship, believe that she saw him as something more than a fantasy man in uniform?

He stood with such force, his chair scraped across the wood floor and toppled over. Just then Sara rounded the corner. His gaze flew to her face. Her jaw dropped when she saw the pained look in his eyes.

Stomach knotted, and heart pounding, he held the notebook up and cocked his head. "So this is all I am to you? Research?"

When she linked her fingers together and hesitated, he tossed the notepad back onto the table. He huffed and shook his head. "And here I thought you were different from the rest. I thought you were a woman who could finally see the man beneath the uniform. I guess I was wrong." With that, he turned on the ball of his foot and stormed past her.

Sara angled her body when Mitch sailed by her. As she watched Mitch storm toward the door, Cassie's warning words suddenly came rushing back to the surface: *He's a playboy, a woman's fantasy. It's the way he likes it.*

Sara's mind raced, piecing together Mitch's words and Cassie's warning. She drew a quick breath as understanding dawned in small increments. It wasn't so much that it was the way Mitch liked it—it was more that it was what he expected from women.

And now, after reading her notes, he concluded that she was like every other woman. Wanting him for the fantasy only and nothing else. But the fact that he was angry with her proved that he cared about her, that it was more than just about fulfilling fantasies, didn't it? That was enough to prompt her into action. She grabbed the notebook from the table.

In her calmest voice, she called out to him, "You didn't flip the page."

Mitch stopped midstride and turned to face her. "What?"

She crossed the floor to meet him. "You didn't flip the page, and I think you should."

Jaw set, features hardened, he stared at her. "Why?"

"I can't deny that I called the Hot Line in search of a hot-topic story and in search of a hot night with you. I'm sure your reasons for answering the phone were the same. A hot night of sex."

He widened his stance and drove his hands into his pockets. "I answered because it was *you*, Sara. *You*. I knew you were only in it for the fantasy, and I was going to give it to you, but deep down I think I always wanted more. And after last night, I thought we connected."

She pressed the notepad into his stomach. "You see, Mitch, I couldn't write the article about fantasy men in uniforms like I wanted. Because the more I got to know you, the more I realized there was more to you than just a fantasy." She gestured toward the paper. "Read it for yourself. I started writing, and all I could get out was how amazing you were." She poked her finger into his chest. "*You*. Mitch Adams the man, not Mitch Adams the fantasy man in firefighter gear."

Conflicting emotions flickered in his eyes before a relieved rush of air exploded from his lungs. "Are you serious?"

When she nodded and offered him a warm, loving smile, his face softened. He crushed his hands through her hair and drew her to him, angling her head. His voice hitched. "Sara, you have no idea how happy I am to hear you say that. I came here today with the intentions of telling you how crazy I am about you, that I want to see where this relationship goes. I know you hate writing for the *Trenton Gazette*, so I wanted to ask you to stay here with me and together we can come up with a fresh, exciting story that *Entice* will love."

Her heart leapt when she gazed at him. There was so much emotion in his eyes that it bored into her soul and stole her next breath. Oh God! She recognized that look. It was the same look she'd seen Cassie give Nick at the restaurant.

He dipped his head, shaky hands touching her all over. His mouth closed over hers. "We need to talk to Nick," he murmured into her mouth.

"Why?" she asked.

"He warned me to stay away from you." His kiss deepened; his hands slipped between her legs. "He said you were a small-town girl and he didn't want me to hurt you. I'd never hurt you, Sara."

As soon as the words left his mouth, the door swung open and Nick and Cassie walked in. "What the hell—"

Mitch broke the kiss and turned to face Nick. After seeing the look on Nick's face, Mitch held his hands up in a halting motion. "Let me explain."

Nick folded his arms. "It had better be good," he said.

Even though Nick had warned Mitch to stay away from her, and his tense body language indicated anger, Sara noticed a somewhat self-satisfied smirk on Nick's face. What the hell was that all about?

"Sara, come here," Cassie piped in.

Mitch widened his stance and tightened his hold on Sara. "Hold it, you two." Sara watched in mute fascination at how Mitch held his ground. He really was her knight in shining armor or, rather, her knight in—and out of—firefighter gear.

"Listen, I'm crazy about her and I have no intentions of hurting her."

Nick's gaze went from Mitch to Sara to Cassie, back to Mitch again. "What?"

"That's right," Mitch said. "I'm crazy about her."

Sara wrapped her arms around his waist.

He's crazy about me!

Nick shook his head in bewilderment, but Sara caught the smug look on Nick's face before he quickly wiped it away. "I think I need to sit down. What the hell has been going on around here for the last few days?"

"What happened," Sara said, her heart overflowing with joy, "is that while you two have been busy with your wedding preparations, I discovered this bad ass really is just a softie at heart."

"Hey," Mitch said, chest puffing out, "cool it, Sara. I have a reputation to keep."

Sara laughed and hugged him tighter. She shot Cassie a look. "You were right, Cassie. You said when I met the right guy, I'd know it. Mitch is that guy, and I know it." She tipped her chin to glance at Mitch. Impatience to hold him, kiss him, and touch him again seeped through her. "Let's go somewhere we can be alone."

Mitch winked at her. "Shall I bring my gear?"

Sara winked back. "You don't need it." Leaving Nick standing there shaking his head in total bewilderment, and Cassie grinning like mad, Sara grabbed Mitch's hand and started toward the back door. Before they could escape to share a private moment together, Dean stepped into the front entrance.

His glance went from Sara to Mitch to Nick, who'd propped himself on the arm of a nearby chair, jaw gaping in awe.

"What's going on?" Dean asked.

Sara glanced at Dean, her gaze panning over the firefighter insignia on his T-shirt.

Mitch grabbed her chin and turned her to face him. "Hey, over here." He scowled at her. "You're mine and mine alone." He closed his hand over hers, dragging her to him.

She grinned, loving how he felt so possessive of her. Loving the way he'd fight for her. "On second thought, maybe you should bring your gear."

"Oh yeah?"

She arched one brow. "Not only do we have more fantasies to explore, but if I'm going to move here and work for *Entice*, I'll need all the inspiration I can get to come up with a new and unique twist for my article."

He laughed and shook his head. "Dear God, what have I created?"

With a seductive sway of her hips, she said, "Come with me, and I'll show you."

SIREN

ONE

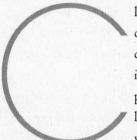lipboard tucked under her arm, Jenna crinkled her brow in concentration and cataloged all the sexy undergarments taking over Cassie's living room. A few days previous, Cassie had asked Jenna to host a lingerie party for all her friends, some of whom just happened to be major players in the fashion industry, and Jenna had been working double time to make things perfect. If things went according to plan, and Cassie's friends were impressed with her latest designs, it could lead to many new and profitable contacts.

Of course, what Nick and Cassie hadn't expected was that every time they entered their living room they'd be bombarded with thongs and negligees. Not that Nick seemed too despondent over that, Jenna mused.

She could hear Cassie in the kitchen trying to usher sexy firefighter Dean Beckman out the back door before the guests arrived at the front. Jenna sighed in relief, thankful Dean wouldn't be around to catch the sexy show.

The last thing Jenna wanted was Dean in close proximity while she showed off her new Siren line. The man turned her into a jittery starstruck teenager and caused her skin to flush with heat and desire without him even trying. Not only were her reactions to his nearness embarrassing at best, but she was certain all her friends had caught her lusting after him a time or two. Who could blame her, though? The guy had a body that would put any male model to shame.

Suddenly, the provocative mental image of a hard-bodied Dean Beckman strutting his stuff in a pair of bun-hugging boxers from her male catalog rushed through her mind.

Jenna let her thoughts wander, picturing a naked Dean standing before her, tall, hard, lethal, and hers for the taking. Her mind raced, as she visualized herself in a barely there teddy from her bestselling collection, and Dean slowly lowering the straps until the skimpy material slipped from her body and pooled at her feet.

Libidinous slut that she was, Jenna bit back a moan as she indulged in her fantasy a second longer—a fantasy that had been invading her thoughts, even in sleep, for the past week or so. Her hand went to her throat, her legs widened involuntarily. She pictured Dean sinking to his knees, his mouth going to her breast, the tip of his tongue making a slow pass over her engorged nipple while his hands slipped between her thighs, climbing higher and higher until he reached her passion-drenched pussy. With the utmost expertise, he'd dip his head, inch open her swollen pink lips, and stroke her with the soft blade of his tongue the way she'd always longed to be stroked. . . .

Oh, my!

As lust rose to the surface and clamored for attention, Jenna swallowed. Hard. If only she had the nerve to live out one of her nightly fantasies with the sexy firefighter from Station 419.

Trying diligently to shake off a burst of heat that suddenly prowled through her, Jenna worked to rein in her lust and gave herself a reality check.

Of course, she couldn't expect Dean to be different from any other guy she'd slept with. The few men she'd slipped between the sheets with cared only about their own needs, their own pleasures. As long as they were inserting object A into slot B, they were happy. No man had ever had the burning desire to take charge of her pleasures, or to drop to his knees and lavish her with undivided attention until she quaked and climaxed in euphoria. Heck, just because she wanted to engage in sex with the lights off didn't mean she wasn't interested in an earth-shattering orgasm, too. She was, after all, a woman with needs.

And fantasies . . .

Blocking all thoughts of men, one in particular, Jenna turned her attention back to the task at hand. She had to ensure the display was arranged perfectly before she unveiled her latest designs.

As Jenna took stock of her new line of red-hot lingerie, she made one final adjustment to the Siren display, making sure each piece in the arrangement was visually as well as aesthetically pleasing to her clientele. Once she was finished, she stood back and smiled.

There, that was better.

"Are you still at it?" Megan asked, sticking her head around the corner.

Jenna steepled her index fingers and tapped them on her lips, continuing her examination. "I just want everything to be perfect before the show begins."

"Stop fussing. Everything *is* perfect," Megan said. With Cassie's black cat, Misty, curling around her feet, Megan stepped farther into the room and glanced at the sexy assortment of lingerie, all arranged by color, style, and line. Under her breath she whispered, "Can you say 'obsessive'?"

Jenna swatted her. "Hey, I heard that."

Megan made a face. Her cute little nose crinkled. "At least it's better than what Sara is calling you from the kitchen."

Jenna folded her arms across her chest, angled her head, and humored her friend. "Let me guess: anal, extreme, fanatical, stubborn, obstinate . . ."

O-kay . . . Megan could stop her anytime now.

Blue eyes sparkling, Megan chuckled and tucked a short blond curl behind her ear. "Yeah, that, and that you need to get laid."

Jenna rolled her eyes heavenward. "I do not need to get laid." Okay, okay, so maybe she *did* need to get laid. Otherwise why would she be drooling like a teething toddler whenever Dean breached her personal space? Heck, who was she kidding? He didn't even have to be in the same room. Just thinking about him had her hormones dancing to the Macarena. Unfortunately, her libido would have to wait. Right now she had a show to think about.

Jenna turned her thoughts to the night ahead. She knew the purpose of the impending event was twofold. One, it was Cassie's way of helping her build clientele and securing new contacts before she expanded her business, and two, Cassie was in search of the perfect negligee for her wedding night, which happened to be a little over a week away.

Jenna glanced at her watch and frowned. Panic mushroomed inside her.

Megan furrowed her brow, concern evident in her big blue eyes. "What is it?"

"I'm just wondering what's keeping Kate."

"Kate?"

"You know, Kate Saunders, Cassie's friend, the model."

Megan nodded. "Oh, right, I remember. The chicky who clung to Dean like dandruff a couple of nights ago down at the Hose."

Tamping down a sudden burst of jealousy, Jenna sauntered to the big bay window and peered out. "What could be keeping her?" she murmured under her breath, twisting back around to face Megan.

"Stop biting your lip and relax. She'll be here," Megan assured her.

"She's over an hour late and the guests are due to arrive any minute. I still have to size and fit her body with the line and style that will best accentuate her shape."

Always one to say the first thing that popped into her head, Megan said, "What shape?" She gave an unladylike snort and waved a dismissive hand. "She's a model. She has no shape. And I really don't know why you had to hire someone in the first place."

Since her friends were always trying to get her to overcome her insecurities, Jenna gave her usual spiel. "An artistic display is far more inspiring, and since my clothes aren't going to strut around the room by themselves, I needed to hire a model."

Megan scoffed. "Smart-ass." She picked up a sexy red thong, walked to the full-length mirror, and held it to her hips. "That's not what I mean and you know it. Why don't you just model the line yourself?" Megan turned sideways, checking herself from all angles. "With all your curves, you have a better body for modeling lingerie than those celery sticks you hire anyway."

Just then the door bell chimed and a noise inside the kitchen gained Jenna's attention. She let out a breath she hadn't realized she was holding. She shot Megan a smile, thankful that she didn't have to rehash their same old argument. How many times did she have to tell her friends that parading her scantily clad body in front of other men and women ranked right up there with injecting herself with the Ebola virus? Heck, who was she kidding? She would choose the Ebola hands down.

Unlike her sexy, athletic friend, Megan, who was confident enough to take a strength training—pole dancing class with a group of other women, Jenna preferred to keep things low-key.

Jenna knew that for all appearances she was a bold, confident business woman. One who'd taken her small town in Iowa by storm when she designed her own clothes and opened her first boutique. Unfortunately, even though she'd shed weight, lost the braces, and discovered contacts, on the inside she was still that chubby little girl who hid behind baggy shirts and droopy drawers. The nickname the boys had given her back in grade school, the same name that had followed her through high school, rushed through her mind. Instead of Jenna Powers, they'd called her "Jenna Bow Wow-ers." It didn't take a brain surgeon to figure out what "bow wow" stood for.

As Jenna made her way into the kitchen, she walked past the floor-length mirror and shot herself a glance. She tossed her long chestnut hair over her shoulders and narrowed her green eyes for a closer inspection. Tonight she'd abandoned her loose-fitting casual clothes and opted for a formfitting business suit, because she wanted to project a professional image. Some might see a tall, curvaceous woman, one with confidence and style, but Jenna saw something entirely different. She could never dispel the image that had been ingrained into her over the years. And at twenty-nine years of age, she assumed nothing or no one could ever change that.

She stepped into the kitchen and scanned the room, noting that Dean was nowhere to be found. She also noted that he'd left behind his unique signature scent—one that turned her knees to pudding and made her feel all hot and bothered inside. She inhaled, letting it curl through her bloodstream, letting it arouse her libido.

Before she did something stupid, like moan, Jenna turned her attention to the waiflike model leaning against the kitchen counter, Cassie by her side, a concerned look on her face. Jenna glanced at how the girl was clutching her stomach and stopped dead in her tracks. Oh, no! This was not good. Not good at all.

"Are you okay?" Jenna asked, stepping close enough to press her palm to the woman's forehead.

"I'm Kate," she said, thrusting a wobbly hand out. "Kate Saunders. Sorry I'm late. I'm not usually late," she rushed on, her glossy eyes unsteady, and her face growing whiter and pastier by the second.

"Kate, you don't look so good."

"I went to a dinner party last evening and I think I might have eaten something that didn't agree with me." Kate swallowed and glanced around the room, panic apparent in her expression. "Um, Cassie, can you help me to the bathroom?"

Cassie set her glass of wine on the table and grabbed Kate by the elbow. "Let's go." A few seconds later, Jenna cringed as the sounds of one very sick Kate reached her ears.

"I guess that settles it then," Megan said, plunking herself into a chair next to Sara, who had a wide grin on her face despite the wretched sounds coming from the bathroom. Of course, Sara hadn't stopped smiling since she'd begun living out her fantasies with Mitch Adams a few days previous.

Jenna's gaze went from Sara to Megan. "Settles what?"

Megan rolled a shoulder. "You're going to have to model the line yourself after all."

Dread washed through Jenna. She narrowed her gaze. "Are you insane?"

"Nope, just a carrier," Megan said, chuckling. She poured a glass of wine and held it out to Jenna. "I don't think you have a choice. Guests will be arriving any minute and there is no time to call in another model."

Jenna accepted the glass, took a much-needed sip, and with a casual nonchalance that she didn't feel, said, "Forget it. I'll just showcase the pieces from the racks."

Megan wagged her finger. "What was that you said earlier, something about an artistic display being more inspiring? Look at it this way, Jenna. If the owner/designer won't wear her own line of clothes, why should they? Are you going to risk your new line flopping because you don't want to put that gorgeous body of yours in a negligee?"

As much as Jenna hated to admit it, Megan was right. Proper presentation was essential for full effect. And if she wanted to ensure contacts and create a buzz in the industry before she officially launched . . .

Jenna suddenly had a lightbulb moment. "Why don't you do it for me, Megan? You get to keep the clothes you wear," she said, adding incentive.

"Can't. I'm on my period and I'm bloated." Megan slunk down lower in her chair and rubbed her stomach for effect.

Jenna cast Sara a pleading look. "Sara?"

Sara threw her arms up in the air. "Wouldn't you know it? I have my period, too. I'd like to help you out, Jenna, but I feel like a big cow." She puffed out her cheeks and mimicked Megan's actions. "Plus, I really think you're the best candidate for the job."

Jenna folded her arms and thinned her lips, casting her friends a sharp glance. All those Nancy Drew books she'd read as a child only added to her suspicious nature. She took a moment to connect the dots. (A) a sick model. (B) both of her friends with their periods. And (C) both of them insisting she model the line herself.

Not that they were responsible for Kate's sudden bout of food poisoning, but still . . .

"What are you two up to?"

"Nothing," they said in unison. "Nothing at all."

Megan hopped up. "Come on, Jenna. I'll help you get dressed."

"And I'll read the cue cards while you model the lingerie," Sara piped in cheerily.

Before Jenna could protest, Megan dragged her into the living room. "Come on. It'll be fun."

Fun?

Skating at Rockefeller Center on New Year's Eve was fun. Swimming with the dolphins at Sea World was fun. Reaching an earth-shattering orgasm with a drop-dead-gorgeous firefighter was fun, not that Jenna knew firsthand, but she could only imagine. But this . . . this modeling stint, not so much fun. Heck, getting struck down by a bolt of lightning actually sounded a hell of a lot more fun to her.

"How about these?" Megan asked, twirling a provocative pair of panties around her finger.

Jenna held her hands up, palms out. "Megan, I don't know about this."

"Come on, Jenna. Just picture the audience naked. It will relax you."

Jenna rolled her eyes heavenward and planted her hands on her hips. "What are you, twelve?"

Ignoring her, Megan said, "Live a little. Have an adventure." She grabbed another pair of skimpy panties. Her eyes sparkled as she examined them. "Ooh, how about these?"

"Whoa. Hold it right there, Megan. Those panties are far too skimpy for me to parade around in."

Megan's grin turned wicked. She held the panties out. "So you'll do it then?"

In spite of herself, Jenna laughed. "Yeah, right after I hang myself."

After giving Nick a lift to the liquor mart, Dean pulled into his friend's circular driveway and killed the engine. He reached for his door handle, but a movement behind the big bay window gained his attention and stopped him cold. The sight of one very curvy, luscious woman—the same woman who'd had his libido in an uproar since she'd arrived in Chicago—drew his focus and rattled him more than dice in a Yahtzee cup.

Jenna.

His thoughts scattered like dust in the wind and his body grew needy at the mere sight of her. Earlier in the evening, after catching a glimpse of her lush backside as she leaned over a stack of lingerie, he thought he'd go mad with the need to fuck her. Ever since he'd set eyes on her, his mind had been swimming with naughty, delicious ideas. Ideas like how good it would feel to cradle that magnificent ass of hers while she stood before him in one of her most daring, most provocative pieces.

Dean sucked in a sharp breath and shifted in his seat, his raging hard-on causing him a great deal of discomfort as it fought to break free from its zippered cage.

Something about Cassie's friend from Iowa had reminded him

that all work and no play had made for some very interesting—and very scandalous—fantasies of late.

Jesus, what he'd do to see her in that sexy red-hot teddy from her new line. What was it she called it again? Oh yeah, the Siren line. Siren, all right. One glimpse of that barely there lingerie had all his sirens going off without warning. He could only imagine how he'd react if he actually saw the little spitfire in that sexy getup. He'd likely blow a fuse and cause a citywide blackout.

Not that he ever expected to see her wearing the red teddy, however. Jenna had barely spared him a glance since their first meeting. Not only did she take to him like a cat to water, but she also went out of her way to avoid him whenever possible. The sexy siren always seemed so agitated when he was around, like his nearness was right up there with a bee swarming by her.

Dean didn't ordinarily let his libido rule his actions, but the thought of seeing that luscious body of hers all decked out in her professional attire, while he imagined, or rather fantasized, about what she wore under it, propelled him into motion.

He twisted around, reached into the backseat, and grabbed two bottles of wine. "I'll help you carry these in." Even though Cassie had ushered him out the door earlier, warning him that the show was for married couples and industry professionals only, Megan and Sara seemed to have other plans. He wasn't sure what they were up to, or why they'd asked him to stop back later, but he sure as hell wanted to find out.

Nick shot him a knowing glance and snatched the bottles from his hands. "If I let you through that door, Cassie will have my balls."

Dean snorted and slapped Nick on the back. "I hate to break it to you, Nick, but she already has your balls."

Nick slapped Dean in return. "Don't worry, pal. Maybe an intelligent, sexy woman will want your balls someday, too." The crazy son of a bitch flashed a smart-assed grin, his voice full of laughter.

Dean held his palms up. "Every girl I've ever been with has tried to *crush* my balls."

Nick's grin broadened. "Maybe they just weren't the right girls for you."

"Maybe, maybe not," Dean said, rolling one shoulder. "Either way I'm off relationships." He ran through his motto: Keep it light, keep it simple, keep it sexy. Casual sex he could handle, but relationships, forget about it.

Nick reached for the door handle, but before he climbed from the passenger seat, he said, "One of these days you'll get it, Dean. You'll know what I'm talking about. The right woman will come along and you'll be down on your knees in record time."

Dean had no problem going down on his knees. In fact he loved going down on his knees. As long as it had nothing to do with a marriage proposal.

"You have no idea what you're talking about," Dean said, shaking his head adamantly. "I'd rather take matters into my own hands than be shackled to the old ball and chain." Grinning, he rubbed his palms together, emphasizing his point. "No woman is going to run my life and dictate my every movement." He'd had enough of that possessive behavior from Kate Saunders, the model Cassie had set him up with months ago. Even though they'd broken up, she still hung out at the Hose and clung to him like dryer lint. The truth was he had more important things on his plate, like finishing his psychology thesis if he wanted to move beyond active duty to counseling fellow firefighters injured on the job.

Nick cast him a skeptical glance and then took note of the time. "Shit, I gotta go. We're running late and I hate for Cassie to worry."

Groaning, Dean snagged the rest of the bottles from the backseat and murmured, "Talk about pussy-whipped." With little time to spare before he made his way to the station, he climbed from the driver's seat, slipped his keys into his front pocket, and hastily made his way to the back entrance.

They found Cassie standing at the door anxiously awaiting their arrival. Once they stepped inside, she quickly grabbed Nick's hand and ushered him into the living room. "What took you so long? The show is almost over and I need your help to pick out the perfect negligee for our wedding night." She winked at Nick. "Not that it's going to be on long."

Over his shoulder, Nick cast Dean a wry grin. "Now that's what I'm talking about."

Dean threw his head back and laughed out loud. Smart-ass son of a bitch!

After depositing the wine on the counter next to the cheese and fruit trays, Dean popped a strawberry into his mouth and followed Nick into the living room. When he rounded the corner and took in the vision before him, his brain nearly shut down.

Sweet Mother of God!

What he expected to see was Jenna all decked out in her business attire. What he saw instead left him with the inability to form a coherent thought.

Scented candles, strategically placed around the room, gave off a soft, romantic glow and set the stage for seduction. His body began trembling with pent-up need as he watched Jenna parade around the room in a sexy red negligee—the same negligee that had been invading his thoughts for the last few hours.

The silky fabric clung to her flesh like a second skin and show-cased her supple figure to perfection. Unlike the other waiflike girls he'd dated, Jenna was the epitome of lush femininity. Soft, round, and luscious in all the right places. The kind of woman he could take to his bed and keep there forever. Now why in the hell had it taken him so long to figure out just how much he loved a curvy woman?

He bit on his strawberry and momentarily ignored the juice drib-bling down his chin. Craning his neck for a better view of Jenna, he let his gaze wander, taking pleasure in the sight of her luscious, half-naked body. Wavering candlelight bathed her body in a seductive glow and glistened on her flesh. Jesus, the woman had a body made for sex.

With him.

Right here.

Right now.

He swallowed his strawberry and wiped his mouth with the back of his hand. Damn, what he'd do to bite into a ripe berry and drip the sweet nectar all over her perfect body and then lave it clean.

Rosy nipples puckered beneath the thin fabric and drew his focus. Suddenly it took effort to think and breathe. As he devoured her from afar, a rush of sexual energy hit him so hard he faltered backward. Shifting his stance he drove his hands into his pockets and leaned against the doorframe. Without question, she was the most beautiful woman he'd ever set eyes on.

There was nothing he could do to deter his cock from rising to the occasion. A low growl of longing crawled out of his throat and gained the crowd's attention. Jenna angled her body, her gaze brushing over the room. When her green eyes locked on his, she stopped midstride. Her mouth formed an O, but no sound came out. A soft red hue traveled up her neck and colored her cheeks. For a minute he wondered if that sexy red blush had also reached her nipples. He licked his lips, his mouth watering to find out.

Body aching to join with hers, Dean stood there, gauging her reactions, tracking her every movement, thinking about how good she'd feel between his legs.

They stared at each other for a long moment, and then something in her gave. Equal amounts of surprise and pleasure raced through him when Jenna swept her gaze down the length of him, her perusal pausing briefly around the vicinity of his crotch. Holy hell! Her visual caress ignited his blood to near boiling and threw him off guard. Jenna had the ability to set him on fire with just one smoldering look.

He was barely able to leash his control when her pretty tongue snaked out to moisten her plump, red-painted lips.

Mmmm . . . more red. That particular shade was quickly becoming his favorite color.

Dean pulled in a quick breath as Jenna's eyes traveled back up to meet his. In that instant, when their gazes collided, they shared a long heated look—one that screamed of passion, sex, and long, lusty nights.

Sweat collected on his brow and it took every ounce of strength he possessed not to cross that room and ravish her, caveman-style.

As sexual awareness leapt between them, Jenna drew her bottom lip between her teeth and folded her arms over her chest, covering her milky cleavage. Even though her actions said one thing, the unbridled desire burning in the depth of her eyes and the hardening of her nipples told an entirely different story. An X-rated one to be exact.

Out of nowhere a burst of possessiveness rocketed through him and shook him to the core. He cleared his throat, rattled. Where had that come from? He hadn't anticipated how deeply the heat flaring in her eyes would affect him, on all levels. Suddenly his very well-rehearsed motto ran though his mind, but despite that, every instinct in his body warned him that a night of wild sex with Jenna would be anything but casual.

As silence stretched on, his gaze left her face, his body registering every delicious detail as he panned her curves. Chestnut curls were piled high on her head, exposing the length of her long sensuous neck. Dean dragged in a huge breath. That was where he wanted his mouth. Right where her creamy neck melted into her collarbone. Everything in him ached to touch her, to taste her, to fuck her hot little body.

His glance traveled lower and settled at the apex between her bare legs, to the thin scrap of material that barely covered her pussy. He moistened his lips. His nostrils flared. His balls tightened and his cock hardened to the point of pain. He clenched and unclenched his fingers, fighting the natural inclination to cross the room, throw her over his shoulders, and haul her upstairs. His entire body ached to lay her out buffet-style, tug aside that silky pair of panties, and press his hungry mouth over her pussy until she cried out in euphoria.

At that moment, sheer force of will was all that had kept him upright. He needed to get her somewhere private. Fast. Because all he could think about was sinking to his knees—in record time—diving into her sweet cunt and pleasuring her like he'd never pleasured another.

Oh, yeah. Now that was what he was talking about.

TWO

A hush fell over the crowd as Jenna stood stock-still, imagining a hard-bodied Dean standing stark naked in the doorway, sinewy muscles flexed, bronzed flesh glistening with perspiration and desire . . . *for her.*

"Damn you, Megan," she whispered under her breath while she visualized the crowd naked. Well, not the whole crowd, just one man in particular, actually.

Moisture pooled between her thighs as her lascivious body beckoned Dean's from across the room. Although she tried to stay focused on the task at hand, the man simply drove her to distraction. She became totally preoccupied by his blatant masculinity and how he'd managed to turn her from a businesswoman into a libidinous slut in record time.

He stood there, leaning against the doorjamb and looking like sex incarnate. Flustered, Jenna folded her arms across her chest and diligently tried to blink away the delectable image of that lethally honed body stripped naked, hers for the taking.

Shifting from one leg to the other, she bit down on her bottom lip hard enough to draw blood, wondering if he could see her aroused nipples.

With a roomful of people watching, she knew she really needed to pull herself together. But how could she possibly strut around half-naked while her cunt throbbed for the man standing across the room, looking so damn sexy he made her mouth water.

Her eyes traveled up his body and met his glance. He gave her a look that suggested he knew her every little secret, her every fantasy, and he was more than capable of fulfilling them. Her mind raced, conjuring last night's sexual solo act, while she pictured him doing just that.

She swallowed past the lump in her throat, wanting nothing more than for Dean to take her upstairs, turn the lights out, and rid her of the unnecessary barrier of clothes separating skin from skin, while he took charge of her pleasures and indulged in every sinful fantasy she had. A burst of heat coiled through her and warmed her body from the inside out. She could feel color crawl up her neck and stain her cheeks.

A noise in the crowd brought her attention back around to the task at hand. She summoned every ounce of control she had and forced her rubbery legs to move.

With her professional demeanor somewhat back in place, she strived for normalcy and sashayed across the floor, showcasing the sexy red negligee. Unfortunately, knowing Dean was in such close proximity proved too much of a distraction.

Her legs quivered, her skin came alive, and her vision went a little fuzzy around the edges. She exhaled slowly and willed the room to stop spinning. One more piece to go and then she could get the hell out of her revealing new line and back into her business suit before she did something telltale, like throw herself at Dean and really make an ass of herself. The truth was, the man had never even given her a second glance since she arrived in Chicago. Obviously she wasn't even his type. He probably gravitated more toward women with long, lithe figures—toward someone like Kate Saunders, the lingerie model. Undoubtedly she'd be his perfect complement.

Unable to help herself, she cast him another glance. Sensual overload set her loins on fire and gave her pause. When she tried to resume her pace, her legs failed her miserably.

Just when she thought things couldn't get any worse, the room turned upside down. Arms flailing, Jenna shrieked and reached for something concrete to grasp on to, refusing to embarrass herself further. What she didn't expect was for that *something* to be *someone*.

"Whoa," Dean said, catching her before she fell to the floor, tits up. One strong arm slipped around her back and pinned her body to his. Densely packed muscles pressed against her breasts and made her nipples tingle and tighten in euphoric bliss. As she tried to right herself, her hands automatically snaked around his neck like a scarf and her fingers burned as they touched his bronzed flesh.

Cradled in his muscular arms, she shifted, until the two of them were joined hip to hip. She could hardly believe how good his rock-solid body felt wrapped around hers, how good their groins felt mashed together. Suddenly, her mind raced with indecent thoughts. Thoughts like how the only things separating her passion-drenched pussy from his cock were a measly pair of jeans and a thin pair of silky panties. She shuddered involuntarily.

He pitched his voice low, his eyes turned serious, his tone genuine. "Are you okay?"

He dipped his head, bringing his mouth to within a hairbreadth of hers. His warm, strawberry-soaked breath caressed her cheeks and aroused all her senses. With just one tiny flick of her tongue, she'd be able to taste those sensuous lips of his and finally discover if he tasted as good as he looked.

His hand connected with the small of her back, intimately. His warmth seeped under her skin, burning her body from the inside out. She felt like a wild animal in heat, and her skin broke out in moisture, as goose bumps pebbled her flesh.

Jenna knew she needed to disentangle herself before one of the other firefighters in the room grabbed an extinguisher and hosed her down like a carnal beast.

Groaning, she straightened and stepped back, removing herself from the circle of Dean's arms. She drew a rejuvenating breath and worked to banish her lascivious thoughts.

She tried to keep her voice steady but her words spilled out like a leaky faucet. "Yes, yes, I'm fine. Just lost my footing for a second. Must be my new shoes. Thanks. Thanks so much."

Dammit, woman, stop babbling.

She stepped back and wobbled on her heels, completely over-whelmed by his intimate touch and the way it filled her with heat.

Dean made a swift move, gripped her elbow, and hauled her to him, once again joining them chest to chest, hip to hip. His nearness made her breathless and melted her brain cells. Never in her entire life had she felt such powerful sexual stirrings.

His hand slid down her back and hauled her impossibly closer. His corded muscles were bunched, and his gaze flew to her face. She glimpsed a fierce protectiveness in his dark eyes before they softened and locked on hers. "Are you sure you're okay?" When he furrowed his brow with professional concern, her insides went all gooey, like a warm chocolate-chip cookie straight out of the oven. "Maybe I should check that ankle." He brushed a loose strand of hair from her face, and in that instant, something deep in her soul told her that not only was Dean the kind of guy who'd take charge of a woman's pleasure, but he'd be eager for it, too.

Reminding herself she had a captive audience watching her every move, she drew a sharp breath and locked her knees to avoid collapsing.

"I'm okay," she whispered with effort, her hands falling to her sides. She rolled her ankle to prove her point. "Nothing broken."

When Dean leaned forward, his hot breath caressed her neck. Heat and desire ambushed her pussy and scattered her ability to form a coherent thought.

"You sure? You look a little flushed."

The deep timbre of his voice flustered her even more, and his raw virility did the craziest things to her libido. Since a reply was beyond her ability at the moment, she simply nodded her head in response.

He brushed his thumb over her cheek. "I have to go," he said, his voice deep and sensuous. "I'll be at the firehouse."

Why was he telling her that? Damn, if only she could think straight, if only she could breathe. "Okay," she whispered, thrilled to find her voice still functioning.

His grin appeared slowly, looked sexy; his voice was like a rough whisper. "If you have any other emergencies, Jenna, I'm your man."

Emergencies? What other emergencies did he expect her to have? And why was he telling her this? And how could he expect her to think straight when he let her name roll off his tongue like that? Like he was tasting it, savoring it.

She opened her mouth to ask what constituted an emergency and why he thought she was clumsiness personified, but then slammed her mouth shut, answering her own unasked questions. After she'd been stumbling around like a bumbling idiot all week, it was no wonder he expected more emergencies. And with all the candles burning around the room, he probably expected her to set the house ablaze.

With a suggestive edge to his smile, he said, "You know the number." Dean stepped back and disappeared around the corner, out of her line of vision.

Number? What number?

Before she had a chance to comprehend Dean's parting words, Megan stepped up beside her, grabbed her hand, and squeezed. "Are you okay?"

"Yeah." Jenna nodded toward the floor. "It's these damn new shoes. The heel must be loose or something."

Megan grinned like the Cheshire cat. "The shoes, huh?" she asked, tossing her a knowing smile.

Jenna furrowed her brow, annoyed at her friend's perceptiveness. "Yeah, the shoes," she bit out. Without giving Megan the chance to press for more information, Jenna tugged on her hand and said hastily, "Come on. I have one more outfit to go and then I'm going to bury myself under a rock."

"Don't worry about it, Jenna. I think Dean has that effect on all women. Every chicky in that room wanted to be rescued by him." As Jenna ushered her down the hallway, Megan cast a glance over her shoulder. "And all those other women in there are married."

When they stepped into the bedroom, Jenna reached for the last piece in the line, a sexy red bustier, and wondered why she found the thoughts of Dean with another woman so disconcerting.

Damn him.

Blocking those thoughts from her mind, she turned her back to Megan, removed the negligee, and pressed the bustier to her chest. "Can you help me tie this?"

Megan stepped up behind her and tied the silky lace bindings together. Tight.

Jenna took shallow breaths and fidgeted. "Not so tight. I can hardly breathe. Can you loosen it?"

"We don't want it to fall off." Megan stepped back without honoring Jenna's request, despite her labored breaths.

Jenna fanned her face. "We also don't want me to pass out from lack of oxygen."

Megan pulled the door open and, with a wave, urged Jenna to join her in the hall. "Come on, you look gorgeous. One strut around the room and then I'll get you out of this."

Unfortunately, one strut around the room became thirty minutes later. Once Jenna finished the show, and before she had time to get changed, she was bombarded with questions and orders. After covering her body with a long cotton robe, she easily slipped into professional mode and discussed business with other industry professionals.

As the crowd dwindled away, she went in search of her friends, needing desperately to get out of the constricting bustier. She found Megan, Cassie, and Sara in the kitchen, all gathered around the delicious looking fruit and veggie trays.

She crooked her finger at Megan, gesturing for her to follow. "Can you help me?"

Arms wrapped around Nick's waist, Cassie piped in. "Great show, Jenna. We're all going to head to the Hose for a celebration and a game of pool. As soon as you get changed, we'll go."

As Jenna took in the loving couple, a burst of envy whipped through her and caught her off guard. Whoa, that came out of nowhere. Especially since Jenna had never thought about love or long-term relationships before. Okay, so maybe she had thought about it a time or two, or a billion, but she'd always tamped down those thoughts and turned her attention to her career. And the truth was, the self-absorbed men in her small hometown were far from marriage material.

Marshaling her emotions, Jenna crinkled her nose. "You all go ahead. I need to do a bit of paperwork first, and then I'll catch up with you." Jenna turned her attention to Megan and ruffled the lapels of her robe. "Can you help me get out of this thing?"

Megan waved her hand. "Go ahead. I'll be right there." She popped a chocolate-dipped strawberry into her mouth and reached for another. Jenna eyed the fruit tray, her stomach grumbling from hunger, reminding her she'd skipped dinner in her quest to perfect her lingerie display. Not that she could swallow anything now, with the damn bustier still on. It'd likely get stuck in her windpipe.

As Jenna moved down the hallway, her thoughts returned to Dean, and she recalled the way her body had reacted so easily, so readily to him. It amazed her that she craved him with a fierce intensity unlike anything she'd ever felt before. Out of nowhere a shiver prowled through her and tingled all the way to her toes, reminding her she was a woman with needs.

And fantasies . . .

She slipped into the bedroom, secured the door behind her, and flicked on her bedside lamp. In search of a loose-fitting outfit while she awaited Megan's rescue, she rifled through her closet, but the sound of an engine roaring to life in the driveway drew her attention. Jenna took two measured steps toward her window and peered out just in time to see her friends pile into a car and disappear down the driveway.

Eyes wide in disbelief, she banged on the glass pane. "Dammit, Megan." How could her friends have forgotten about her, leaving her there to expire from lack of oxygen?

Jenna hastily crossed the room, grabbed her suitcase, and flung it onto her bed. The old bedsprings grated and made an ungodly sound. She tore through her supplies in search of her trusty sewing kit. If she couldn't get the damn bustier untied, she'd cut herself out of it. After a thorough search turned up nothing, she angled her head and glanced at her nightstand, to the spot where she'd left her cell phone. When her gaze settled on a small white business card, her pulse leapt into gear and her libido roared to life.

Was that what she thought it was?

Surely it wasn't.

She whisked the card off the table, turned it over in her hands, and read the print. She gulped air.

Oh God.

It was.

Her heart picked up tempo, while her palms moistened. As she stroked her thumb over the numbers, her body tightened and burned with desire. Her pussy clenched and throbbed in heated anticipation, urging her to call . . . *the Hot Line.*

A low groan crawled out of her throat, her legs widened involuntarily, and one hand slipped in between, touching the swollen spot that quaked the most, attempting to quell the hot restlessness deep inside her before she shattered into a million tiny pieces. Her hands spent a long time between her legs, working to release the long building tension.

Before she reached an orgasm, her cell phone rang and jolted her back to reality. Startled, she sucked in air, but the constricting lingerie prohibited her from filling her lungs. The bustier hampered her breathing, and frustration welled up inside her, although at the moment she was pretty certain her frustration had more to do with the unanswered ache between her legs than it did with the tight bustier.

Feeling light-headed from lack of oxygen, she picked up her cell phone. "Hello?" She sounded breathless, even to herself.

"Jenna, is that you? You sound odd."

Upon hearing Megan's voice, Jenna blurted out, "Are you trying to kill me?"

"What are you talking about?"

"You tied this bustier so tight I can hardly breathe and then you skipped out without helping me get it off." Jenna could hear pool balls banging in the background. She immediately thought of Dean and the way she'd watched him the previous evening while his strong athletic body circled the pool table. Her body heated in remembrance. Warmth flared through her, and for a brief moment, anger segued to passion.

The sound of Megan's voice brought her attention back around. "Hmmm . . . that definitely sounds like an emergency to me," Megan said, humor evident in her voice.

Jenna sat on the edge of the bed, trying to take deep belly breaths. "It is an emergency. If you don't get over here and get this thing off me, I'm going to pass out."

"Then maybe you should call the Hot Line. I hear they can handle all kinds of . . . *emergencies*."

Her gaze flew to the card as Dean's words came rushing back: *If you have any other emergencies, I'm your man.*

"Megan," Jenna said, her voice raising an octave, "did you plant this card in my room?"

"Card? What card?"

Exasperated, Jenna threw herself back onto her bed. "You set this whole thing up, didn't you?" God, didn't Megan realize the sexy playboy firefighter was completely out of her league?

Megan gasped, as though appalled by her accusation. "Would I do something like that?"

"You are so dead, Megan."

Megan chuckled and lightened the mood. "You want him. He wants you. I'm not seeing any reason for murder here. In fact, I think you'll be thanking me in the morning."

Jenna flew to her feet. "Who said he wanted me?"

"If you weren't so busy drooling over him, and running in the opposite direction all week, you would have noticed that he has the hots for you too, chicky. It's clear to everyone but the two of you that you both want each other."

Jenna gulped in air and paced around the room. "Are you serious?"

"Hell, yeah, I'm serious. Now call that number and you'll see what I'm talking about."

Silence reigned as Jenna took a moment to wrap her brain around things. She perched on the edge of her mattress and sorted through matters. *Dean wanted her?*

"Make the call, Jenna," Megan pressed. "Live a little, have an adventure, get yourself laid. Deep inside you there is a sexy siren just waiting to break free. Let her come out to play before you implode from sexual frustration, and in the morning, I want all the juicy details."

The last time Jenna listened to Megan's advice and had an adventure, she'd found herself half dressed in a roomful of strangers. Lord knows what would happen next time. She'd probably find herself half dressed in a room with just one stranger—a stranger who could fulfill every wild fantasy she'd ever had, and some she didn't even know she had.

O-kay . . .

Jenna swallowed past the lump in her throat and croaked out, "Good-bye, Megan." As her gaze slid to the card once again, her breath came in a ragged burst, her libido pulsing with the promise of things to come.

Without censor, her mind took her on an erotic journey, leaving her to wonder what it would be like to experience the lust, passion, and mind-blowing sex like other women experienced, wondering what it would be like if the sexy firefighter from Station 419 appeared at her door, ready and able to handle all her emergencies.

Every sinfully delicious . . . *emergency.*

She studied the card longer, committing the number to memory, and worked to extinguish the flames lapping at her thighs. Of course there was one surefire way to accomplish such a task. One very scandalous way to be precise.

Not that she'd ever dial the Hot Line, however. She liked sex— loved it even—but she would never be so bold as to call in a playboy firefighter to help extinguish the flames of desire licking a path up her thighs. It was something she'd never, ever do. Not in a million years.

No way.

No how.

She drew in air, but the lack of oxygen circulating through her bloodstream made her dizzy and prompted her into action. Jumping to her feet, she reached around her back and fumbled for the lace.

Her efforts proved futile. Frustrated, she planted her hands on her hips and began pacing around the bedroom looking for something, anything to help her.

She caught her reflection in the mirror. Outwardly, she looked like a sexy siren, a wanton seductress—a seductress who wouldn't hesitate to call a firefighter to her rescue.

If you have any other emergencies, I'm your man.

Jenna stopped midstride and considered her dilemma a moment longer. Did a too-tight bustier constitute an emergency?

She bit down on her bottom lip, Dean's parting words drumming in her head. She wasn't really considering calling him to her aid, was she? Lack of oxygen had to be clouding her judgment.

Once again her gaze panned over the numbers. She let her mind drift, remembering the erotic way his seductive strawberry-flavored breath caressed her nape like an intimate kiss. Suddenly, frustration morphed into desire, leaving her warm, wanting, and *hungry*—for a hard-bodied firefighter.

As her fingers curled around the card, she drew a fueling breath and mustered all her courage.

Because heaven help her, she was going to do it!

Psychology textbooks in hand, Dean made his way into the firehouse kitchen, dropped down into a chair, and planted his elbows on the long oaken table. He felt sexually frustrated and unable to dispel the image of a sexy siren parading around the room in a skimpy red negligee. He buried his face in his palms. Biting back a groan of longing, he angled his body, enabling him to better hear the special phone kept in their sleeping quarters, should it ring.

Even though Jenna had barely spared him a glance over the past week, there was no denying that tonight she'd made up for her lack of interest. He saw the desire in her gorgeous green eyes and felt the way she'd beckoned him from across the room. When their bodies collided, and skin connected with skin, everything in her reached out to him.

The sound of Brady Wade's voice pulled him from his musings. "Coffee?"

Shaken from his fantasies, Dean glanced up to see Brady hovering over the stove, and at his feet his chocolate Lab, Jag, salivating over the delicious smells. Dean nodded and then inhaled.

"What's cooking?" he asked, his own mouth watering.

Brady wiped his hands on his apron and went to work on the coffeepot. "Your favorite. Chicken cacciatore for dinner, and since strawberries are in season, strawberry pie for dessert."

Strawberries . . .

Dean groaned and shifted uncomfortably in his chair. His gaze went from Brady to their sleeping quarters back to Brady again.

Never one for subtleties, Brady got right to the point. "Waiting for a call?"

Dean rolled one shoulder and said in a noncommittal tone of voice, "No. Yes. Maybe. I don't know."

Dammit.

Brady leaned against the counter with a knowing grin on his face. "Well, well, I never thought I'd see the day."

Dean narrowed his eyes, digesting Brady's cryptic words. "What day?" he asked, annoyed that Jenna had reduced him to a hormonal teen-ager who could barely see straight, let alone hold an adult conversation.

Brady smirked. "I never thought I'd see the day that sworn bach-elor Dean Beckman would fall so hard for someone."

Dean scoffed and arched a brow. "You're out of your frigging mind."

Brady rolled his eyes. "Uh-huh," he said, sounding unconvinced. "I wonder if it could be love at first sight."

"Like fuck," Dean said. "I don't believe in such a thing."

Feeling antsy, Dean hoisted himself from his chair, walked over to the counter, and popped a strawberry in his mouth. Not his brightest move, apparently. The taste immediately brought back memories of Jenna and how he yearned to drip sweet strawberry juice all over that lush body of hers and then lick her clean, every groove, every nook, every hidden valley. A slow burn gravitated south. His cock hardened to the point of pain.

He purposely stepped behind the island counter in a maneuver that enabled him to hide his raging erection. No need to show off the hard-on he was sporting. Nope, no need of that at all. The truth was, what he really needed was one wild night between the sheets with Jenna. To fuck her out of his system once and for all. Then he'd be able to move on and get back to completing his thesis.

Redirecting the conversation, he shot Brady a dubious look. "Besides, what do you know about falling hard or love at first sight? I haven't seen you with a woman in ages. You spend all your free time in this kitchen. Not that we don't appreciate that, mind you," he added with a grin, "because we do."

Brady drummed his fingers on the counter, waiting for the coffeepot to fill. "Oh, I know all about such things, my friend."

Dean angled his head and waved his hand, offering Brady the floor. "Yeah, you want to enlighten me?"

At the sound of the beep, Brady twisted around and filled two mugs with coffee. "I'm crazy about someone," he said, handing Dean a cup. "And she's crazy about me, too. She just doesn't know it yet."

With a nod of his head, Dean gestured toward the CPR training doll. "I hate to break it to you, pal, but Blow-up Betty doesn't count. Besides, I think she's smitten with Christian."

"Speaking of our newest rookie," Brady said. "I heard he really had your back when you guys were out on a call the other night."

"Yeah, he's a real stand-up guy. Definitely a guy I want on my team."

"I guess it's time to initiate him into the brotherhood."

Dean grinned. "Leave that to me."

As Dean sipped his coffee, Brady turned the conversation back to him. "So tell me about her."

After a long pause, Dean gave a resigned sigh and said, "It's Jenna Powers." Jesus, just saying her name out loud fired his blood and rendered him senseless. Rattled by the way she threw him off balance, Dean shook his head. "She's been getting under my skin all week."

"No shit, Sherlock."

Dean's head came up with a start. "What?"

Brady nodded toward the textbooks strewn across the kitchen table. "And you're supposed to be the intuitive one." He threw his arms up in the air. "Come on, Dean. It's obvious. You've been walking around here all week like a lovesick puppy. Everyone knows it but you. I guess in your case love really is blind."

"Not love. Lust," Dean clarified. "The woman's got a killer body."

"And you know this how? She walks around in baggy clothes all the time, downplaying her figure."

Dean paused, unable to deny Brady's observations. As Dean knocked around that thought, Brady lifted a brow and said, "Which raises the point that maybe your attraction to her goes beyond the physical and maybe your interest goes beyond a night of wild sex. Have you ever thought of that?"

Ignoring Brady's sudden epiphany, Dean shifted his stance after recalling the sight of Jenna's hot little body in a barely there negligee. "If you'd have seen her tonight, you'd know what I was talking about."

The bell on the stove chimed. Brady shut it off and tossed his words over his shoulder. "Grab a couple of plates. Dinner is ready."

Dean reached into the cupboard and grabbed two plates. The sound of the phone ringing in the other room stopped him dead in his tracks. His pulse leapt. He sucked in a tight breath. Heat spread like wildfire through his body. The phone rang a second time, jolting him out of his carnal stupor.

"You want me to get that?" Brady asked, smirking.

Dean shoved the plates at Brady. "Fuck off," he grumbled good-naturedly. He listened to Brady's laughter as he negotiated his way to their sleeping quarters, double time.

When he glanced at the caller ID, heat and desire rocketed through him. He whipped the phone from the cradle and shot a look around the room, ensuring his privacy.

He lowered himself onto his bunk. "Hello."

"Dean?" Jenna's voice sounded low, rough.

Breathless.

His body buzzed to life at the sound of her deep, sexy tone. "Yeah."

Jenna cleared her throat. "Hi."

His heart thudded and he closed his eyes against the flood of heat rushing south. "Hi," he finally managed in return. After a moment of silence, he pitched his voice low and practically whispered, "I'm glad you called."

"Yeah?"

He heard the surprise, the excitement, and the anticipation in her voice.

"You told me to call if I had any other emergencies."

So he had. Damned smartest thing he'd ever said. Inhaling, he scrubbed his hand over his chin, praying they were on the same page here.

"What kind of emergency are you having, Jenna?"

"I'm not sure it's the type of emergency you handle."

"You might be surprised at the types of emergencies I handle." He heard her breath quaver and then there was a noise, like she was licking those plump red lips of hers.

"Well, I've sort of found myself in a terrible predicament."

"Why don't you just tell me what the problem is, what kind of emergency you are having, and how I can be of assistance?" He could think of a million ways to assist her, but he wanted to hear her say it, to ask for it.

Her chuckle was soft and low. "Well, it's a bit embarrassing," she stalled.

"Tell me, Jenna," he urged.

Her hesitation only lasted a second, and then she said, "I'm having a clothing emergency."

Dean drew in a deep breath as his mind took him on an erotic adventure. One that involved Jenna, a sexy red negligee, and a bowl full of juicy, ripe strawberries.

He shifted. Jesus, he was in total fucking agony here. He tried for casual but his voice betrayed him. "What kind of clothing emergency?"

She gave an edgy laugh and he heard the bedsprings sound in the background. "It seems I've gone and knotted the lace on my bustier, and now I can't get it off."

Dean bit back a moan as he visualized Jenna sitting on her bed dressed in a sexy bustier—her beautiful breasts pushed together, her nipples tight, her milky cleavage beckoning his tongue.

"I see," he said around a low, throaty groan. "Is the knot too tight to untie?"

"Uh-huh."

"Hmmm . . ." he murmured, sorting through his options, every delicious one of them. "You were right to call me, Jenna. This is definitely the type of emergency I handle."

"I knew you'd be the right man for the job, Dean." Her voice was full of need.

Sexual frustration welled up inside him. Fingers trembling, he balled them into fists. "I believe the only thing we can do is cut you out of it."

Once again he could hear her lick her lips. "That's exactly what I was thinking, too," she replied, echoing his sentiments.

"So that's why you called me, then? To come over there and cut you out of your bustier?" For some unfathomable reason, he needed to hear her say it, needed to know she wanted to fuck him as much as he wanted to fuck her.

Arousal edged her voice. "Actually . . ."

"Yeah?" he rushed out, his cock pounding against his zipper, clamoring for attention.

She blew out a shaky breath. "Actually, it's so hot in here, it feels like flames are licking up my thighs. It's quite possible that I set the house ablaze with all the burning candles. You might want to bring your . . . *hose*."

His heart skidded to a halt.

His blood pressure soared. His mind shut down.

Sweet Mother of God and all good things holy!

He bounded off his bunk. "Jenna?"

"Yeah?"

"Sit tight. I'm on my way."

THREE

it tight.

How the hell was she supposed to sit tight? In a few minutes, the man of her dreams—or rather, her *fantasies*—would walk through that door and cut her out of a very revealing, very seductive bustier. And after she had acted like a sexy siren on the phone, Dean wouldn't expect anything less from her in person.

In all honesty, her boldness surprised even her. Maybe Megan was right, and deep inside her existed a sexy siren, a wanton seductress just waiting to break free.

Jenna's flesh broke out in a sweat as she paced around the bedroom with her pussy quivering in heated anticipation. Good Lord, her pussy was actually quivering—in heated anticipation.

Unbelievable!

Then again, calling a sexy firefighter to her rescue was right up there in the unbelievable section, too.

Jenna cracked her bedroom window, listening for sounds of an approaching vehicle. Less than twenty minutes later, she heard gravel crunching beneath rubber tires. She flicked off her lamp and moved to her window.

Camouflaged by darkness, she glanced at the street below. Her pulse leapt when she spotted Dean climbing from his car. As he shut the driver's-side door quietly, he angled his head upward. Dark eyes sparkled and a wicked, self-assured grin curled his lips. He had to be the most confident man she'd ever met, and his assuredness made her feel wildly out of control. No man had ever made her feel that way before.

Without haste, Jenna dropped the curtain and stepped back into the shadows, wondering what the hell she'd gone and gotten herself into.

Heart racing, she took a moment to remind herself how much she wanted this. How much she wanted to experience the lust, the passion, and the mind-blowing sex other women experienced.

Just once . . .

Heavy footsteps on the stairs gained her attention. Dean inched open her door without knocking. Light from the hallway spilled inside and fell over her scantily clad body.

Dean took one predatory step forward. His overwhelming presence dominated the small bedroom. The desire reflecting in his eyes told her all she needed to know. Megan was right: Dean wanted this just as much as she did.

Desire and need moved into Jenna's stomach. She drew a shaky breath and moistened her lips. Heat pooled between her thighs when her gaze panned the length of him. He was so goddamn hot that her pussy ached to swallow his cock.

As she took pleasure in the sight of his tall, hard body, her skin moistened. He was dressed in a pair of jeans and a knit navy sweater that showed off his toned body. She watched transfixed as he scrubbed his hand over the stubble shadowing his jaw, his lusty eyes seeming to undress her. She could see his pulse beating at the base of his throat, double time, as he continued his slow perusal. It both thrilled and surprised her to know she had this effect on him.

Restless, edgy for his touch, she shifted from one leg to the other. Like a wild animal, he made a guttural noise low in his throat.

By God, he looked so feral, so wild, so hungry. He licked his lips, his gaze brushing over her body like he was going to eat her alive.

And heaven help her, she was going to let him.

She stood before him, warmth and desire stirring her blood, making her forget everything but this moment and this wild man.

He pointed at her with his index finger and made a circular motion. His voice was controlled. "Turn around, Jenna," he demanded, taking charge of the situation as though he knew what she wanted and just how to give it to her.

Jenna tried to keep her focus. "Have you brought scissors?" she asked, with a desperate edge to her voice as she turned her back to him, and inched her body deeper into the shadows, uncomfortable with the way the bright hallway light exposed her body.

Without answering he moved farther into the room. Sexual tension hung heavy in the air as he closed the distance between them. He stood only inches from her, crowding her, his body close but never touching hers. His breath was hot on her neck, raising her passion to new heights. She could feel his heat and his lust reaching out to her. Jenna inhaled his warm spicy scent, letting it seep into her bloodstream and wrap around her like a silken cocoon until she thought she'd go mad with desire.

Dean ran his fingertips along the back of her neck. Jenna shivered in response.

"It seems we have a problem, Jenna." His warm breath caressed her skin as he spoke in a hushed tone.

She angled her head to better see him. Soft rays drifting in from the hallway provided sufficient light to glimpse the lust, passion, and something else—something that looked like mischief burning in his eyes. Jenna swallowed past the knot in her throat and willed her legs to keep her upright.

"We do?" she asked, striving for some semblance of control as cream moistened her panties. "What kind of problem?"

Dean's brow puckered into a frown as his fingers traveled lower to play with the knotted lace as he addressed her concerns. "You see, in my haste to come to your rescue, I forgot to bring scissors." He pressed against her and she could feel his rock-hard cock indenting her back.

Jenna gulped and worked to form a coherent sentence. She nodded toward the open door and shifted, pressing harder against his erection. Her telltale actions would let him know just how much she wanted this . . . wanted *him*. "Maybe there's a pair somewhere in the house."

Hands trailing over her skin with the utmost care, he brushed aside her suggestion. "No time to search."

"No?" she asked, wiggling again.

A low growl caught in his throat as his groin pounded against her ass. A tremor racked her body. "Afraid not," he bit out between gritted teeth. "You see, your skin is on fire, and with your air flow so constricted, you could be in real danger of passing out. There is no time to waste."

Jenna nibbled her bottom lip and worked to take in air. Her deep, labored breath was emphasizing his point. "I see," she said. "What will we do?"

"No worries. All is not lost."

"No?"

His voice turned serious and he sounded professional. "No, I have one other option."

"What is it?" she asked over her shoulder, playing along.

He paused for a second, as though considering the dilemma a moment longer. "Well, it's a bit drastic, but under the circumstances, I don't see any other choice."

"Drastic?"

He pressed his lips close to her ear and murmured, "I'm afraid I'm going to have to rip it off you." With his hands on either side of her bustier, he gave a quick tug, which released the pressure and allowed her to breathe easier. She heard a few metal clasps give way and sprinkle to the floor.

When he groaned, her cunt clenched in euphoric bliss; the nerve endings in her clit screamed for attention. Lord, she'd never been more excited in her life. A small gasp of pleasure rose from her throat, conveying without words just how much his take-charge attitude thrilled her.

She clutched the bedpost, bracing herself. "But surely there must be another way," she challenged, calming her emotions. "This just seems so . . . *barbaric.*" Her heart leapt, and her breasts tightened to the point of pain.

His voice took on a hard edge, exciting her even more. "There is no other way. If you have a problem with that, you're going to have to take it up with my captain later. Right now I'm the only man on the scene and it is my duty to do what I deem necessary," he said, sounding impatient, on edge.

With her body trembling, she drew a calming breath and closed her eyes. "I fail to see—"

Her words fell away when Dean sank to his knees behind her. His face brushed over her backside; his hands spanned her waist, pinning her in place.

The room spun before her eyes when his lips brushed over the small of her back and began a downward path, until he reached her quivering thighs. His movements were sensual, seductive, determined. Warm fingers slipped between her legs and urged them apart. Lust stole through her as she handed her pleasures over to him completely.

"I'm afraid these panties might hamper my efforts. I'll have to remove them first."

Her whole body shook with excitement. "Are you going to have to rip them, too?" she rushed out, not bothering to mask her enthusiasm. She arched her back, her actions and desires transparent.

His low chuckle made her body quake. Deft fingers caressed the silky patch covering her soaked mound before curling around the thin lace. His dark hair brushed against her skin and sent shivers skittering through her. She bit her lips and felt her body flush hotly.

"Hmmm . . . why are they so damp, Jenna? Have you attempted to extinguish the fire yourself?" With one sharp tug, he ripped her panties from her hips.

"Oh, my," she murmured in a whisper.

"Answer the question, Jenna," he commanded in a soft voice. Leaning back on his heels, he tucked her panties into his pocket.

"Yes," she admitted honestly, recalling the way she'd touched herself only minutes earlier. Pushing her finger deep inside her pussy in a quest to take the edge off before she splintered into a million pieces.

He *tsk*ed, grabbed her hips roughly, and spun her around to face him. The ardent darkening of his eyes elevated her blood pressure and prohibited her from thinking straight.

Her entire body reacted to the pure desire shimmering in his gaze as he gave her a disapproving shake of his head. "Don't you know such things should be left in the hands of a professional?" He exhaled slowly so that his warm breath bristled her damp hairs, making her next breath nearly impossible.

Dean cast a glance her way and gently slid his finger over her cunt, teasing her sex lips open, dipping into her liquid heat. Jenna whimpered as a fine tremor rippled through her.

"Now that I'm down here, it is apparent that I'll have to deal with this emergency first. The flames between your thighs are reaching dangerous proportions." He urged closer, his hands touching her in aroused eagerness. Was it just her imagination or had she seen a flash of possessiveness in his eyes when he gazed up at her? "You were right to call for *my* services and *my* services only, Jenna. Not only am I the right man, but I'm the only man properly equipped for this job."

Before she could reply, Dean leaned into her and inhaled the tangy scent of her arousal as it filled the room. A surge of warmth flooded her veins. When he gripped her hips tighter, she angled her head and looked into his dark, passion-filled eyes. Her pussy quaked and cried out for his attention.

The tip of his tongue caressed her inner thigh and drew her focus. The tantalizing sweep sent shivers of pleasure racing through her. In no time at all, the room grew thick with the scent of her excite-

ment. The warmth of his mouth ignited her flesh. Desperate for him
to release the pressure brewing inside her, she gyrated against him.

His fingers left her hips and traveled lower, until they reached
her puckered clit. He gave it a quick, light brush and then parted
her drenched folds. Jenna felt a rush of moisture between her legs.
Dean dipped into her creamy essence and brought his finger to his
mouth for a taste. Excitement flared in his eyes and he moaned his
approval.

"You're very wet, Jenna. But not wet enough to extinguish this type
of fire, I'm afraid." He licked his lips, leaned forward, and breathed a
kiss over her pussy. "I believe the moisture from my tongue is the only
thing that will help put out these raging flames."

She moaned deep in her throat. Delicious warmth spread over her
skin, his words nearly taking her over the edge. How was it possible
that he was so in tune with her needs and desires?

The pad of his thumb pressed against her clit, and he circled
it slowly. Jenna lost herself in the sensation. Sweat beaded on her
half-naked body. She loved the way he touched her with such single-
minded determination and the way he cared about her desires.

She thrust her pelvis forward—his artful manipulation was taking her to magical places. Places she'd never been before, places she
feared she'd never go again. Undulating against him, she gave a lusty
groan and raked her fingers through his hair.

His mouth found her clit. He nibbled, licked, and sucked, drawing
her engorged nub between his teeth, lavishing her with his undivided
attention. His pleasure was apparent in the way he moaned in delight
and spent a long time ravishing her like a wild, primal animal.

Changing tactics, he eased back and caressed her with the soft
blade of his tongue, stroking her with the utmost care, the utmost

expertise. It suddenly occurred to her that for the first time in her life, a man was stroking her the way she'd always longed to be stroked.

His thumb breached her opening, teasing her with its width but never offering her more than an inch. His slow seduction did the most torturous, exquisite things to her libido. She rolled her tongue around a dry mouth and widened her legs farther in a silent invitation.

"Please . . ." she begged.

Before he allowed her to tumble into an orgasm, he reached behind her back, and with one quick tug, he tore her bustier from her body.

Jenna sucked in a tight breath as it fell to the floor, forgotten. Warm hands closed over her breasts, toying with her distended nipples until her cries of pleasure filled the air. She closed her fingers over his, loving the way her swollen breasts fit into his strong hands. After a long moment, his palms left her chest and followed the path of her curves to the valley between her legs. Once again his attention drifted back to her pussy.

"Open your legs wider," he growled, taking charge of her pleasures.

She loved the way Dean understood her needs, her desires . . . *her fantasies*. He was so intuitive, so unlike the other men she'd had sex with.

After she obliged, he licked her clit and pushed two thick fingers all the way up inside her. The stab of pleasure she felt had her teetering on the edge of oblivion.

She moaned. He growled. Need consumed them both.

His fingers pumped in and out of her, taking her to where she needed to go. Jenna took deep, gulping breaths. Her heart slammed inside her chest with the approach of an impending orgasm. Her throat tightened.

"I'm . . ." was all she managed to choke out.

Dean glanced up at her. "Come for me, Jenna. Let me taste you." His words brought her to the edge.

Once again Dean's tongue sifted through her silky strands and laved her clit, his fingers picking up the tempo. She gripped his shoulder, her nails digging into him, leaving her mark. A whimper of relief sounded in her throat as her sex muscles clenched and contracted with enough force that she almost blacked out. Dean gripped her hips and moaned as her liquid heat drenched his mouth.

Once her tremors subsided, Dean slid up her body and gathered her into his arms.

The fire temporarily controlled, but by no means extinguished, her sigh of delight filled the room. "I was quite right to call for your services, Dean. You were definitely the man for the job," she whispered.

Dean offered her a warm smile before his lips found hers for a long, lingering kiss. His tongue swept inside her mouth to tangle with hers. His fingers stroked the small of her back, then dipped down lower to tease her ass.

When his strong fingers inched open her cheeks, her body tightened and tingled and ached for him all over again. She gyrated against him.

"You're insatiable," he murmured, "just like I knew you would be." Dean pushed against her so that she could feel his cock. Everything inside her throbbed and ached to lick him, to suck him, and to pleasure him in return. She spread her legs wider.

"Dean?" Her mouth watered, her body shook.

"Yeah," he breathed the words into her mouth.

She touched her pussy. "I still feel hot, deep inside me." Good

God, she hardly recognized her voice, hardly believed how bold she was.

"That's because you're not out of the woods just yet, Jenna." His deep, sexy tone raised her passion to new heights.

"No?" When their eyes met, sparks of desire flew between them.

He slipped a hand between her legs and stroked her folds. His dark eyes flared with lust. "Sometimes embers can smolder long after the fire is out."

His words wreaked havoc on her senses. When he found her clit, she swallowed. "I had no idea."

He nodded. "It's true, and there is only one way—and one piece of equipment—that will allow me to get deep enough to really soak those embers." He offered her a sexy wink and said, "It's a good thing you told me to bring my *hose*."

Excited at the prospect, Jenna drew in air, but was unable to fill her lungs. The man sure had a talent for knowing exactly what she wanted. Her whole body broke out in a sweat.

Just then her stomach grumbled, alerting Dean to her ravenous state. Although at that moment she was more ravenous for his "hose" than she was for food. They both chuckled, but her laughter quickly died away when she caught the mischievous look in his eyes.

"What?" she asked.

"Don't move," he said. "I'll be right back."

When Dean inched the bedroom door open farther, spilling more light into the room, Jenna became acutely aware of her nakedness. Never one to be comfortable in her own skin, she quickly crawled under the bedcovers. A moment later footsteps on the stairs heralded his return.

Dean stepped back into the room with a bowl of strawberries

in one hand and flicked on the lights. Surprise registered on his face when he spotted her tucked under the covers, the sheets pulled to her chin.

She crinkled her nose and bit down on her bottom lip. "Would you mind turning the lights out?"

He hesitated for a second before honoring her request. After flicking off the light, he made his way across the room. He placed one strawberry in her mouth and perched on the edge of the bed. Warm fingers brushed her hair from her forehead. Moonlight spilled in through the window, providing her with enough light to see the concerned look in his eyes. Her heart tightened. A barrage of emotions rushed through her.

"What is it?" he asked.

She shrugged and strived to make light of the situation. "I just prefer the lights off."

He pitched his voice low and stroked her cheek. "But I want to see you, Jenna. All of you. Naked. When I slip my cock inside your sweet pussy, I want to see your face, your eyes, your mouth, and your breasts. I won't have it any other way."

She opened her eyes wide, alarmed. "I never thought it would be a problem."

By small degrees, his body tightened, and he inched back, away from her touch. "Oh, it is a problem, a big problem." In a motion so fast it took her off guard, he stood and glanced toward the door.

She gulped, her heart sinking to the bottom of her stomach. "You're going to leave because I want to fuck you with the lights off?"

Brow furrowed in concentration, he grew quiet for a moment, as though sorting through matters. She could almost hear his mind race but had no idea what he was thinking. After a long, thoughtful moment, he glanced at her. With his voice full of conviction, he said, "Yes."

Time seemed to stand still as his athletic gait carried him toward the bedroom door. But he didn't leave. Instead he rooted through the pile of lingerie that she'd modeled earlier. "And you're coming with me." Holding a sexy red teddy poised on the end of his fingertips, he walked back to the bed and offered her his hand.

She narrowed her gaze, scrutinizing him. What the hell was he up to? She opened her mouth to ask but he cut her off and said, "I'm afraid that once again, drastic measures need to be taken."

FOUR

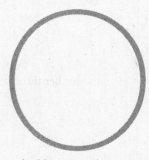h yeah, under these circumstances, Dean knew drastic measures were definitely in order. Jenna's request to kill the lights before they fucked had shocked him at first, but after he reflected on her actions all evening, and the way she'd kept her body draped in darkness, understanding had begun to dawn.

Intuitive intelligence told him that on the outside she was a bold, confident career woman, yet underneath all that, she was plagued with insecurities. He knew exactly what he had to do to help her embrace her sexuality and show her that she was as sexy as she was smart.

As he considered his outlandish plan a moment longer, his gaze panned over the woman before him. The truth was, Jenna had a fantasy-inspired body that erotic dreams were made of. He knew firsthand. And said hands had the calluses to prove it. So why on earth did she keep her femininity hidden?

He wasn't sure but he planned to get to the bottom of her self-doubt and shyness. He also planned to help her discover and embrace another side of herself—a sexy side that he'd glimpsed while he fucked her with his hands, his mouth, and his tongue.

Dean gripped her hand and pulled her to her feet. Her body collided with his. As his fingers slid through her hair, he angled her head and moistened his lips. Lust hit him like a high-voltage jolt, urging him to turn the lights out, join her on the bed, and fuck her out of his system once and for all. He quickly banked his desires and took a moment to compose himself, refusing to let his lust rule his actions. He had other, more important matters at hand.

Dean inched back and drove his fists into his pockets. It was time to show this sexy woman just how desirable she really was. He nodded toward her red negligee. "Go ahead and get ready."

Once she was dressed in a pair of jeans and a blouse, lingerie hidden beneath the clothes, he gripped her hand and led her through the house. Silence fell over them as they made their way to his car. To break the quiet, Dean flicked on the radio and negotiated his vehicle out of the driveway.

After they reached the freeway, he shot Jenna a glance. Hands folded on her lap, she worried her bottom lip. She'd been so quiet, so lost in her own thoughts since they left the house. Everything in him softened and tightened at the same time as he took in the sight of her. Longing shot through him, and he felt a curious shift in his gut. He closed his eyes briefly and made a silent vow to make tonight good for her . . . so damn good for her.

Needing to reassure her, he closed one hand over hers and said, "We're going to this club I know."

She forced a smile. "I see." She paused and then asked, "So why the red-hot teddy then?"

He squeezed her hand. "Because it's my favorite and you look damn sexy in it. Even if I can't see you in it, I know you're wearing it, and I can fantasize about it, can't I?" Jenna smiled and looked down, a soft red hue crawling up her neck.

Dean touched her chin and brought her gaze back up to his. Her hair fell over her eyes, shadowing her expression. He brushed it away and tucked it behind her ear. "You are the hottest fucking woman I know, Jenna. And I'm going to prove it to you."

Ignoring her dubious look for the time being, he concentrated on the directions. Less than a half an hour later, Dean pulled up in front of Risqué, a private club on the outskirts of town.

A few months back, after putting a fire out in one of the upstairs bedrooms, he'd been presented with a VIP pass—one he had not used. Had no desire to, really. Until now. But tonight . . . tonight he planned on making up for lost time.

Jenna read the sign, her eyes scanning the establishment with interest. "What is this place?"

Dean killed the ignition, released his seat belt, and cocked his head to get a better look at her. The sight of her wet lips beckoned him. He leaned forward, caging her between his body and the door. She pressed against him, as though seeking his heat, his contact. Her hands raced over him with hunger, generating warmth and need inside him. He loved the way she touched him, the way her body felt against his, and how she felt right in his arms.

Giving in to impulse, Dean dropped a soft kiss on her mouth. When their lips met, her sweet, delectable scent reached his nostrils and filled him with hunger. He inflated his lungs with her aroma, shocked at the way her feminine fragrance wreaked havoc on his senses. His tongue found the warmth of her mouth. Unexpectedly, fierce possessiveness exploded through him and rattled him right to his core.

He softened his voice, wanting to tell her the truth about where he was taking her, but not wanting to scare her off just the same. "It's a private club"—he paused briefly and then added in a hushed tone—"where private things happen."

He noted with satisfaction that her expression was one of curiosity, intrigue. She raised an eyebrow. "Tell me, Dean. What kind of private things?"

He eased away. "I'd rather show you, instead." Without waiting for a reply, Dean climbed from his car, circled it, and opened Jenna's door.

When she gave him a hesitant look, he held his hand out to her and chose his words carefully. "Trust me, Jenna."

She stepped from the car and joined him on the sidewalk. Moonlight spilled over her gorgeous body and glistened in her seductive green eyes. She moved into his open arms, offering herself up to him completely, putting her trust in his hands.

He dragged her into his embrace, and in that instant, when her arms tightened around him, Dean realized just how much he liked her and how much he wanted to know everything about her: her likes, her dislikes, her dreams, her desires, and what incident in her past had caused her to feel so insecure about herself sexually. Perhaps it was the psychologist in him that reached out for such answers.

Or perhaps it was the man.

Either way, tonight he was on a mission, and nothing or no one would stand in his way—not even Brady's voice ringing loud and clear in the back of his head, questioning whether his interest in her went deeper than one night of wild, animal sex.

With Jenna tucked under one arm, Dean pulled open the huge oak door and stepped into the spacious foyer. A few feet away another set of double doors stood before them, blocking the world out and guarding the patrons' privacy inside. The sound of music and voices just beyond those security doors reached his ears. He glanced up to see a camera poised on them. A man's voice came in through an intercom system.

"Can I help you?"

"Dean Beckman, VIP."

"Present your card to the window to your left please."

Dean flipped open his wallet and held his card up to a two-way mirror.

Jenna pressed against him. "Why all the security?" she whispered.

He put his mouth close to her ear. The way she trembled beneath his touch filled him with pleasure. "Security ensures privacy," Dean whispered back.

"Please sign in," the man said. "And don't forget your mask."

After signing them in, Dean reached into a treasure chest and pulled out two masks. A jeweled gold eye mask for her and a silver Casanova Mardi Gras eye mask for him. Once they donned their disguises, a buzzer sounded and Dean pulled open the security door. When they stepped over the threshold, Dean felt Jenna's body tighten in his arms. He twisted sideways to gauge her responses to the erotic scene before them. She stilled, with surprise registering in her eyes, and her jaw dropped as she darted a quick glance around.

Shocked silence lingered. He remained quiet, letting her absorb her surroundings. As though she were taken aback, a sound caught in her throat. Her tenuous grip on his arm tightened and he could feel her tension. She drew a deep, shaky breath, let it out, and then turned to him.

"Dean, what is this place?" Her voice sounded alarmed, but the excitement in her eyes didn't go unnoticed by him; it told him all he needed to know. Somewhere deep inside her existed a sexy siren, and with a little bit of coaching, maybe he could get her to come out to play. Once again Jenna panned the room, awareness dawning on her face.

Dean followed her gaze, taking in the sight of numerous disguised couples, all in various stages of undress, dancing, kissing, and engaging in other, more intimate activities, while making no attempt at discretion.

With its invitation-only membership, the classy establishment catered to the elite of the elite. Chicago's high-society members paid dearly to maintain their confidentiality while engaging in . . . *private affairs*. Dean had been gifted with a courtesy VIP card to ensure their privacy remained intact after the fire.

The area was tastefully decorated in warm cranberry hues and plush upholstery, with soft lighting that gave a modicum of privacy. For those wishing for complete seclusion, the upstairs loft housed fantasy theme rooms.

Dean felt a shiver race through Jenna's body. "I've never seen—"

After looking over the crowd, her voice fell off and suddenly, out of nowhere, he felt his whole world shift. He tightened his hold on her. "Come on, let's get a drink." With determined strides, he cut a path across the dance floor until they came to a private booth in the back.

Jenna sat. Dean slid in next to her and summoned the waitress.

Shifting in her seat, Jenna adjusted her mask and eyed the dance floor.

A few feet away a barely clad couple made no qualms about their desire for each other. Exhibitionists that they were, they danced to the music, their bodies rocking together, her back to his chest, soft ass to hard groin, hands roaming freely as they moved sensually to the seductive beat.

Dean studied Jenna's reactions. Equal measures of surprise and delight crossed her gorgeous face. She spent a long moment watching the couple, lost in the erotic show. Dean gathered her in tighter. She fairly trembled in his arms. Obviously the sexy act had flustered her as much as it had him.

She swallowed, her face taking on a ruddy hue. Her voice sounded hoarse, labored, and aroused. "Clubs like this don't exist in my small hometown. Good God, I feel like a voyeur."

He shrugged. "You're supposed to. People come here for lots of reasons. To watch. To be watched." He wondered which one she liked more.

"So why do *you* come here, Dean?"

Before he had time to answer, the waitress arrived with a bottle of champagne and two glasses. Dean filled their flutes and handed Jenna one. She took a big gulp. Dean bit back a chuckle.

"Thirsty?"

"That's one way to put it."

He pulled her impossibly close. Her green eyes sparkled with sensuality as they locked on his.

Unable to help himself, he leaned forward and pressed his lips to hers. Her eyes dimmed with desire; her mouth opened in invitation. With hunger consuming him, his tongue swept inside her mouth and tangled with hers in an animalistic mating dance. She tasted sweet, seductive, and sinful, like fine champagne. His whole body trembled with pent-up passion. A need he couldn't seem to assuage whipped through him. Jesus, he ached to return to the valley between her legs, to taste her liquid silk, to push his cock into her and fuck her until he ingrained himself on her and erased the memory of every other man she'd been with. She made a sexy sound and shifted, her hands going to his shoulders, touching him with intimate familiarity.

A moment later, she pulled back, breathless. "Whew," she murmured.

He grinned. "I can't seem to control myself when I'm around you." He cupped her chin, then let his hands wander. He pulled her against his chest, unable to get her close enough.

She glanced up at him and waved one hand around, redirecting the conversation. "So you never did tell me why *you* come here."

He fingered the soft material of her blouse, ignoring her question and deciding to get right to the point. "Tell me something, Jenna. Why do you design sexy lingerie but hide your sensuality behind baggy clothes?" He felt her body stiffen. She looked past his shoulders. Dean shifted, forcing her gaze back onto him. "I want to know."

She didn't bother to deny it. "Why do you want to know?"

"Because it's important." *She* was important.

After a long moment she folded her hands in her lap and gave a resigned sigh. "You're a pretty perceptive guy, Dean."

"I like to think so. After studying for my psychology degree for the past four years, and finishing up my thesis, I like to think I know a little something about human nature."

"Thesis?"

"Yes, I want to go from active duty to counseling fellow firefighters emotionally scarred on the job." He turned the conversation back to her. "So talk to me, Jenna. Why the insecurities?"

She rolled one shoulder and tried to make light of things. "After being teased relentlessly as a child, I'm just not comfortable with my body."

He touched her cheek and softened his tone. "Why were you teased?"

"Because I was chubby, and I had braces and glasses. Not a beauty-pageant candidate, for sure."

"I see," he said, when everything began to make sense. He squeezed her hand in reassurance. "You're not that girl anymore, Jenna. You're a strong, smart woman, with a body any man would die to touch. And something tells me beneath all those baggy clothes exists a sexy siren just waiting to break free."

She arched an inquisitive brow. "So that's why you brought me here tonight?"

"Yes," he admitted honestly. "With your disguise on, you can be whoever you want and do whatever you want. No one will ever know."

"You'll know."

"Precisely."

That earned him a smile. She looked past his shoulder and moistened her lips. He could tell her mind was racing a million miles an hour as she contemplated his sexy plan.

He stood and caught hold of her hand, ready to take her on a journey of self discovery. "Come on." He gave her a minute to entertain the idea, to get used to it, and then said, "Are you game?"

She pointed a finger toward the dance floor and crinkled her nose. "You want me to go out there and get naked?"

He grinned. "For now, we'll just dance."

"And later?"

"Later is up to you."

She sucked in air and let it out slowly. "These are definitely drastic measures, Dean."

He cocked his head. "Sometimes drastic measures need to be taken, Jenna," he reassured her.

She became quiet for a long, thoughtful moment and then something in her expression changed. "Dean."

"Yeah?"

She met his gaze unflinchingly and he could tell she was gathering her courage. "I'm game."

Jenna was ensconced in Dean's embrace when they stepped onto the dance floor. She could hardly believe she was doing this, but she had to secretly admit seeing all those other couples engaging in various sex acts really excited her.

Sidestepping other couples, they moved to the center of the room. Dean's actions tonight had touched her down deep. He could easily have fucked her with the lights off and walked away, both getting what they wanted. But Dean refused to take her that way. No man had ever cared much about her pleasure or had taken such drastic measures to see her naked before.

Which left the question, why had Dean?

Not that she thought his "drastic measures" would work. As much as she'd like to let go of her insecurities, after twenty-nine years of hiding her body, she just didn't think she had that in her.

Thick muscles bunched as Dean's hands snaked around her body and splayed over the small of her back. He tucked her in tight against his body, his lips close to her mouth. Her pussy came to life when he gave her a look that conveyed his hunger, his desire . . . *for her.*

A shiver racked her body and a throaty purr resonated in her throat. Blocking out the crowd, they held each other for a long moment, bodies moving in sync, both lost in each other's touch.

"I like the way you move," Dean whispered. His hot breath on her neck made her dizzy with desire.

A short while later, a couple sidled up beside them, their moans of pleasure drawing both Jenna's and Dean's focus. Jenna angled her head; Dean followed the motion. Wearing a black Lone Ranger face mask, the man seductively peeled off his partner's blouse, exposing her gorgeous body. His hands went to her breasts. She moaned and thrust her chest out as he kneaded her supple skin. Heat and desire tightened and moistened Jenna's flesh. Cream pooled between her thighs, proving how much she actually enjoyed the sexy performance.

As she watched them perform, she wondered what it would be like to fuck a guy while others watched. As she considered it further, her nipples quivered and her body trembled. How deliciously interesting. Was it possible that she had exhibitionist tendencies but was too inhibited to embrace that side of herself?

Dean must have felt her response. "You like that, Jenna?"

When she nodded, he growled and melded their bodies together by pulling her up against him.

He nodded toward a table near the corner. "Look at those two."

She licked her lips and angled her head to watch a man ram his cock deep inside some woman's cunt. Mercy! A groan crawled out of her throat.

"Does watching them fuck make you hot?" Dean asked.

She pushed her pussy against him. "Uh-huh" was all she managed.

"Maybe you'd rather be watched than do the watching."

She drew a deep breath in response to the heat that ambushed her pussy. Her legs wobbled slightly, but it was enough for Dean to notice. She knew her body's reactions answered his question.

"I see," he said, grinning. Joined hip to hip, they began rocking to the beat, the hardening of his cock alerting her to his arousal. He dipped his head, his dark hair falling forward, fringing his mask.

"You feel so fucking good, Jenna," he whispered into her mouth.

Ignoring all those around her, she shifted her hips and gyrated against him, desperate to feel him inside her. "You feel good, too."

Dean groaned and pushed his knee between her thighs, spreading her legs wider. The gleam in his eye turned wicked. He nodded toward the couple beside them and narrowed his gaze on her. "Be careful, Jenna, or you just might get more than you bargained for out here." He was testing her and she knew it.

Lust settled in her stomach. Her blood pulsed hot. Fueled by her need to touch him, she ran her hands over his biceps, loving the way his muscles bunched and clenched beneath her eager fingers. The sudden, overwhelming need to rip off his clothes and feel his naked body pressed to hers made it damn near impossible to stand. As though reading her mind, Dean inched back and peeled off his sweater to reveal a formfitting T-shirt. His arms flexed, showcasing his finely tuned body.

With excruciating slowness, he grabbed her waist and pulled her to him. Anchoring her body to his, he began to palm her curves—the warmth of his hands scorching her skin.

"I want you so much it's killing me," he said, his voice nothing more than a strangled whisper. "Tell me you want me, too," he demanded. She'd never heard such need, such intensity from a man before. It was both frightening and exhilarating to her.

"I want you, Dean," she murmured honestly, desire claiming her full attention.

His lips closed over hers so that his mouth could devour her with hunger. Her body convulsed, crying out for so much more. Consumed with need, she ravished him in return, her body language indicating exactly how much she wanted his touch. He pushed his tongue into her mouth in a demand that she give herself over to him as he feasted on her. His erection pressed hard into her stomach. She quaked, aching to take his cock into her mouth, to lick, suck, and taste every inch of him.

He eased back. "Let me look at you." After a moment he let out an agonized groan and said, "You're so beautiful, Jenna. The most beautiful woman in the room."

In that instant, when she met his glance, her entire world spun before her eyes and something blossomed deep inside her. There was something about the mix of tenderness and heat in those dark eyes. It made her feel like the most alluring, seductive woman alive.

Once again his gaze surfed over her curves. Confidence growing, Jenna stood there proudly, allowing his gaze to pan her curvaceous body with longing in his eyes.

He drew her mouth to his and kissed away her reserve. "Let me see you, Jenna, all of you," he coaxed. "Your body is beautiful and should be showcased," he reassured her.

She was so caught up in the moment, her hand went to her blouse. Senses on overload, she undid the top button, exposing the lace on her red teddy.

Dean swiped at his brow, his breath coming in ragged bursts. He gazed at her with pure desire. "Look around, Jenna." She did as he requested, taking note of the many eyes on them . . . *on her*. She trembled with excitement. "You're beautiful in every way." He brushed his thumb over her lips and added, "On the inside, and on the outside. Every man in here wishes he could be in your sweet pussy tonight." He pulled her back to him, crushing her body to his.

Jenna swallowed, realizing that it wasn't all the men in the room gazing at her that gave her confidence and made her feel seductive and bold, it was this man, and this man only. He made her feel special, beautiful, and *siren sexy*.

With Dean murmuring soft words of encouragement, she felt herself grow bolder with each passing second. She'd never been comfortable in her own skin before, so she was surprised at just how confident Dean had made her feel in such a short time.

"No one here knows you, Jenna. You can be whoever you want tonight and do whatever you want."

She wanted—no, *needed*—to do this for him. For her.

With her inhibitions ebbing away, she pushed through her insecurities and embraced her sexuality. "Dean," she managed to get out, too far gone, too caught up in the moment to think straight.

"Yeah?"

"I think I'm ready."

His hand stroked her breasts, his thumbs brushing her nipples, causing them to harden and swell. "Ready for what, babe?"

In a flood of bolstered confidence, she waved her hand around the dance floor. "For more than I bargained for." She widened her stance and her hands went to her buttons.

As soon as the sexy, bold words left her mouth, air rushed from his lungs. "Jenna," he whispered in a soft tone, his eyes burning with desire.

She inched her blouse open farther, affording him a view of her sexy red negligee. Wild with need, she said, "Dean, I want you. I want you on top of me. Underneath me. In front of me. Behind me. Inside me." Her shirt spilled to the floor as her gaze dropped to his crotch. "But right now, where I want you most, is in my mouth."

She felt his body tremble and watched his throat work as he swallowed. He put his mouth close to her ear. "You want a lot of things, Jenna." She shivered beneath him. He inched back and looked into her eyes. "So tell me, can I have the one thing I'm asking for?"

Her tongue made a slow pass over her lips. In whispered words, she said, "I wouldn't have it any other way."

FIVE

ean was no longer able to fight down his carnal cravings. He shackled Jenna's wrist and practically dragged her across the dance floor.

While keeping pace with him, she asked, "Where are we going?" The lust in her voice urged him on.

"I need to get you alone. Fast."

Dean rushed up to the bar and retrieved a card key to one of the upstairs lofts. A few minutes later, they found themselves locked away in a private bedroom. Richly decorated in soft colors and plush fabrics, the room was designed for seduction. A huge king-sized bed dominated the space, urging them to live out their every delicious fantasy.

Dean shifted his attention to Jenna and watched her walk to the lamp. Eyes alive with anticipation, she flicked it on, bathing herself in a golden glow. With the lamplight pouring over her half-dressed body, she came back around to stand before him. Her mouth thinned provocatively before her fingers went to her zipper. His hungry eyes left her face and traveled lower, to watch the seductive way she slipped her pants to her ankles and kicked them away. She stood there, radiating confidence, embracing her sexuality. Dean's heart slammed in his chest.

As he took in her voluptuous curves, he began trembling from head to toe. He stood perfectly still, observing her. The thrill of self-discovery was apparent in her expression.

She crooked her finger, her gaze dropping to his crotch. While he continued to bask in her sexual awakening, her pretty tongue slid over her lips, signaling her intent. "I want you, Dean. All of you." The soft, seductive whisper of her voice drew him toward her.

With a predatory advance, he was on her in seconds. "I want to taste you," she murmured into his lips as they closed over hers. He kissed her, long and hard and with all the passion inside him.

Jenna inched back and slid down his body. He tore his T-shirt off and tossed it away as her fingers went to his zipper. She released the button and drew his pants and shorts to his ankles, releasing his throbbing cock. As she took in his girth, her eyes widened in delight. She closed her hands over his shaft. Her fingers felt warm and smooth and so damn good on his naked flesh.

When she spotted the juices pearling on his slit, Jenna moaned deep in her throat. Her hands continued stroking the length of him, caressing him with the utmost care. Overcome with desire, he wobbled and blinked the room back into his vision. He could barely keep his focus, let alone remain upright. Marshaling his control, he let his hands go to her head, where his needy fingers raked through her hair as he fought to hang on to his composure.

The wet tip of her tongue brushed his engorged cock, lapping at his cream. Her furtive touch evoked myriad sensations and emotions inside him. A moment later, she teased his throbbing cock between her lips.

Her warmth closed around him like a silken sheath. She rocked forward until his bulbous head hit the back of her throat. The onslaught of pleasure weakened his knees.

Dean threw his head back and growled. "Jenna . . ." he choked out with effort. "I'm never going to last if you keep that up."

She tilted her head back to look at him. "I've been dying to taste you, Dean. It's all I've been able to think about."

Small hands slipped between his legs, cupped his balls, and gave a gentle squeeze. Dean drew in a sharp breath. She filled him with such raw need. Unable to help himself, he began to undulate forward, fucking her hot, slick mouth with much force. He wanted to control himself—he really did—but her moans of encouragement and the way she worked her hands over his cock had his libido raging out of control.

He pitched forward and pulled her hair back, watching the way his cock slid in and out of her hungry mouth. He'd never seen a more beautiful sight in his entire life.

Pressure brewed inside him. His body ached for release. Senses exploding, he fisted his fingers in her long hair. Christ, he had difficulty remembering how to breathe. A moment later his stomach tightened, his cock thickened, and his world turned upside down. He stilled his movements with a growl and released his seed inside her mouth.

She spent a long time between his legs, milking his every last drop, continuing to lave him with her tongue. Her soft moans of delight and the way she took great care in pleasuring him nearly shut down his brain.

Licking moisture from her lips, Jenna stood. Dean drew a calming breath. "You have one hell of a mouth, Jenna," he said, his hands spanning her waist. She melted against him, pressing her breasts to his chest and murmuring against his throat.

He needed to touch her, to taste her, to fuck the hell out of her all night long. He glanced toward the bed and noted the bottle of champagne and bowl of fresh fruit.

Mmmm . . . strawberries. His mind raced. Oh yeah. Now it was his turn to remedy a longing that had been plaguing his dreams. His whole body shook just thinking about it. He swallowed a tortured moan.

Needing to get her naked, to do delicious things to her body, Dean reached behind her and, in one swift move, ripped her teddy from her back.

She gasped in surprise. "Dean—"

Without taking his eyes off her, he let his hand go to her panties. What he felt nearly drove him to his knees. He loved knowing how wet he made her. "You're drenched, Jenna. Did sucking my cock make you wet?"

Nodding, she gave a breathy, intimate moan and moved shamelessly against him. She shot him a smoldering look. "Are they too wet to peel off?" she asked, her voice hopeful.

Understanding her needs, *her fantasies*, Dean snapped the elastic and ripped off her passion-soaked panties. Pleasure danced in her eyes. His chest tightened.

Once he had her sufficiently naked, he commanded in a soft tone, "I want you on that bed, with your legs spread for me. There's something I've been dying to do, too."

She quickly obliged. He studied the seductive sway of her ass as she crossed the room, pulled the sheets down, and positioned herself on the mattress. Heart racing, Dean advanced purposely and perched on the bed beside her. He took in the sight of her gorgeous naked body. His mouth went desert dry and once again his cock began to thicken with need. His fingers trailed over her skin, touching her body gently, stroking the underside of her breasts. His hands journeyed lower, to her stomach, to her hips, between her legs. He dipped a finger into the moisture between her thighs and wet his parched lips.

Jenna writhed restlessly and spread her legs farther. Her uninhibited responses to his touch nearly dissolved his composure. Everything in him urged him to surrender to his desires, climb over her, and fuck her. Hard. Until they were both sated and drained. But he marshaled his urges. He needed to make this great for her.

Dean reached into the fruit bowl and grabbed two strawberries. He popped one into Jenna's mouth and bit into the other. He trailed the chilled berry over her flesh. Goose bumps exploded on her skin as he dragged the fruit over her lips and her neck, then moved lower until he reached her breasts. He poised the strawberry over Jenna's nipple and squeezed. Sweet nectar dripped over her smooth, milky skin and pooled between her heavy mounds.

She tossed her head to the side, her fingers gripped the sheets. "Oh my," she whispered. The pleasure in her voice excited him.

Bombarded with primal hunger, Dean bent forward and circled his tongue around one puckered nipple, the soft blade lapping at the succulent juice, rehydrating himself while washing away the stain of red from her heated skin.

His thirst temporarily quenched, he pulled her hard bud into his mouth and sucked until her nipple swelled and throbbed in bliss. As he turned his attention to her other breast, offering it the same attention, Jenna cried out and quaked beneath him.

Eager to taste her sweet feminine cream, he climbed onto the bed, nestled himself between her legs, and shifted his focus to her drenched sex. He parted her twin lips, exposing her ripe pink clit, and squeezed more juice onto her pussy. When the cool red nectar touched her heated clit and trickled downward, tickling her, she bucked forward.

"Oh, Dean, that feels incredible."

Leaning into her, he made a slow pass with his tongue. That first sweet taste of her honeyed heat had him salivating for more. "Mmmm . . . you're the sweetest thing I've ever tasted, Jenna."

Her flesh suffused with color. She pitched her hips forward and a moan caught in her throat. Dean inhaled her delicious scent as the urgent need to feast on her whipped through his blood and set him into motion. Without preamble he buried his face in her sex. He pillaged her with his tongue, the warmth from his mouth stoking the fire inside her. Circling his thumb over her inflamed clit, he drove his tongue inside, making sweet love to her with his mouth and fingers until she whimpered with pleasure.

He could feel her tension mount and an orgasm pulling at her. Dean increased the pressure on her clit, knowing just what she needed and just how to give it to her.

Dipping into her wet cunt, he pushed two fingers up inside her, stirring her heat. Stroking deep, he controlled the pace, depth, and rhythm until she writhed and cried out for more.

Impatience laced her voice. "Dean. Please. Now . . ." she begged, her words fractured.

Ready to let her tumble over, Dean sank a third finger inside her.

"I . . . I . . ." she murmured, her voice trailing off as a shudder ripped through her entire body.

He continued to indulge her with his tongue. "That's it, babe. Give me everything you've got." As soon as the words left his mouth, her sweet juices flowed like a broken dam. She bucked forward, giving herself over to her orgasm, as his fingers and tongue took delight in her powerful climax. He paid homage to her clit by drawing it into his mouth, nurturing her orgasm, prolonging it, stretching out the rippling waves of ecstasy for as long as possible.

Her nails dug into his shoulders. She took deep gulping breaths while her muscles tightened and clenched around his fingers in climactic ecstasy.

Dean held her for a long moment. Once she finished riding out the last fragments of her orgasm and her waves had fully subsided, he slid up her body and put his mouth close to hers. Her warm smile turned his heart over in his chest.

He smoothed her hair from her face. His eyes locked on hers. "Tasting your sweetness has made me hard all over again. I believe I need to fuck you, Jenna." Hunger consuming his thoughts, he pressed his cock between her slick thighs. She wiggled until his tip probed her opening.

She flicked her tongue over his lips and moaned. Passion grew in her eyes. Her mouth curved enticingly. "Yes, I believe you do." Dean heard the raw ache of lust in her voice.

Fierce need ripped through him. Jenna snaked her hands around his neck and pulled him to her, until his body crushed against hers. Their mouths met. Control obliterated, they exchanged hungry kisses. Moisture broke out on their bodies and sealed them together.

The need to fuck her made him fairly mad. He quickly sheathed himself, then gripped one silky thigh. Lifting her leg, he tucked it around his back until her calf hugged his hip. The erotic position spread her sex wide-open.

She pressed her mouth to his and whispered, "Fuck me, Dean."

Groaning, he plunged into her hot cunt. His lips crashed down on hers, swallowing her gasp. His tongue darted into her mouth, seeking her heat as he savored her satin warmth. Pleasure forked through him as her body rocked against him, matching his every thrust.

Tight pussy muscles gripped his dick and drew him in deeper. He pumped harder and faster, his balls slapping against her backside. With his cock stretching open her tight walls, he rode her hard, as though leaving his mark, claiming her. It was almost frightening to him the way he needed her.

He rotated his hips, his thick cock caressing her sensitized G-spot, drawing out her next orgasm. Driven by sheer hunger and desperation, he plunged faster, ramming her. She shifted beneath him, driving him impossibly deeper. Her shallow pants and cries told him she was close.

Desperate to give her everything she needed, he slipped a finger between them and pressed his thumb against her clit. Her sex muscles clenched and vibrated around his cock as another rippling climax tore through her. A whimper escaped her lips.

His own orgasm was only a stroke away. The pressure was building, coming to a peak. When her mouth found his again and she kissed him hard, he felt the first erotic pulse of ecstasy. Throwing his head back, he gave himself over to his orgasm. His primal growl rumbled like thunder. His body pulsed and throbbed with the hot flow of release.

He stayed inside her for a long time, just needing to hold her.

Once he caught his breath, he climbed in bed beside her and gathered her in his arms. Jenna snuggled closer to him and rested her head on his chest. The feel of her eyelashes fluttering against his skin caused him to shiver. He grabbed the sheets and covered them both. As he cradled her in his arms, he noted that he'd yet to sate the hunger inside him.

An easy silence descended upon the room as they both retreated to their own thoughts. Dean let his eyes drift shut. He relaxed against her, listening to her breathing level off and soften. A short while later, Jenna broke the comfortable silence.

Lifting her gaze, she stared into his eyes. "Thank you for bringing me here, Dean, and thank you for taking me on a journey of self-discovery. I believe your 'drastic measures' were successful."

Quiet confidence radiated from her eyes. "I have no idea what you're talking about, Jenna. This wasn't about you." He jabbed his thumb into his chest. "This was all about me and my ploy to see you naked. I should be the one thanking you."

She chuckled easily and wiggled in closer. "Oh, okay then. You're welcome."

Suddenly a deep contentment settled in his bones. It occurred to him that, for the first time in his life, he had a feeling of completeness. He idly stroked Jenna's hair and tried to keep his voice light. "What are your plans for tomorrow?"

Again, she tipped her head to look at him. She pursed her lips in thought. "Well, we're still finalizing the bachelorette party plans, and then after that, the girls and I go for a dress fitting. Later on, in the afternoon, I believe we're heading out to do some exploring."

"Oh, I see." He paused and then asked her, "What are you doing tomorrow night?"

"I'm having drinks with one of the clients I met during the fashion show."

"After that?" he pressed, sounding like a possessive lover. The one thing he'd always run away from.

Imagine that.

"After that, I'm free."

When she didn't ask his plans in return, his stomach sank. Really, wasn't that what he always wanted? A woman who wanted casual sex only and had no interest in dictating his every move.

Even though she hadn't yet agreed to go out with him again, he said, "I'll pick you up at eight."

"Aren't you on shift tomorrow night?"

"Yeah," he said, not bothering to elaborate or tell her that they were far from over.

Not only was it time to initiate the rookie into their brotherhood, but it was time to show Jenna that he was capable—and more than willing—to fulfill *all* her sexy fantasies.

Especially her exhibitionist ones.

After giving Dean a good-bye kiss at the back door, Jenna quietly stepped inside the house and made her way to her bedroom. With her mind racing and her body still humming, she could hardly wait to see what tomorrow night would bring. If it was anything like tonight, she knew she was in for one hell of a wild ride. Her body quaked in anticipation.

She washed up in the bathroom, then flung herself on her bed, exhausted but excited just the same. She felt a little guilty that she was here in Chicago for her best friend's wedding only to find herself counting down the hours until she could be with Dean again.

Before drifting off, she gifted herself another moment to think about that couple fucking at the club and wonder what it would be like for someone to watch her: Dean sinking his cock inside her while they had an audience enjoying *their* sexy show. She trembled right down to the tips of her toes. Until tonight, until she'd shed her inhibitions and embraced her sexuality, she'd had no idea how much that prospect excited her.

After a night of great sex, her body shut down quickly, and she fell into a dead sleep. Later, upon awakening, she was swept out of the house by the girls. The daytime hours flew by in a flurry of prewedding activities. Nighttime drinks with a future client went well, and Jenna now found herself alone in the house, pacing restlessly while she awaited Dean's arrival.

Since he was taking her to the firehouse—to do God knows what—she wasn't sure what to wear. She settled on jeans, a T-shirt, and a sexy pair of strappy sandals. Underneath, she wore a thong and a bra from her Siren collection, just in case. . . .

Impatience thrumming through her, she stepped outside and inhaled the fresh summer air while she waited. She walked around the pool and listened to the children playing a few yards down. When she heard a car pull into the driveway, she rushed around the corner.

The gorgeous sight of Dean coming toward her, looking all warm and sexy in his jeans and T-shirt, filled her with need.

His smile was slow and seductive. "Hey, babe." He pulled her against his chest and planted his lips on hers. "Are you all ready?"

"I'm all set." As they made their way to the car, she asked, "What's going on at the firehouse?"

He shrugged. "I thought you might like a tour," he said casually, but the mischief in his eyes told another story.

They talked quietly during the drive there. A short while later Dean pulled into the parking lot and shot her a seductive grin. "This is the station," he said.

She laughed. "Wow. Nice. I never would have guessed."

He chuckled, his eyes widening in mischief. "Want me to show you around?"

"Sure, I'd love a tour."

Dean shot a glance at his watch. "Come on." Hurrying, he climbed from the car and circled it to meet her.

He placed his hand on the small of her back and led her inside. After giving her a quick tour, he guided her out back, to where the fire truck was parked.

His sexy grin made her toes curl. He pulled her in close and brushed his lips over hers. He gestured toward his truck. "I thought you might like to see my hose."

She played along, noting the way her pussy grew wet in anticipation. "I'd love to see your hose, Dean."

"Actually, I thought maybe you'd like to climb onto the roof with me. The view is great."

Excitement coiled in her belly. He wanted to fuck her on the roof of his truck. How totally scandalous! Feeling bold, she slipped her hand between their bodies and cupped his cock. "I'm not really interested in the view."

His body trembled and she could feel his dick thicken. Strong hands pulled her T-shirt out of her jeans. "Tell me something, Jenna. Are you wearing my favorite teddy underneath this?"

She nodded toward the truck. "Why don't we go up there and you can find out for yourself?"

Wasting no time, Jenna went up the ladder first, Dean tight on her heels.

"Hmmm, I kind of like this view," he teased, his face only inches from her ass.

Once she climbed onto the truck, she glanced around, noting that the tall brick buildings surrounding the firehouse gave them a modicum of privacy.

Dean threw a blanket down, dropped to his knees, and dragged her to him.

He pitched his voice low. "I haven't been able to stop thinking about you," he said as his mouth found hers.

Her palms raced over his body in her eagerness to feel his cock inside her again. "Me, neither."

With gentle hands, Dean peeled her T-shirt off. His eyes widened in approval when he glanced at her lacy red bra. "You're so fucking sexy, Jenna."

She had to admit she loved this new uninhibited side of herself. In record time, Dean had made her feel so confident, so gorgeous, and so proud of her body. She in turn tore his shirt off, needing to touch and feel his hard muscles.

He laid her out on the blanket and leaned on his side to face her. "So when you were thinking of me, what were you thinking about?" he asked, his thumbs brushing her nipples.

Jenna arched into his touch and moaned. "Mmmmm, that feels good."

"Were you thinking about me doing this?"

"Yeah," she said.

That and so much more.

Dean pulled the bra cups down to expose her breasts. He leaned in and flicked his tongue over her hard bud. "Were you thinking about me doing this?"

"Uh-huh," she managed, all the while writhing beneath him.

Dean trailed his hand down her stomach until he reached her jeans. He pulled them open. "How about this, Jenna? Were you thinking about me undressing you?"

She angled her head to see his smoldering eyes. "Oh yeah."

Dean lifted himself up, tore off the rest of his clothes, and climbed between her legs. Her mouth watered when she saw his magnificent body and impressive cock.

He pulled her pants off, leaving her panties behind. "Mmmmm, nice." Warm fingers brushed over her soaked cunt.

"I can tell by your wetness that you were definitely thinking about me doing this."

When she lifted her hips, he slowly pulled her panties off, then tucked them into the pocket of his jeans. He leaned forward and licked her. The first sweet touch of his tongue had her spiraling out of control.

"Tell me, babe, were you thinking about my tongue on your clit?"

"Yes," she cried out and widened her legs to give him better access. He swiped his tongue over her pussy a second time and she nearly convulsed.

"Were you thinking about my fingers inside you?" He drove two fingers all the way up inside her, both his thumb and tongue lavishing her clit with attention.

She found it was harder and harder to draw in air. "Yes."

"Were you thinking about me ramming my cock into you?"

She whimpered, aching for him. Delirious with need she whispered, "More than anything."

"Now tell me, Jenna, were you thinking about someone watching while I fucked you?"

Oh God!

She came. Just like that. Her muscles clenched; come flooded his hand.

A noise on the side of the truck drew her focus. Her lids flew open. She gasped and tried to cover herself.

"You have a beautiful body. Don't hide it." Dean pulled her hands away and placed them at her sides.

A guy dressed in firefighter gear stood over them. "Sorry, Dean. You told me to meet you here for some initiation. I didn't realize I was busting in on you."

"This is your initiation, Christian. Have a seat."

Surprise and delight registered on Christian's face as he glanced at Jenna. When he said, "My pleasure," a shiver stole through her.

Jenna tensed. Her gaze traveled from Dean to Christian and then back to Dean again. "What—"

"We're a brotherhood, Jenna. We work together, we play together, and sometimes we pleasure women together." He urged her thighs apart.

Her head was spinning and her entire body quaked. Dean pulled open her lips and swirled his finger through her thick heat.

"And sometimes, my sweet Jenna, it takes two firefighters to put out the flames."

Her skin grew tight, needy. Fire licked over her legs and she damn near erupted a second time just thinking about it. "Are you serious?" She heard the raw ache of lust in her voice.

"Of course. Trust me, Jenna. I *know* what you want and I *know* how to give it to you. Tonight I'm going to pleasure you and I'm going to make all your fantasies come true. Every single one of them"—He reached for his jeans, pulled a condom out of his pocket, and sheathed himself—"even if it takes all night."

Her blood ignited. She gulped, her glance going to Christian, who looked so goddamn sexy in his gear. He slicked his blond hair back. His eyes darkened with desire when they met hers.

"First Christian is going to watch while I fuck you," Dean said, playing out her fantasy.

Her heart pounded with excitement. Need spiraled through her, fueling her hunger. She could hardly believe this was happening. Every nerve in her body came alive. She thrust her pelvis forward and began panting heavily.

Dean knew. He knew her secret fantasies, probably long before she did.

"And later?" she squeaked out.

"Later is up to you."

Before she could formulate a response, Dean climbed between her legs and, in one swift movement, sank his cock all the way up inside her.

"Oh Jesus," she cried out as his thickness filled her completely. She heard Christian let out a low growl and watched the way he shifted for a better view.

Pleasure like she'd never before experienced welled up inside her. She caught her bottom lip between her teeth as Dean pumped harder. His hunger for her seemed so carnal, so raw. Groaning, he buried himself inside her, driving every delicious inch of his huge cock into her wet pussy until his movements reached a fever pitch. She moaned and palmed his corded muscles. Their aroused scents filled the air.

With a hungry gleam in his eyes, Christian rubbed himself, making no qualms about how much he loved watching *their* sexy show. She shivered with delight, knowing how excited their fucking made him.

The stab of pleasure between her legs gained her attention. Her muscles bunched as Dean's cock hit her hot button. Her erotic whimper filled the air.

"That's it, babe. Drip all over my cock," Dean crooned to her.

She bucked against Dean, forcing him deeper. A moment later she shuddered with an orgasm ripping through her. The second she came, Dean pulled his cock out and pressed his mouth to her cunt, lapping her sweet cream. "You taste so fucking good."

She saw Christian lick his lips.

Impulse flooded her. Entirely caught up in the moment, she reached for Christian. He slid in beside her. "Do you want to taste?" she asked.

He nodded and bent forward. In tandem, the two men licked her. One tongue was rough, one soft. One worked her clit while the other dipped into her swollen opening. She angled her head to watch. She reached down and touched Dean's shoulder, needing to feel him. Someone slipped a finger inside her. Her body trembled at the sensation. Another finger joined the mix, and she could feel the rippling waves of another orgasm take hold. She sucked in a tight breath. Unhinged, a climax tore through her and she shattered over them both.

"God. Dean. Yes," she cried out in ecstasy.

Dean glanced up at her. The passion in his eyes filled her with warmth. Her heart tightened. She was falling so fucking hard for him.

"You take her breasts, Christian. I need to finish fucking her."

Christian wrapped his gorgeous mouth around her distended nipple and sucked while Dean drove his cock back into her pussy.

Christian's hot mouth felt like fire on her flesh. Her dry throat cracked as he flicked her with his tongue and cupped her in his palms.

"Jesus," Dean said, ramming into her, "you're so tight, I'm not going to last." He slammed into her a few more times, stilled, then pumped his come up inside her.

When Christian pulled back, Dean collapsed on top of Jenna. She wrapped her arms around him and fought to think.

"Dean, that was . . . *unbelievable.*"

His mouth curved and he shot Christian a glance. The two exchanged a knowing look before Dean turned back to her. "Oh, did you think we were done?"

Just then Christian stood and pulled off his jacket. Her pulse leapt.

Dean brushed his lips over hers. "Because if you did, you'd be wrong."

SIX

Morning was upon them as Jenna pulled off her shoes and crept through Cassie's kitchen alone. She'd given Dean a kiss at the door and her lips still tingled in delight. The sound of Megan's voice stopped her before she could make it to her room and collapse in a heap of one sexually satisfied woman.

"Just getting in?"

She glanced up to see Megan hovering over the coffeepot, a knowing sparkle in her big blue eyes.

"Uh-huh," Jenna said, hardly able to wipe the smile off her face. She still could not believe that Dean had fulfilled her deepest, darkest fantasies and had turned her into a wanton seductress in record time.

"Coffee?"

"Love some," Jenna said, taking a seat.

Megan put a cup of coffee in front of her, sat across the table, and narrowed her gaze, assessing Jenna. She threw her arms up in the air. "What's with you and Sara anyway? A few good rolls in the hay and now you're smitten."

There was no point in denying it. Jenna was crazy about Dean. Plain and simple. Who wouldn't be crazy about a guy who went to drastic measures to pleasure her?

Jenna scoffed and waved her hand right back. "Like you wouldn't be?"

"That's right. I wouldn't be. After my messy divorce, I don't plan on ever falling for anyone ever again. Sex, yes. Anything else, forget about it." She softened her voice. "I knew Dean had it bad for you in the bedroom department, but has he fallen for you, too?"

"It's doubtful."

Megan leaned back and sipped her coffee. "Why?"

"Because he's a playboy, Megan. A playboy who takes women to private places. A playboy who does 'scandalous' things.' She shivered just thinking about it. "This wild affair is just about fulfilling fantasies."

"By the look on your face, I take it he's been doing a fine job fulfilling yours."

"Oh yeah."

Megan's eyes lit up hopefully. She quirked a brow. "Would you like to share all the juicy details?"

"Maybe later."

"Are you going to see him again?"

"Yeah, tonight we're going to dinner." Jenna took a few sips of her coffee and then stood, knowing she needed sleep more than she needed caffeine. "But right now, I need sleep."

"Jenna."

"Yeah." Jenna stopped at the doorway and turned to her friend.

"I bet he feels the same way about you."

Jenna exhaled loudly. Too bad she wasn't a betting woman.

Hours later, after awakening from her nap, Jenna set into motion. She enjoyed a fun day of sightseeing with her friends, did some last-minute wedding preparations, and finally found herself in the bathroom, giving herself a once-over in the mirror.

The sexy silky blue dress Megan had helped Jenna pick out that afternoon hugged her curves and made her feel feminine and sensuous.

There was no doubt about it. Deep inside her a siren existed. It just took the right man to unleash her.

She looked at her watch at the same time the kitchen door opened. She glanced up to see a very handsome Dean. Dressed in a pair of casual pants and a sweater, he oozed masculinity. His dark hair looked damp from a recent shower. Dean panned her body in return and then advanced toward her, closing the gap between them.

He put his mouth close to hers. "You do know we're going to dinner, right?"

Jenna furrowed her brow. "Yeah, why?"

He gestured with his head. "And that's what you're going to wear?"

Her stomach tightened. "You don't like it?"

"Just know this, Jenna. If you're going to sit across the table from me dressed like that, I can't be responsible for my behavior."

Jenna chuckled, pleased at his reactions and the way he made her feel.

He gave a low whistle. "If I ravish you under the table, it's entirely your fault."

She shivered and took a moment to consider things. There was no denying they were physically attracted to each other. But that didn't mean he wanted more, right? Then again, why would a guy like Dean go through so much trouble by taking her to Risqué and helping her overcome her insecurities if he didn't care? And why would he arrange to have Christian join their little party so the two of them could fulfill her secret fantasy? Was it possible that his interest in her went deeper?

Did she dare bet on it?

Pushing those thoughts to the recesses of her mind, she said, "I'm all set."

"Good. I'm starving." The look in his eyes told her it wasn't food he hungered for.

Less than twenty minutes later, she found herself seated in a cozy corner table at Chez Frontenac, Lucien Beaufort's restaurant. She glanced around. "I love this place," she said. "Megan is going to be so jealous."

Dean smiled. "Lucien is a fabulous chef."

"So is Megan. I just hope she gets her big break sometime soon."

Just then the waiter came to take their drink order. Dean ordered a bottle of wine, and after the man left, he turned his attention to her. His eyes darkened and smoldered as they locked on Jenna.

"You look beautiful tonight, Jenna."

"You make me feel beautiful," she said in return.

Dean reached out and closed his hand over hers. The warmth of his fingers scorched her skin. Her entire body came alive. Her sex muscles fluttered. Dean shifted his chair closer to her, his hand going to her knee.

He cleared his throat. "What we did last night—it was pretty fabulous."

"Yeah, definitely fabulous."

"And the night before, at Risqué. You were wild."

She closed her eyes for a second and shivered in remembrance. "It was quite a place."

Dean nodded in agreement. "If I had known how great it was, I'd have gone there sooner. Then again, you're the only girl I ever wanted to take there."

Her heart leapt. She was thrilled to know that Dean wasn't a regular at Risqué, and even more thrilled that she was the only girl he'd ever taken there—the only girl he ever wanted to take there. It amazed her how special he made her feel.

He sidled closer, a torn look in his eyes. "I want to be a gentleman, Jenna, and engage you in meaningful conversation while we share a romantic dinner. But at the same time, all I can think about is taking you home to my place and spending the rest of the night between your legs."

She shivered. "I don't want you to be a gentleman, Dean."

"Good. Take your panties off for me."

She widened her eyes. "Are you serious?"

"Yeah, do it and hand them to me under the table."

Reaching down, Jenna slipped her panties off and slipped them into Dean's waiting hand. He shifted in his seat and tucked them into his pocket.

"I think you're getting a nice little collection of my designer panties," she teased.

"Soon I'll have a pair from every line," he returned, offering her a lopsided grin.

Before she could respond, the waiter arrived with their wine. As the wine was being poured, Dean's hands climbed higher up her thighs. Jenna felt her face flush and her whole body quiver with need. Dean exchanged words with the waiter, but Jenna couldn't comprehend them, not with Dean's fingers brushing over her damp curls. When she widened her legs, Dean dipped into her heat.

Oh. Good. God.

After the waiter left, Dean glanced at her. His playful grin turned wicked, his fingers pressed deep into her. Within seconds, she was on the brink of an orgasm. The man sure knew his way around her body.

"You're a very naughty boy, Dean," she managed around the lump in her throat.

"I told you that I couldn't be responsible for my actions with you dressed like that." His gaze went to her cleavage. He licked his lips. When his thumb found her clit and circled slowly, the world around her faded. She gripped the table and orgasmed right there. Her sex muscles clenched and pulsed around his fingers. She heard his soft growl of delight.

"God, that feels so good," she said breathlessly.

"Well, well, what a surprise to see you two here without the rest of the bridal party." The sound of a woman's voice snapped her back to attention. Dean's hand slipped from between her legs. Jenna straightened and smoothed her dress.

"Hello, Kate," Dean said, annoyance in his voice.

Jenna glanced up to see Kate Saunders, the lingerie model. "Hi, Kate," Jenna piped in and worked to keep her voice steady. "I'm so glad to see you're feeling better."

"Thanks." Kate shrugged her thin shoulders. "I only had a mild case of food poisoning. Some of the other guests at the dinner party were much worse off." Her mouth twisted like she'd sucked a lemon.

Her hand went to her chest. "But after what *I* had to endure, the health inspectors had better stick to their word and shut down All Seasons Caterings."

Jenna paused, wondering why that name sounded familiar.

"Do you two know each other?" Dean asked.

Kate eased her long, lithe body into the chair next to him. "Not really. I saw her hanging around the Hose with Cassie and the other bridal party members, and I was supposed to do a lingerie show for her the other night." Kate flashed her lashes at Dean. "Would you like to formally introduce us?"

Dean glanced at Jenna. "Kate, this is Jenna Powers, my date. Jenna, this is Kate Saunders." He angled his head toward Jenna, offering Kate his back. "Now, if you'll excuse us, Kate, we were——"

Kate cut him off. "What he failed to say is, 'This is Kate Saunders, my girlfriend.' Or, rather, ex-girlfriend." She put her fingers over her mouth. "Oops, excuse my slip."

A pang of jealousy whipped through Jenna's blood. Even though she had no claim on Dean, she still didn't like the way Kate mauled him or threw around their past relationship, wearing it like it was some sort of badge.

Jenna stood, wanting to go freshen up, needing a moment to pull herself together. "Actually, if you two will just excuse me for a second . . ."

"Jenna, wait," Dean said.

"It's okay. It sounds like you two have a few things to work out." With that, she made her way into the washroom.

After splashing her face with water, and taking a few minutes to compose herself, Jenna dried her hands and turned to leave. With any luck, Kate would be long gone by the time she made it back to Dean.

As she pulled open the door, she came face-to-face with Kate. "Kate," she greeted her, attempting to step around her.

Kate backed up, but didn't let Jenna pass. Hands on hips, Kate panned her eyes over Jenna, making her feel self-conscious in her revealing, body-hugging dress, with no panties beneath.

"No baggy pants and sweatshirts tonight?" Kate asked, a derisive twist to her lips. "Dean sure did a fine job with you."

Jenna's head shot up. "What are you talking about?" she asked.

Kate's eyes opened wide in both surprise and delight. "Come on, Jenna. Do you mean to tell me you didn't know?"

"Didn't know what?" Jenna asked through clenched teeth.

"Why, you're just a psychology experiment, sweetie."

Jenna's mind raced, recalling her conversation with Dean at Risqué, and how he was working on his psychology thesis. Surely not . . .

Kate waved her hand over Jenna's body. "Goodness, Jenna, just look at you. You can't possibly think he'd want you."

When Jenna didn't answer, Kate put her hand to her mouth. "Oh, my goodness, you really thought he'd chosen you over me. You're an experiment, sweetie. It's simply in his nature to help people."

Just then Dean came up behind her. Eyes enraged, he grabbed Jenna by the elbow and hauled her to him. "It's not like that."

Kate's high-pitched chuckle grated on Jenna's last nerve. "Go ahead, Dean," Kate encouraged. "Tell her she's nothing more than an experiment to you." Her gaze panned Jenna's silky blue dress. "An experiment gone wrong by the looks of things."

Stomach clenching, Jenna tipped her head to meet Dean's gaze. Without warning, old insecurities rushed back to plague her. Her mouth opened, but her words caught in her throat. When she looked deep into his troubled eyes, her world shifted. His brow furrowed in concern as he held her gaze.

As she gauged his expression, it occurred to her that what she saw was a man who cared a great deal about her needs, a great deal about her desires, and a great deal about her. A man who cared enough to take her on a journey of self-discovery, fulfill all her secret fantasies, and offer her a gift no man had ever offered her before: sexual self-confidence.

Suddenly Megan's words rushed through her mind: *I bet he feels the same way about you.* The second she looked into Dean's eyes, she knew he reciprocated her feelings. The way he gazed at her told her everything she needed to know.

She glanced at Kate. A beautiful woman on the outside, no question about it. It was too bad that, with her, beauty really was only skin-deep. Dean had shown Jenna that she was both. Beautiful on the inside and on the outside. And the look in his eyes gave her the courage to do what she was about to do next.

She drew a breath and considered Kate's question. Did Jenna really think Dean would choose her over Kate? "Yes, I think he chose me," she said with confidence. She put her hand on Kate's shoulder and gave her a little push. "Now, if you'll excuse us, we are in the middle of a romantic date."

When Kate gasped in outrage, Jenna turned her back, giving Dean all her attention. He let out a slow breath and gathered her into his embrace. "Thank you," he whispered. "You are an amazing, beautiful, confident woman, and I'm absolutely crazy about you."

After he dropped a soft kiss on her mouth, she inched back. Her heart beat so hard in her chest she thought it would explode. She could hardly believe the man of her dreams—*and fantasies*—was as crazy about her as she was about him.

"Dean, I feel the same way about you."

He tugged on her arm and looked at her with smoldering eyes. "Come on. We need to eat. Fast."

Chuckling, Jenna asked, "What's your hurry?"

"I need to get you home."

"Oh, but I thought you were starving," she asked, teasing him.

"Someone once told me that when I met the right girl, I'd be down on my knees, in record time. Jenna, you make me want to be down on my knees, in more ways than one."

Her heart leapt in her chest and she stopped midstride. "I think we should skip dinner."

His lips curled. "Yeah?"

"You see, Dean, now that you've unleashed my inner vixen, my siren side, you have no idea what you're in for."

He circled his arms around her waist. "I can't wait to find out." Making no attempt at discretion, he pressed a hungry kiss to her mouth.

Feeling like the bold, seductive woman she really was, she said, "I think you should take me home, strip me naked, and get down on your knees." She pushed her hips into him. "Then I think you should spend the rest of the night fucking me."

She felt his whole body shake. "One condition," he said.

"What's that?"

"I get to fuck you tonight, tomorrow night, and every night after that."

She inched back and smiled at him. "Dean." She paused and brushed his hair from his forehead. "I wouldn't have it any other way."

FLASH FIRE

ONE

rritated, Megan snapped her cell phone shut with much more force than necessary and glanced around the kitchen table. "Great," she blurted out to her friends. "That was Bare Entertainment calling to inform me that our exotic dancer can't make it." She gave a heavy sigh and threw her arms up in the air. "Apparently they overbooked the one and only Dick Diamond."

Jenna groaned and finished her last sip of coffee. "With a name like that, it's no wonder. Can we find someone else?"

The ever-resourceful Sara grabbed the phone book and began flipping through it. "I'm sure it shouldn't be too much of a problem." A moment later she said, "Ah, here's one." Eyes gleaming, she tapped her index finger on the page. "Naughty Boyz, featuring the much-coveted Naughty Nate." She grinned. "Hey, he's no Dick Diamond, but I'm sure we can't go wrong with a guy called Naughty Nate." She dialed the number and pressed the phone to her ear. "If this doesn't work, I'll keep trying." Phone book in hand, Sara twisted around and stepped into the other room, where it was quieter.

"Keep trying what?" Cassie asked, coming around the corner to join them at her table.

"Our entertainment just canceled," Megan said. Removing a purring Misty from her pajama-clad lap, Megan pushed to her feet, walked to the fridge, and grabbed a bottle of dill pickles. "I'm afraid we might have to resort to watching Jenna stare off into space while she dreams about Dean." Megan came back to the table and snapped her fingers in front of Jenna's eyes, bringing her focus back to them. "Hello, earth to Jenna."

Grinning, Jenna smacked Megan's hand away, then glanced at her watch. She nibbled her bottom lip, a familiar habit.

Megan raised an inquisitive brow and handed Jenna the jar. "Going somewhere?"

Jenna twisted the lid off and passed the jar and lid back. "I'm meeting Dean for a late dinner."

Megan shot her a sidelong glance and fished a pickle from the jar. "Uh-huh, and I'm still waiting for that thank-you."

"For what?" Jenna tossed her a miffed look. "For nearly killing me by asphyxiation?"

Undaunted, Megan adjusted her pajama pants higher on her hips and reclaimed her chair. "*And*," she said, dragging out that one word, "you never did share all the juicy details."

Jenna reached for a strawberry and held it poised over her mouth. "Oh, they were juicy, all right, Megan," she said before drawing the berry in with her tongue. "But you'll never know how much."

Feigning a shiver, Megan grabbed the bowl and wrapped protective arms over it. Around a mouthful of dill pickle, she said, "Jesus, Jenna, have you been abusing this delicious fresh fruit? You know, as a sous chef, it's my duty to investigate all produce mistreatment. So kindly tell me all the details," she said in her most authoritative voice, "and I'll let you know if I have to report you to the food police."

Jenna chuckled and stole another glance at her watch.

Megan pushed the bowl away. "Go," she said, waving a dismissive hand. "Go have dinner with Dean. Enjoy yourself. Sara is taking off shortly to meet with Mitch anyway. Apparently they have to do some 'research' "—Megan paused to make air quotes around the word—"for her *Entice* article."

The grateful look in Jenna's eyes made Megan smile. While Megan herself had no desire or plans to ever walk the matrimonial path again, she was happy that her friends had all recently fallen in love. And truthfully, she wasn't jealous at all. Okay, okay, so she might be a bit jealous that her friends were all getting laid and she wasn't.

Even though she'd recently encouraged Jenna to call the Hot Line—heck, the woman had been ready to implode from sexual buildup—deep down Megan really wasn't into one-night stands, which was probably why she married the first guy she'd slept with. Thanks to the nosy blue-haired bingo buff living in the apartment next to them, everyone in Trenton knew what a disaster that turned out to be.

Her ex had been sweet, sensitive, and oh so wonderful when they met. Until she married him. Then, after the honeymoon period, he became a lazy house hippo who wanted to be catered to day and night. Megan learned the hard way that when something looked too good to be true, it usually was.

Even though she wasn't into sex with strangers, she somehow suspected that hunky firefighter Brady Wade could have her singing to another tune. Or talking into the microphone, at the very least, she mused. Yup, with just one smoldering look, the man could have her shedding her panties and swinging on his firefighter pole like a bur-lesque showgirl—and she wasn't referring to the pole in the firehouse, although that came with its own sexy possibilities. . . .

Jenna made her way to the door. "Are you sure?" she asked, pulling Megan from her carnal stupor.

Megan waved her hand and grabbed another pickle. "Yes, go. We're quite capable of figuring out the stripper situation without you, chicky," she assured Jenna with a click of her lips.

"I sure hope so," Cassie piped in, winking playfully at her friends. "All my other gal pals are expecting great things from you three wild women."

After Jenna left, Sara came back in the room and plunked herself into a chair. "Not good," she said.

"No?" Megan crinkled her nose in dismay and held the jar out to Sara, offering her a pickle.

"Nope, not good at all," Sara repeated, taking the jar from Megan's hand. "No one can seem to do anything with only two days' notice." She rolled one shoulder. "Go figure."

Megan puckered her lips, planted her elbows on the table, and blew a deflated breath. "I'm sorry, you guys. It was my responsibility to book the exotic dancer. I should have had some sort of backup plan."

"It's not your fault, Megan," her friends said in unison, consoling her.

After a long moment Sara said, "There must be something we can do."

Megan plopped the rest of her pickle into her mouth, pressed her palms to her eyes, and shook her head. "I cannot believe that in all of Chicago we can't find one man available and willing to take his clothes off for us."

"I'm willing." The deep masculine voice came from behind them. Megan didn't have to turn around to know who it was. She'd recognize that seductive tenor anywhere. His rich tone moved like lightning through her bloodstream and had her libido sizzling like a fiery flambé.

Twisting in her chair, Megan came face-to-face with Brady Wade, the sexiest firefighter she'd ever had the pleasure of setting her eyes on. Her pulse leapt. Her hands moistened. Her pickle lodged somewhere deep in her throat. Holy. Shit. Was he serious? Because if he was, then not only had she solved her dilemma, God had finally answered her prayer to see that sexy firefighter nekkid!

Cassie angled her head and scoffed. "Forget it, Megan. He's Nick's best man. I don't want to see him naked."

Without censor, Megan blurted out, "I do." Oh damn. Had she just said that out loud?

Brady's knowing grin broadened. Megan's stomach clenched, her pickle rising to the occasion, attempting to see what all the commotion was about. She swallowed hard before gifting Brady with an unpleasant view.

Brady Wade. Lord, talk about sex appeal. The guy was smoking hot and had her hormones disco dancing in a way they'd never disco danced before. Of course, she could easily attribute the attraction to her lack of sexual activity since her divorce two years previous.

Flames spread through her like a flash fire explosion as she took a moment to register every scrumptious detail of the guy before her. As Brady stood in the doorway, his huge, well-toned body practically blocked the light from the other room. With his soft hazel eyes, a light sprinkling of hair on his face, and his mussed, sun-bleached blond hair, he always looked like he'd just tumbled out of bed. She wanted to tumble right back into it with him.

Megan took a huge fortifying breath and tamped down her lusty thoughts. This was not the time to be indulging in one of her rich sexual fantasies. That would come later, while watching him strip at the bachelorette party. She bit back the maniacal laughter and resisted the urge to rub her hands together, Jekyll-style.

The truth was, if they didn't take him up on his offer to dance, it could blow the party, except at this moment she had to admit, there really was only one thing she was interested in blowing. . . .

As she continued to take pleasure in his "I can go all night long" athletic physique, his roguish good looks, and his surfer-boy charm, it occurred to her that not only was Brady nipple-hardening sexy, but he was willing and *able* to help her out in a crunch. And dammit, she was willing to let him.

She was a regular humanitarian.

But still, she should have sex with him. Just sex. Wet. Wild. Sloppy. Sex. He looked like a guy who was up for that. She'd just have to make it clear from the git-go that this was a no-strings-attached affair. Not that she expected him to have a problem with that. Not at all. Brady had one-nighter written all over him. He was just the kind of guy who'd indulge in a little good old-fashioned slam-me-up-against-the-wall-and-fuck-me-wild sex.

Jesus, was it getting hotter in here?

Unlike her friends, however, she was not about to fall for a sexy firefighter. Fall *on* him, yes. Ride him hard and put him away wet, yes. But fall for him?

Uh-uh.

No way.

"I think it should be someone outside the bridal party—don't you agree, Megan?"

Dammit, she'd been so caught up in her dirty little thoughts, she couldn't comprehend Cassie's words. She had two choices here: She could agree with Cassie, or she could ask her to repeat the question, letting everyone in the room know that her thoughts had careened off track the second Brady had made an appearance.

Yeah, like they didn't already know that! Sheesh. Still, there was no need to embarrass herself further.

A third option just popped into her mind. Ignoring Cassie altogether, she grabbed the jar of pickles from the table and hopped out of her chair. "Want one?"

Brady grinned and shook his head. "No, thanks. They have garlic in them."

Megan glanced at the jar and noted that Sara had tightened the lid back on. "So."

He cocked his head. "*So* . . . if I kiss someone, I don't want to taste like garlic."

Megan arched a brow and worked to open the lid. Her efforts proved futile. "Well, I just so happen to know that if two people *both* eat garlic, then the tastes cancel each other out. Sort of like two negatives make a positive."

"So if you eat one"—he pointed his index finger at her—"and I eat one"—he paused to jab his thumb into his chest—"and we kiss"—he wagged his finger back and forth between them—"there'd be no garlic aftertaste?" Hazel eyes glistened playfully as they met hers.

Nope, no garlic aftertaste. Just moist panties and nipples hard enough to cut through glass.

When Brady's hungry gaze panned over Megan, she became acutely aware that she was dressed in a pair of hip-hugging pajama pants and a thin cotton T-shirt. Passion smoldered in his eyes when his glance settled on her midriff. His gaze lingered on the exposed skin near her navel, where her T-shirt didn't quite meet her bottoms.

Sex-deprived nymphette that she was, her body responded to the heat in his gaze. She resisted the urge to squirm right into his arms. Instead, she squeezed her thighs together, the action creating heat and friction at the juncture between her legs. Cripes, if she didn't soon gain control of her raging hormones, she was going to set off the smoke detectors. She swallowed a tortured moan, noting that this was the first time in a long time that she had felt such powerful sexual stirrings.

She gave an edgy laugh. "That's right," she managed to get out as the air around them charged with sexual tension. "No aftertaste."

A moment later Brady said, "Well, when you put it that way, then maybe I will have one." He moved into the kitchen and, with two easy steps, closed the gap between them.

Easing into her personal space, he took the jar from her hand, opened the lid with ease, and withdrew a pickle. He slipped it between his lips.

Coming unglued, Megan stood there slack-jawed, watching that gorgeous mouth of his draw the elongated pickle inside. Her mind raced and saliva pooled on her tongue, imagining what it would be like to draw a similarly shaped body part of his between her lips. Her body grew tight and needy. Her internal temperature rose.

She gulped for air.

As her sex muscles fluttered, liquid heat dampened her pajama bottoms. Brady took that moment to redirect the conversation. "When and where is this party?" His tongue snaked out to wipe the juice from his lips.

Megan's brain stalled, making it nearly impossible to comprehend his words. "What party?"

She heard Cassie and Sara chuckling obnoxiously behind her. Dammit, she was going to throttle them both. She marshaled her lascivious mind and got herself a clue.

"Oh, the bachelorette party," she said with an ease that belied her emotions. Making light of her forgetfulness, she slapped her palm to her forehead and said, "I have so many things on the go, I don't know where my mind is half the time."

Like hell she didn't. Her mind was centered on the rather large package before her. Or, rather, on the large package centered between his legs. She forced her eyes back to his face, tucked a temperamental blond curl behind her ear, and took a moment to compose herself.

She smiled and said, "It's Thursday night. In a private room at the Hose. Are you free?"

"Forget it, you two," Cassie piped in.

They ignored her.

Brady's reckless grin turned wicked. "I'm free."

Okay, something about the way he said that sent shivers skittering through Megan. She needed to sit. She really, really needed to sit. Megan retreated, taking a distancing step back, but before she could collapse into her chair, Brady grabbed her arm and hauled her toward him.

He caught her off guard, and her body collided with his. Jesus he smelled all warm and woodsy. Strong and virile. Like a real man. An outdoorsy kind of man. The kind of man who'd like to go on long hikes with her and make love in the wilderness instead of sitting at home, demanding she cater to his every whim. Hmmph, like she'd ever do that!

Which was, of course, why she was divorced today.

Mouth curling upward, she tipped her chin and arched a questioning brow. When she saw the dark desire in his eyes, her smile fell from her face. "What—"

His nostrils flared as he pressed her body against his. A mixture of heat and fire curled around her when his fingers touched her cheek. Intimately. "I just want to test your theory." His voice sounded husky, rough.

Her breath came in a low rush. "My theory?"

Without waiting for Megan's brain to catch up, he cupped the back of her head and angled her mouth. Warm lips closed over hers, taking her by surprise. With desire clouding her judgment and fire singeing her blood, her lips opened in invitation. She moaned and widened her legs, welcoming him into her mouth and anywhere else he so desired.

A tremor raced through her as she reveled in the exquisite, tantalizing flavor of his mouth. He tasted warm, sweet, and very masculine. In fact, he tasted like seconds—thirds, even.

As she entertained the idea, she went up on her toes, her body melting against his like hot wax on a candle. Flames surged to the surface as her sex muscles quaked with need. She moved against him and felt his erection. More precisely, his very big, very hard erection. Her pussy grew slick with excitement. Her body thrummed in anticipation.

The onslaught of pleasure dissolved her composure and had her body gearing up for the good old bump and grind. Not that any bump and grind with her ex had been good. But this sexy Adonis was not her ex—oh no, not by a long shot. Megan had no doubt that if they slipped between the sheets, not only would Brady know his way around her body, but he'd know how to work all her little buttons. And no frigging way on the face of this earth would he think fellatio was something you ordered off the dessert menu at Applebee's.

She burrowed closer and deepened the kiss. Brady groaned low in his throat and dipped his tongue inside her mouth for a slow exploration. Her breasts pressed into his muscular chest. Her nipples puckered. Had she been wearing panties, they'd have been soaked.

Strong hands slid down her neck and caressed her skin. A soft purr caught in her throat as her flesh absorbed the heat of his thick fingers.

Good Lord, there they were, standing in Cassie's kitchen, trading wet, heated kisses like it was the most natural thing in the world for them to do. And the only thing keeping her from jumping his bones and showing him a few other *natural* things they could be doing was the audience of two behind them.

A short while later, Brady inched back and licked his lips. Staring down at her, he gave a slow side-to-side shake of his head, his mussed hair falling forward, cloaking his handsome face. Grinning, he gave a needy, not quite satisfied sigh.

"Well, I'll be damned. You were right, Megan. No garlic aftertaste." She could hear the amusement and arousal in his voice.

With the sweetness of his mouth still lingering on her tongue, and her body still shaking from that mind-numbing kiss, she gasped for her next breath and worked to recover her voice.

"Nope, just moist panties and tight nipples," she blurted without thinking.

Even though she lacked the censor gene, she really needed to curb her outbursts when Brady was around. She stepped back from the circle of his arm.

His eyes smoldered like hot lava. "Oh, and just so you know, Megan. If you do decide you need me after all, I don't plan on getting totally naked."

When disappointment crossed her face, he gave a soft chuckle. His warm breath caressed her flesh. A shiver traveled all the way down to her pussy. He angled his head, his hands going to his forehead. Thick fingers brushed back tousled hair and gained her attention.

"I reserve those shows for private," he added.

She sucked in air, her mind drifting. Visions of herself locked away in a secluded room with Brady, while he danced and stripped for her, caused her body to flush from head to toe. A strange noise crawled out of her throat, and there wasn't a damn thing she could do about it.

"And, Megan."

"Yeah?"

"When you're ready for that, you know the number."

Maneuvering his body to prevent Megan's friends from seeing his raging hard-on, Brady exited through the back door and made his way to his truck. He knew he had to get the hell out of there before he gave in to his lusty urges, dropped to the floor, and dragged Megan down with him, all the while ignoring the fact that they had two sets of curious eyes locked on them.

Okay, so he had to admit: It was a little bold and presumptuous of him to just kiss Megan like that, right there in the middle of the kitchen floor with her closest friends watching. Not only was it a little presumptuous—it was downright cocky. Megan easily could have pushed him away. By rights she should have. Although he was damned pleased she hadn't. But hey, nothing ventured, nothing gained, right?

Normally he wasn't so aggressive, but he wanted to show her that when their lips met, sparks would fly. And indeed they had. He felt the way Megan had responded to his kisses, the way she'd allowed herself to get lost in his touch.

When he walked into that kitchen and spotted her sitting there, looking as sexy as sin in her untied, loose-fitting pajama bottoms, it was all he could do to control his primal urges.

With his cock thickening to the point of pain, he'd fought the compulsion to draw her curvy body to his, to tug her low-slung pants down farther, and drop a kiss on her lush mouth while his hands dipped into her sweet cunt.

There was nothing he could do, however, to keep his gaze from wandering to the exposed skin at her midriff. Honestly, he'd never met a sexier woman, or hungered for anyone quite the way he hungered for her.

His mind shifted through all the things he wanted to do to her body, using his hands, his mouth, and his cock. But the first thing he wanted to do was dip his tongue into her sexy belly button and then trail it lower, until he tasted the sweetness between her legs.

As he negotiated his car into traffic, he afforded himself one more minute to recall the way she'd quivered when he'd pressed his cock into her hip. Fully aware of his arousal, she moved restlessly against him and moaned. The husky desire in her voice had filled him with need, letting him know that she was as wild about him as he was about her.

Brady's cock grew another inch just thinking about her now. He shifted uncomfortably in the driver's seat and gripped the steering wheel harder.

He certainly wasn't about to apologize for ravishing her either, not when they both had enjoyed it so much. And the truth was, he wasn't nearly done with her. Oh no, not by a long shot. His parting words made it loud and clear that he wanted her, and that he was leaving the ball in her court.

Like he'd told his buddy Dean just the other day, he was crazy about a woman, and she was crazy about him, too. She just didn't know it yet.

Soon enough she would come to him, when she was ready. He just hoped it was sooner, rather than later—because the last week had been agony for him. Total fucking agony. Every time the special phone in the station rang, his pulse leapt in his throat and heat rocketed through him like a runaway freight train. Unfortunately, much to his dismay, Megan had yet to call.

Since she wasn't willing to make the first move, Brady was left with no choice. He'd gone to Nick's house tonight fully intending to give the sexy spitfire a little incentive.

Fortunately, Megan had presented him with the perfect opportunity to gather her in his arms and cover her fleshy lips with his. Never one to let an opportunity pass, he took full advantage of the situation and kissed her with all the pent-up lust inside him, proving that the chemistry between them was most powerful, and not to be denied.

Ever since he'd set eyes on her, he knew he wanted to get to know her better, and not just in the bedroom. Over the course of the week, during the wedding rehearsals and intimate gatherings, it became apparent just how much they had in common, just how good they'd be together.

Unlike the women from his social circle, this small-town girl shared his love of the outdoors, his love of animals, and his love of cooking. Not only was she feisty, and bright, but her quick wit and smart-ass attitude made him laugh.

With her well-defined body, it wasn't hard to tell Megan was athletic. Even though she was toned and tight, she was feminine and soft just the same. She had full, round breasts, a nice sway to her hips, and a lush backside that Brady ached to cradle in his palms.

Now the trick was to convince her to take him for a test drive. Since she'd yet to call the Hot Line, he knew he had his job cut out for him.

Soon enough, with the right persuasion, she'd come to him, and when she did, he planned on proving to her how good they could be together. Over and over again, if need be.

Good thing he was a patient man.

Leaving the ball in Megan's court, and biding his time until she made the next move, Brady drove to the station. He found Nick playing a game of solitaire at the card table, Jag asleep at Nick's feet.

"Hey," he said to Nick. After petting his dog, Brady dropped into a chair and asked, "How's it going?"

Nick glanced up, studied Brady for a moment, and gave a resigned shake of his head. "Not you, too?" He snatched his water bottle from the table and held it to the light. "Jesus, there must be something in the water."

Brady grinned. "And here we all thought Dean was the intuitive one in the bunch. Yet he was the only guy who didn't know he'd fallen, and fallen hard."

Nick arched a questioning brow. "Megan, I presume."

Brady moistened his bottom lip, the delectable taste of Megan still alive on his tongue. He took a moment to savor her sweetness and scrubbed his hand over his jaw. Her light floral scent lingered on his skin. He inhaled, dragging air into his lungs.

"None other," Brady confirmed, working to marshal his arousal.

Nick angled his head and made a face that suggested Brady had no idea what he was up against. "I think you've got your work cut out for you, pal."

"I was thinking the same thing." He paused and asked, "What do you know about her?"

Nick shuffled the cards and rolled one shoulder. "Probably not a lot more than you do. She's a sous chef, anxious to open her own restaurant, and she's divorced."

Okay, that one took Brady by surprise. "Divorced?" He took a minute to process the information.

"Yeah, I thought you knew. It was a couple of years ago, and from what I understand, it was a pretty messy breakup. Cassie said Megan hasn't dated anyone since."

Brady paused for a moment to consider that tidbit of information a second longer. As he mulled things over, he had a sudden epiphany. There was no disputing the fact that he wanted Megan and she wanted him. Tonight's passionate kiss had proven that. Obviously her failed marriage had left her reluctant to get involved with anyone again, or to call the Hot Line for a night of hot, passionate sex.

Brady nodded his head. "Megan never mentioned it, but it sure explains a lot."

"Such as?"

"*Such as* . . . her reluctance to call the Hot Line."

Nick laughed and gifted Brady with an amused look. "Maybe you just don't do it for her, Brady. Have you ever thought of that?"

Brady tossed him a cocky grin. "See, that's just it. She needs to call the Hot Line so she can see just how much I can do it for her."

Nick snorted and then divvied up the cards. "Cassie did mention something about Megan's ex being a real asshole. I think the term she used was house hippo, whatever that means. I guess after the honey-moon stage he turned into a complete jerk, expecting Megan to cater to his every whim. My guess is he destroyed her belief in happily ever after." Nick shrugged. "It's obvious she doesn't want to find herself in that situation again."

A burst of anger shot through Brady. "Asshole," he said under his breath.

He stared at his cards and took another moment to sort through matters. No doubt after her disastrous relationship, Megan had lumped all men into the same category: lazy guys who wanted to be catered to. He fisted his hands, his blood burning hot. To think her ex would treat her like that infuriated him. A smart, sexy woman like Megan deserved a hell of a lot better. She deserved someone who would appreciate her. He wanted to be the one to show her that.

His mind raced, crafting a plan to prove he cared about her and her needs—a plan that would also show her he was nothing like her ex. As he settled on the perfect solution, his heart beat in a mad ca-dence, eager to put his idea into motion.

He knew exactly what he had to do.

He'd cater to *her* every whim.

The minute he got her alone, he planned on addressing her every desire, her every fantasy, taking his time to pleasure her like she'd never been pleasured before.

His muscles began to vibrate as he pictured her naked body spread out on his bed, his mouth on her lips, her breast, her clit as his hands traced the pattern of her curves. His cock probing her drenched open-ing until she begged him to take her, over and over again. He shifted uncomfortably in his seat, his dick clamoring to do just that.

When morning came, he'd cater to all her other needs. He'd run her a warm bath and serve her breakfast in bed, followed by a round of dessert, if she was so inclined.

"Jesus," he murmured under his breath, his cock swelling to the point of no return.

Needing to release some tension, he tossed his cards down, climbed from his chair, and grabbed his basketball from his locker. "How about a game of twenty-one?"

Fuck, he needed something to occupy his hands until Megan's call came in. Then again, maybe letting off some steam in a hot shower might help him make it through the next few hours. Because if she didn't call soon, he was going to go off like a goddamn grenade.

TWO

With Jenna and Sara off on their dates, and Nick at work, Cassie and Megan were the only two left at home. Fortunately—or unfortunately, depending on whom you were asking—they'd managed to track down an exotic dancer for Thursday night's show. Megan could certainly understand why Cassie had no desire to see Nick's best man naked. But, damn, what about Megan's desires? Talk about a blown opportunity. How the hell was she going to get a glimpse of Brady's gorgeous, well-toned body now?

By calling the Hot Line, of course.

Megan was yawning and thinking about making her way to bed early when Cassie poked her head into the kitchen. "I have to head over to the station for a minute. Want to come?"

Megan shrugged, no longer tired. Clearly the thought of glimpsing Brady decked out in his firefighter gear had given her a second wind. She tried to keep the enthusiasm from her voice. "Sure. Why not? I have no other plans." She waved her hand. "Plus I'd love to see Brady's dog, Jag," she said breezily.

Cassie shot her a knowing look, then rolled her eyes heavenward. "Jag? Oh please, Megan. You're as transparent as cling wrap."

Megan scoffed and shrugged her shoulders. "What? I like animals," she said, unable to keep the maniacal grin from her face. Not only had she been born without the censor gene, but she'd also been born without the cloaking gene. She wore her emotions on her sleeve, and there wasn't a damn thing she could do about it.

"Just give me a sec to get freshened up." Megan took a quick minute to splash on some makeup and fluff her short blond hair. After changing out of her pajamas and into a pair of jeans and a short-sleeved blouse, she met Cassie at the door.

Once they were on the highway, Megan turned to Cassie, curiosity getting the better of her. "So what's Brady's story, anyway?"

Cassie took a sip of cola and put it back into the dash tray. "He's one of the nice guys, Megan." She angled her head and met Megan's glance. "And, as you and I both know, those nice guys are few and far between."

Megan chewed on that bit of information for a minute. So Brady was nice *and* hot. What a lethal combination—a combination that would attract a lot of women, no doubt. For a minute she wondered if he had his own harem—or if he was a regular participant in the Hot Line. Not that it mattered to her. It didn't. Because what he did in his free time was none of her business. But still . . .

"What does he do for fun?" Megan asked.

"Well, he loves to cook, loves animals, and loves the outdoors. The four guys often take off on the weekends. They either go fishing—you've already heard Mitch's fish tales," she chuckled and continued, "or they go mountain biking. Sometimes in the winter they go snowmobiling. Brady has a cottage just north of us."

Megan pursed her lips. Sounded like fun. Her kind of fun. "Hmmph, he sounds too good to be true, Cassie."

"Maybe. I guess you'll have to find that out for yourself."

Maybe Megan would.

Or not.

Megan mumbled under her breath. "He probably has his mother down in the deep freeze."

Cassie laughed out loud. "Such a pessimistic attitude."

Megan flashed a smile and folded her arms across her chest. "That is not a pessimistic attitude, by any means. That is an 'I don't want to have my ass frozen in anyone's deep freeze' attitude."

Cassie chuckled. After a quiet moment she said, "Look Megan. I'm not going to tell you what to do—you're a grown woman. I do know what you've been through with your ex though, and trust me, not all men turn out to be assholes like him. Maybe you should give Brady a chance." She gave Megan a wink and lightened the mood. "He sure seems to want it."

With that advice, Megan turned her attention to the radio and flicked through the stations. A short while later, Cassie pulled her compact Honda into the parking lot at the station. When Cassie spotted Nick playing ball outside the big garage doors, a warm loving smile crossed her face. "He's one of the good guys, too, Megan."

Megan's heart turned over in her chest when she saw the love shining in Cassie's eyes.

"So are Mitch and Dean," Cassie added. "They're a family. A brotherhood. Where they all look out for each other."

A wide smile crossed Nick's face as he waved to Cassie and made his way to the car. They were so obviously perfect for each other. Megan felt a pang of envy. She once thought she had fairy tale love like that. But look how that "happily-ever-after" had turned out.

But still, just because she had no intention of walking down the aisle again, it didn't mean she wasn't up for a hot roll in the hay with a sexy firefighter.

Her gaze drifted to the basketball net in time to see Brady—a bare-chested Brady, that is—go in for a layup.

Her thoughts careened off track.

Her breath caught in her throat.

Her libido jumped as if it had just struck gold.

As she took in his broad shoulders, sculpted muscles, and rock-hard abs, she had to roll her tongue back into her mouth.

O-kay . . . this was way better than seeing him in his firefighter gear. Waaayyyy better. Now how could she go about getting him to remove those low-slung jeans?

By calling the Hot Line, she knew.

All righty, then . . .

Brady tucked the ball under his arm and started toward her. The floodlights overhead bathed the parking lot in a fluorescent glow, providing sufficient light for her to see the moisture glistening on his bronzed skin. His long legs ate up the cement walkway in record time. Talk about eye candy, she mused. The kind she'd like to pop in her mouth and savor until sunup. A week from Thursday.

Gaze riveted, Megan watched his hair billow in the summer breeze. With long, even strides, he moved across the parking lot, his body exuding the confidence of a man who knew what he wanted and how to get it.

He scrubbed a palm over the bristles on his chin. "Mmmm . . ."

Megan moaned and shifted her stance. Moisture pooled in her panties. Brady was pure carnal delight. He did the most interesting things
to her libido. She flushed from the top of her head right down to the
tips of her toes just from looking at him. For a moment she wondered
if her blond hair had turned fiery red from heat and desire.

"Why don't you take Nick's place and go shoot a few baskets with
Brady?" Cassie said. "I have to steal him away for a few minutes."

Instead of answering her friend, Megan stood there taking pleasure in Brady's athletic gait while her hormones played an aggressive
game of leap frog. As she once again thought about exploring a brief
affair with him, heat ambushed her pussy, scorching her in a way it
never had before. For a moment she had difficulty remembering how
to breathe. The idea of having a hot affair with him was simply scandalous.

Megan could feel flames licking at her thighs, a flash fire threat-
ening to overtake her. Lord knew if she didn't do something soon to
extinguish the heat she was feeling, the fire station was going to go up
like an inferno.

His eyes full of desire, Brady stepped into her personal space. His
earthy scent assailed her senses. He held the ball out to her. "You want
to play a little one on one?"

Oh God, those innocent words held so many innuendoes. Her
mind raced with the possibilities. Her eyes locking on his triggered a
craving deep inside her. She licked her lips as they itched to get reac-
quainted with his.

Her voice hitched. "Sure, but I must warn you that I played var-
sity in high school."

His reckless grin turned her insides to Jell-O. He widened his
stance, forcing her to work overtime to keep her eyes from drifting

downward. His hand touched hers and lingered an extra moment as he passed the ball. "Then I consider myself duly warned." He waved toward the net. His perfect teeth flashed in a smile. "Ladies first."

Her shoulders rolled as she relaxed into conversation. "And here I thought chivalry was dead," she said.

He fell into step beside her. His sweet-scented skin curled around her like a powerful aphrodisiac. He chuckled easily. "Hang with me for a while, Megan, and I'll show you chivalry isn't dead." He winked at her. "I believe in ladies first, second, and third."

Oh. My. God. Yes.

It was official. Her libido *had* struck gold.

Dribbling the ball, Megan made her way to the net with a shirt-less Brady keeping pace beside her and his words ringing loud and clear in her brain. How the hell did he expect her to concentrate on the game with his promise of triple orgasms dancing in her head?

He jogged ahead, positioning himself in front of her, providing her with an unobstructed view of his magnificent body.

He gave her a lopsided grin. "Just don't think I'm going to go easy on you because you're a girl," he said, a gleam in his eyes.

Heck, she didn't want him to go easy on her. She wanted him to go *hard* on her. Perhaps she should let him know that. "I'd never want you to hold back, Brady. I'm sure I can take all you can give." She bounced the ball through her legs, showing off her ball-handling skills.

Her words brought passion to his eyes. "You think so?"

She puckered her lips in defiance. "I know so."

"So if I play my hardest, you think you can keep up?"

She bit back a grin. "Not only can I keep up, but I can probably keep going long after you're finished." Megan was pretty sure they were no longer talking about basketball. She was also pretty sure surfer boy here had the stamina of a stallion and could long outlast her any day. Especially since she'd been out of practice for the last couple of years.

His soft chuckle made her wet. "Perhaps we should make a wager."

Her glance went from Brady to the net, back to Brady again.

Damn, he was hot.

Never one to back down, she gave a casual shrug. "Perhaps we should."

His eyes darkened with lust. "If I win, and you lose, then you're mine for one hour."

She gulped for air. Uh . . . how exactly was that losing? "And if I win?" Did she get him for a whole hour, too? Damn, talk about giving a whole new meaning to a little one on one.

"Well, what do you want?" Brady asked.

Megan kept the grin from her face. "I do have some laundry to do."

Brady laughed out loud. "You want me to do your laundry?"

"No, I was just thinking out loud." She crinkled her nose in thought. With a casual nonchalance that she didn't feel, she said, "I supposed if you get me for an hour, then it's only fair that I get you for an hour."

Dear God. Brady Wade. Hers. To do with as she pleased. For one whole hour.

Hell, yeah! She really had to win this. Then again, losing had its appeal too. . . .

"Deal." Brady held his hand out to her.

She switched the ball over to her left hand and shook his hand with her right. The warmth of his flesh ignited a fire inside her and bombarded her with desire. A deep ache between her legs drew her focus. She took a moment to rein in her lust and strategize her next move. Okay, all she had to do was dribble the ball around him and do a layup. Easy-peasy. She'd done it a million times before. Then again, she'd never had a sexy, half-naked firefighter blocking her path before, derailing her concentration.

Truthfully, not only would it be impossible to get around that huge, rock-solid body of his, but his near nakedness was throwing her off her game. And from the way she stood there ogling him, she suspected he knew it.

Well, two could play his game, she mused. She wasn't without her own feminine wiles. In her most sultry voice she said, "My goodness, it sure is a warm night." She undid the top two buttons on her blouse and dragged a finger over her throat, trailing lower until she felt the swell of her breasts. As if on cue, Brady's gaze dropped to her cleavage. With his attention diverted, she dribbled around him and went in for the layup.

She shoots. She scores.

Brady grinned and cocked his head. He gave a low, throaty chuckle. "So that's the way we're going to play it, is it?"

She threw him the ball and rolled her eyes. "It's the big ones who are always the slowest," she teased. "This is going to be a cake walk."

Brady grabbed the ball and gave her a sly grin. God, she loved that sexy grin of his.

Megan positioned herself in front of him. Guarding the net, she reached out and palmed his stomach. Okay, maybe that wasn't her brightest move. The second her hand came in contact with a row of densely packed muscles, a shiver stole over her. Brady took advantage of the situation, rolled around her, and took a jump shot.

"That's a three-pointer, Megan." He caught his rebound and tossed her the ball.

"Hmmph," she groaned, ignoring the look of victory on his face. "Lucky shot."

Switching tactics, Megan turned and put her back into him. Her plan was to bump him backward, but unfortunately, hitting that rock-solid body was like hitting a brick wall. One bump into him sent her flying forward. She lost her balance and hit the ground with a thud. Arms and legs spread wide, she groaned. Shit, that hadn't gone quite as planned.

Within a second Brady was at her side. "Megan, are you okay?"

She rolled to face him and touched his stomach. "Damn, Brady, what are you packing?"

He glanced at her apologetically. His knuckles brushed her cheek and pushed back a strand of hair. "God, Megan, I'm so sorry." The emotion in his voice took her by surprise.

His gaze panned her body. "You ripped your jeans, and your knee is bleeding."

She went up on her arms for a better look. Bits of gravel were embedded in her leg. Ugh . . .

Crouched on his knees, Brady cradled her leg in his hand. He bent forward for a closer inspection. "Let me take care of this for you." When he lifted his head and met her gaze, her heart nearly stopped. The compassion and warmth she met there did the weirdest things to her.

He adjusted his body and scooped her into his arms. His nurturing side sent myriad emotions rushing through her bloodstream. It had been a long time since someone had taken care of her and she had to admit that she rather liked it.

As Brady packaged her in his strong arms, his long legs made quick work of the parking lot. "Let's get you inside." He pulled open the firehouse door and carried her through the threshold. Her libido roared to life as he pulled her in tighter. She sank into the warmth of his magnificent body as he hustled her down the long corridor. Her skin flushed hotly and she wondered if he felt the desire rising in her.

With his expression both tender and sensual, he pitched his voice low and said, "I need to remove the gravel and cleanse your cut."

Remove the gravel.

Cleanse her cut.

Give her an orgasm.

Or three.

Really, the possibilities were endless.

A wheezing sound crawled out of her lungs.

His voice softened again. "Are you okay?"

"Yes," she lied.

Bypassing the others, Brady carried her through the locker room and into a private-shower area. He locked the door behind them while she studied her surroundings, taking note of the decor. Gray-and-white marble tile covered the entire shower area, floor to ceiling, wall to wall. She noticed a small cabinet tucked away in the corner, out of spray range.

Gesturing with a nod toward the built-in perch beside the shower hose, Brady said to her, "Have a seat."

"Uh, my clothes will get soaked."

His gaze darkened. He moistened his lips. He jammed his

hands in his pockets, pulling his low-slung jeans down farther, gifting her with a nipple-hardening view of his sexy oblique muscles, which just happened to be one of her favorite male body parts. He narrowed his gaze. "Yeah, I guess we should do something about that."

Hormones on overdrive, and needing desperately to quell the restlessness inside her, Megan reached for her button, eager to shed her pants and see where that led them. Even though she'd never engaged in a one-night stand, she wasn't inhibited sexually. She was merely deprived sexually. And by God, it was about damn well time she did something about it.

Brady stopped her. "Here, let me. It might be easier if I pull them over your cut."

"Okay." Her voice came out a little rough.

Brady dropped to the floor before her and worked the button free. With the utmost care, he eased her jeans down her legs. As she took in the length and thickness of his fingers, her heart hammered. She could only imagine how good they'd feel inside her. Shaky hands gripped his shoulders for support. Her nipples began to tingle and the incessant ache between her legs demanded attention.

Brady stepped back and turned the shower on. Megan eased herself onto the perch and stuck her leg out.

"Are you comfortable?" The sincerity in his eyes tugged on her emotions.

Brady was so sweet, so caring, and so damn sensitive . . . so different from her ex. Megan drew a long breath and gave herself a quick lecture. This wasn't about relationships or marriage. It was about a cut knee and orgasms. Yes, "orgasms" with an "s," as in plural. He'd promised her three.

She shifted, her body aching for his touch. "Yes. I'm comfortable."

Pulling a professional face, he removed the nozzle from the hook, tested the water and then let the warm stream spray over her knee. After a minute or two, he grabbed a washcloth from the cabinet and cleansed the area. She watched in speechless fascination as he took care of her, the same way he would anyone under his professional care.

She found that damn sexy.

When he glanced up at her, his eyes were dark and hungry. His jaw clenched and unclenched. "There you go. I think you'll be fine."

Oh no, she was far from fine. She cleared her throat. "Are you sure?"

She met his glance, her eyes conveying without words what she wanted—no . . . what she *needed*. As though he understood her desires, Brady dragged the nozzle higher on her thighs, his fingers following the path. Without taking his gaze off hers, he spread her legs and tipped the showerhead toward her. The soft spray sluiced over her flesh as it drenched her silky underwear. It felt erotic, stimulating. Her soaked panties pressed against her sex. Her clit puckered and throbbed in response. Blistering heat exploded in her veins and she ached to feel his cock inside her.

"Oops. I accidentally wet your panties." His voice caressed her all over, and the bulge in his pants told her he was equally aroused.

"Brady."

"Yeah?"

"They were already wet."

The way Megan lifted her hips provocatively off the marble perch had his body reacting with primal need. Heat, desire, and passion whipped through his blood, so it was all he could do not to tear off her panties, pull her onto his lap, and drive his cock deep inside her. Moisture broke out on his skin; his hands shook with need.

She gave him a smoldering look, then leaned forward, her mouth hot against his ear. "See for yourself," she said in a breathless voice.

Lust hit him so hard he nearly toppled backward. Brady roughly tugged her panties aside and pressed a finger into her heat. Megan threw her head back and sobbed with pleasure.

Holy fuck. She was so tight and so fucking hot. Her sweet cream soaked his skin and nearly shut down his brain. Sex muscles clenched around his finger and he knew she was desperate for release. He was just as desperate for it. He slipped another finger in deep and pumped in and out until her muscles tightened and spasmed. She clutched his hand and held it inside her, while her other hand went to her clit. As she stroked her puckered nub, he rolled the tip of his finger around her G-spot. Her face flushed. Her body vibrated. Her eyes clouded.

"Oh, my God," she cried out. She bucked forward, once, twice, and then came all over him.

Hunger clawed at him. His body trembled and his cock nearly burst through his zipper in an attempt to reach her slick channel. Christ, he needed to release the tension inside him before he blacked out.

Brady lifted her to her feet and hauled her under the warm spray. Her lashes fluttered but her blue eyes were still glossy from her orgasm. He adjusted the overhead nozzle. Water drenched them both. The clothes stuck to their bodies and clung like a second skin.

She blinked up at him through the hair plastered to her forehead. Her eyes glittered with dark sensuality. She looked so damn beautiful standing there in her panties with her wet blouse hugging her breasts.

When her body melted against his, his breathing grew shallow as he marveled at how crazed she made him feel.

He bent forward and gave her a soft kiss, letting her know what she did to him.

A moment later, his fingers went to her buttons, ready to advance their relationship to the next stage. "Let's get you out of this." He heard the impatience in his voice.

She arched into his touch, her mind still two pages behind. "Brady, that was amazing. I've never come so fast before."

"I guess you must have needed it." He cleared his throat, barely able to speak.

She tore at his shirt. "That's not all I need. I've been dying to see you naked since I first laid eyes on you."

He gave a low, rough laugh, pleased as hell at her bold behavior. He stepped back, ripped his wet clothes off in record time and re-joined her under the spray. "You know, Megan, I think that's what I love most about you. You say it like it is and don't hold anything back."

Her eyes widened as they settled on his engorged cock. She licked her lips. "You're so . . . impressive." She sheathed him in her hands and squeezed.

Was that concern he spotted in her eyes? "I'll go easy."

She furrowed her brow. Passion burned in her eyes. "I told you already I don't want easy. I want hard."

He knew it had been a while for her and wanted to take it slow. "Megan—"

She cut him off. "Since I don't hold anything back, I don't expect you to either." She wrapped her arms around his neck and pulled him to her.

His lips crashed down on hers. Their tongues mated as he peeled off her blouse. Her bra quickly followed. Gorgeous breasts pressed into his chest and weakened his resolve to take this slow.

He growled with longing. Brady knew the first thing he needed to do was taste her. He pushed her back against the wall and bent forward, his mouth going to her breasts.

She cupped them in offering. He brushed his tongue over her damp flesh before drawing her taut nipple into his mouth. Her fingers raced through his hair. She gripped his head and held him to her. He sucked her nipple. Hard. The way she wanted it. God, she tasted like heaven. A moment later she moved his head to her other nipple.

Brady inched lower, running his tongue over her stomach until he found the hollow of her belly button. Ever since he'd glimpsed her in her pajama bottoms, dipping into her button was all he'd been able to think about. He slid his hands around her ass and gripped her. His tongue made slow passes over her stomach, poking in and out of her sexy little cleft. Megan shook beneath his seduction. She writhed, opened her legs, and rubbed up against him. As Brady inhaled the sweet scent of her arousal, his body went up in flames.

He trailed his tongue lower, until he reached her hot pussy. He pulled open her lips with his tongue and ran the pad of his thumb over her plump clit.

"Brady," she whispered and sagged against the wall, "that's . . ." Her words fell off.

He inhaled her, then moved in for a taste. At the first touch of his tongue to her clit, she came again, taking him by surprise. She leaned forward and grabbed his shoulders. Her body shook violently. Small whimpers caught in her throat. Jesus, he'd never met a more responsive woman.

He spent a long time lapping up her silky heat. His cock throbbed with need. His desire mounted, his liquid heat spilling from the slit.

"Brady, I need you to fuck me. Please . . ."

Shit! He wasn't equipped. He glanced up at her. "Tell me you've got condoms, Megan."

Her mouth twisted downward, then she splayed her hands on the wall. "Oh no . . ." she whimpered. "You have to fuck me, Brady. You really, really have to. You have no idea how much I need you."

Fuck, he needed her just as badly. His gaze went to the cabinet and he gave a silent prayer. Please let there be condoms in there. Actually, he'd pretty much make a deal with the devil himself right about now.

He inched back. When he did, her hand went to her sex. She slipped a finger into her pussy and began to masturbate. Her boldness excited him beyond anything he'd ever known.

He sucked in a sharp breath. "Hang on, sweetheart." Leaving her writhing against the wall, he rushed to the cabinet and tore into it. His heart raced as he tossed towels and washcloths over his shoulder. He nearly cried out in euphoria when he found a half-full box of condoms tucked in the back.

He quickly slipped one on and rejoined her. He brushed his lips over hers and his fingers widened her opening. She was so small and tight he feared he'd hurt her. Megan reached down and stroked him.

Blue eyes met his. "Please fuck me," she said, her voice full of want.

Brady opened her legs with his, bent his knees, and positioned his head at her slick entrance. His nostrils flared. His blood pounded hot. His bottled-up lust exploded. In one swift motion, he pushed into her, lifting her clear off her feet.

"Yessss," she hissed. She wrapped her legs around his waist to hold him inside her. Brady slipped his arms under her ass and balanced her against the wall. Her heat scorched him, her muscles gripped him hard.

"You're so tight, Megan. I'm filling you up."

With her back to the wall, she rocked her hips forward so that her hard nipples scraped across his chest, her hands clawing through his hair. God, she was so wild, so frenzied. Her eyes blazed with need. "Brady, please stop talking and just fuck me."

The urgency in her voice prompted him into action. "My pleasure." Needing to give her what she wanted and answer the pull in his groin, he began rocking, burrowing deeper, ravishing her with dark hunger. Breath labored, she met his every thrust. Her muscles spasmed and sucked him in deeper. Her sweet syrup scorched his cock. Jesus, he was so close. He clenched his jaw in distress before he completely lost all control.

The fire in her eyes licked over him. Heat colored her skin. She closed her eyes, seemingly delirious with pleasure. Balancing her with one arm, he reached between them and pinched her clit. She gave a broken gasp. He could feel the pressure building inside her, feel her soft quakes. Their eyes met. He plunged deeper.

"Brady . . ." she whispered against his cheek. Suddenly, her body began vibrating and he felt her rippling tightness around his cock.

A rush of tenderness overcame him as he watched her peak. "That's it, Megan. Let go. Drip on my cock."

Panting, she gave herself over to the hot flow of release. Her nails bit into his skin as her heat soaked his cock. She moaned and impaled herself on his erection. "Oh, God, Brady," she whimpered.

Brady drew quick shaky breaths as his cock absorbed each delicious wave of release.

After her tremors subsided, her lips found his. She brushed his hair back and collapsed against him. "Please, Brady. I want to feel you come inside me."

He crushed his chest into hers, and with single-minded determination, he pumped again and again, until he reached the point of no return. He gave a low groan of surrender. Holding her tight, he threw his head back and released deep inside her.

She cried out as he pulsed and throbbed deep in her pussy. "That . . . feels . . . so . . . incredible."

"Sweetheart, you feel incredible," he managed to get out between pants.

A long moment later, Brady inched back and let her legs fall to the floor. He then gathered her into his arms and held her. She nestled against him. Both of them breathing heavy, they just stood there, wrapped in each other's arms. When he felt her shiver, Brady walked backward and pulled her into the warm spray.

She gave a small sigh and tipped her head to meet his eyes. "I really, really needed that." Brady smiled down at her and hugged her tighter. "It's been a long time," she admitted. "Two years to be exact." She chuckled softly, poked her finger into his chest and added, "After one night with you, I just might be able to make it through another two years."

Brady chuckled. "Don't worry, Megan. There's plenty more where that came from."

Her eyes opened wide. "Yeah?"

"Oh yeah." And he was about to prove it. He pitched his voice low. "Let me wash you up." He grabbed her hips, twisted her around, and tucked her ass into his groin. He lathered his palms and began soaping her body. His hands slid over her breasts and her stomach, then between her legs. She moaned and arched into his touch.

"Ahhh . . . is this supposed to be turning me on?" she asked breathlessly. "You're turning me into a sex nymphette. Keep this up and I'll want you to do this to me every day."

Then his plan was working.

She pushed against his cock and he instantly hardened. "I'm just trying to wash you up." When she angled her head to see him, he pulled an innocent face and purposely nudged her clit.

As his erection pressed into her back, she stepped forward, splayed her hands on the wall and tipped her ass, offering herself up so nicely to him. "Please, Brady, I need to feel you inside me, again."

Brady knew there was just no sating their hunger for each other. He stepped back to let his gaze pan over her. Hands pressed to the wall, ass up in the air, her slick pussy was wide-open, still swollen from his cock. He swallowed hard at the erotic sight.

Passion and possession raced through him. Brady quickly sheathed himself and, with one quick push, plunged into her heat.

"Ooohhh," she whispered, rocking back and forth on his cock, "that feels so good."

He wrapped his hands around her waist and pumped hard and deep. She fisted her fingers and bent forward a little more, granting him deeper access.

"More," she screamed. "Harder."

Brady rammed her deep, giving her his entire length and girth. Bending over her back, he practically buried his balls inside her.

Wild with need, she began thrashing against him. "Take the condom off, Brady. I don't want to feel rubber. I want to feel you inside me. I want to feel your cock."

Before he had a chance to honor her request, she came apart in his arms. Her muscles clenched around his dick, and he exploded right along with her.

He grabbed her waist and spun her around to face him. His lips found hers. "You are so wild," he murmured into her mouth.

She gave a satisfied sigh. "You're pretty wild yourself." She wound her hands around his neck and held him close to her.

He brushed her wet hair from her face. His heart pounded in his chest. There was no way he could let her walk away tonight. "Megan, stay here with me."

She glanced around. "Here?"

He chuckled. "Not here in the shower. Here in the firehouse."

"Can I do that?"

He nodded. "I'll make us something to eat, and later, when you get tired, you can go to sleep in my cot."

Her glance settled on her wet clothes. "What will I wear?"

"I keep spare clothes in my locker. You can slip into something."

She grinned. "You think they'll fit?"

"We'll make them fit." He pulled her in tighter. Now that he had her here, he had no intention of letting her go. For the rest of the night, he planned on fucking her over and over again, catering to her every sexual need.

"Come on, sweetheart. Let's go get changed. I'm turning into a prune."

"Umm, Brady, before we go . . ."

"Yeah?"

"You mentioned something earlier about chivalry."

He dipped his head to look into her gorgeous blue eyes. "Uh-huh."

"Something about ladies first, second, and even third."

"That's right. I did."

She nibbled her bottom lip and offered a mischievous grin. "I believe I only counted two," she lied.

"Two, huh?" He chuckled at her playful side.

She shrugged innocently. Her lips twitched. "Yup, only two." She gave him a sexy wink. "Then again, math never was my strong point."

THREE

ood morning, gorgeous."

Megan stretched and opened her eyes. She smiled as her gaze settled on Brady. Eyes dim, hair mussed, and fully clothed, he lay beside her on his cot, looking warm and sleepy. She'd fallen asleep only hours earlier, not that she had wanted to. She enjoyed Brady's company far too much to waste the night away sleeping. But morning was upon them, his shift was over, and she knew it was time for her to make her way back to Cassie's house.

"Good morning, handsome," she whispered back. She snuggled into him and took a moment to recall the amazing night they had shared. Her body quaked in remembrance.

Late last evening, after showering, they'd made their way to the firehouse kitchen, where they'd whipped up a couple of omelets. She had no idea that Brady was such a fabulous cook.

Over their omelets, Megan had spilled jam on herself, which meant another trip to the shower to wash up. The erotic memories of what took place during that little interlude filled her with warmth. Honestly, now that Brady had opened those sexual floodgates, there was just no stopping her.

Last night was the most amazing, incredible, fairy tale night she'd ever had. Too bad morning was now upon her, and it was time to get back to the real world.

When Brady dropped a soft, tender kiss on her mouth, her lids fluttered open. Her gaze met with warm hazel eyes, and something inside her hitched. There was no denying that she felt something deeper for him. How could she not? Brady had been so giving, tender, and attentive last night, taking care of all her needs, inside the bedroom— or, rather, shower—and out. Even though she felt the deeper connection, she refused to go there—to that place where fairy tales turned into bad realities. Right now she just wanted to savor the memories of their great night together and leave it at that.

"Come on, sweetheart. Let me take you home."

She touched his cheek. A warm shiver tingled all the way to her toes. "Brady, last night was great. Really, really great. But there can't be anything more between us. I probably should have made that clear from the beginning."

He shook his head. "I know."

Okay, so he agreed to those terms rather quickly. But wasn't that what she wanted?

Less than a half hour later, still dressed in Brady's flannel pajama pants and a T-shirt, Megan followed Brady out to his truck.

"Are you working again tonight?" she asked. It felt weird, making small talk after the intimacies they'd shared last night.

He nodded and opened the passenger's-side door for her. She offered him a smile. "You really are a gentleman, aren't you?"

He gave her a sexy wink. "Like I said, ladies first."

"Yeah, and second, and third, and fourth, and fifth," she blurted out.

They both chuckled, easing the tension around them. After he backed his truck from the parking lot, his hand snaked out and closed over hers. Never once did he let her go during the entire ride to Cassie and Nick's.

When Brady pulled into the circular driveway, Megan glanced at him. Okay, this was awkward. What did one say after a night of wild sex with a man she'd only recently met, but felt like she'd known for a lifetime? "I guess I'll see you later then."

"At least let me walk you to the door."

She nodded and climbed from the truck. They made their way to the back door. The minute Megan stepped inside, she knew something was wrong. She came up short and Brady crashed into her from behind.

When she bumped forward, his hands snaked around her waist to support her. It reminded her how incredible his touch made her feel.

"Whoa. You okay?"

She assured him she was fine, but that didn't stop him from holding her tight, like he'd always held her in such a manner. He remained pressed to her back, arms around her waist as she glanced at Cassie and Nick sitting at the table. Cassie's eyes were red. Had she been crying?

Megan worked to keep her voice steady, which was hard to do with Brady's arms around her. "What's going on?" Megan asked them.

Cassie blew her nose and said, "It appears the entire staff at All Seasons Catering has come down with food poisoning. It happened a few days ago but they delayed in telling me because they thought they'd be up and running by now."

Megan felt the blood drain to her feet. "Oh no."

Cassie threw her hands up in the air. "The wedding is in four days. Where am I going to get a caterer this late? Finding a dancer was hard enough on such short notice, but getting someone to cook an entire meal for one hundred people will damn well be impossible."

Megan's mind raced with the turn of events. She could do this. If she had the proper facilities and staff, she could pull this off. Her heart beat harder in her chest.

"It's not impossible," she blurted out.

Cassie's eyes lit up in hope. "No?"

"No. I can do this, Cassie."

"You can?"

Still cradling her from behind, Brady said, "And I'll help."

Incredulous, Megan stepped away from the circle of his arms and twisted around to face him. "Really?"

Brady's arms dropped to his sides, and he shrugged easily. "Sure. I'm not without my own culinary skills, you know."

Oh, she knew. He was a man of many talents.

"Where can you prepare the meal?" Cassie asked.

"We can use the firehouse kitchen. It's fully equipped. We might have to rent another oven and refrigerator but that shouldn't be a problem," Brady said.

Nick piped in. "What about kitchen staff?"

Megan spun back around to face Cassie and Nick. "With Brady's help, I won't need any other kitchen staff. We'll just need serving staff at the banquet hall."

"I already have serving staff in place," Cassie added. "I just didn't have any food for them to serve."

"We can prepare the food ahead of time, and deliver it to the hall," Brady said.

Megan turned to Brady. "Brady, do you know where we can rent hot and cold chafing dishes?"

"Not offhand, but we can check the rent-all place down on Main Street."

"Good, we'll do that this afternoon. We also need to go shopping for food supplies. We can prepare the food the morning before the wedding and drop it off at the banquet hall. The serving staff can take over from there."

"Then we'll still have plenty of time to get ready for the wedding," Brady added.

"Right, because no way am I missing the wedding."

As Megan and Brady talked out the details, Cassie and Nick just sat there listening, their heads bobbing back and forth between the two, following the conversation.

It suddenly occurred to Megan that Master Chef Lucien Beaufort would be a guest. "Oh my God," she said.

"What?" all three asked at once.

"I'll be cooking for Lucien Beaufort."

Still sniffing, Cassie stood and plugged the kettle in. "That's right, Megan. You know he's always on the lookout for new talent."

A mixture of excitement and nervousness stole through her. "I'll be cooking for Lucien Beaufort," she repeated.

Brady's soft chuckle wrapped around her. So did his arms. "Don't worry, Megan. We can pull this off. You're going to impress Lucien so much, he's going to beg you to come work for him." He dropped his voice for her ears only. "Then you can move to Chicago, and after a hard night's work, when you're all dirty, you can stop by the firehouse for a long, hot, soapy shower."

Her entire body quaked with the possibility.

His hands cupped her cheeks. "Why don't you go get some sleep and I'll stop by later to pick you up? Then we can work out a menu and go shopping. I need to pick up some supplies for the station anyway." Despite the audience, he dropped a warm kiss on her mouth and then shot Nick a glance. "I'll see you guys later."

With that, he made his way out the door. Megan watched him go. Tamping down a sudden riot of emotions, she turned back to Cassie and Nick. When Cassie opened her mouth, Megan held her hands up in a halting motion. "It was a one-night affair, that's all."

Cassie didn't press Megan any further, and for that, Megan was grateful. Instead, Cassie crossed the room and leaned in to hug Megan.

"Thank you, Megan. I can't tell you how much I appreciate you doing this for me."

Megan hugged her back. "For you, Cassie, anything. But save the thanks until after the food is served. Just knowing Lucien will be dining on my cuisine has my stomach in knots." And knowing Brady would be in that kitchen with her, helping her every step of the way, had the rest of her in knots.

Even though she was tired, her mind continued to race a thousand miles an hour. She made her way to her bedroom for a quick nap before Brady came back for her.

Brady.

The things that man had done to her last night. And the things he promised to do to her again. Her body ignited with memories.

Okay, so the guy was hot, heroic, witty, charming, and skilled in bed. Qualities she never thought she'd find in a man. But that certainly didn't mean she was going to go all soft inside and fall for him.

Exhausted, Brady climbed into his truck and drove out of the driveway. He needed to head back to the fire station to pick up Jag before making his way home to crash for a couple hours. Last night he'd gone without sleep, and this morning he was feeling the effects, not that he would have played the night out any other way.

After cooking and talking with Megan until the wee hours of the morning, she'd slept in his cot while he'd spent his time watching her, caressing her, and enjoying every minute of her company.

His heart pounded harder in his chest every time he relived last night's lovemaking sessions and the frenzied way she wanted him. Her uninhibited responses to his touch had raised his passion to new heights. He loved the way he aroused her until she was delirious with need and the way they were unable to sate their desire for each other. Throughout the night they both continued to take and give until exhaustion finally overtook them.

Brady took a moment to reminisce about the way she gave herself over to him last night, welcoming him into her body. Now he just needed her to welcome him into her heart.

As he flicked on his signal light to pass a slow-moving vehicle, he glanced down and noted she'd left her clothes in his truck. When he picked them up, her unique scent reached his nostrils and aroused all his senses. A sudden rush of emotions made him light-headed and the need to fuck her again filled him with primal possessiveness.

He'd only been away from her for five minutes, but already he missed her heat. Last night when they made love, he knew there was nothing impersonal in the way she touched him. She wanted him as much as he wanted her, but she just wasn't ready to come to terms with it yet.

He ached to take her home with him, to share his bed, to sleep with her in his arms, but he somehow suspected that it was too soon to bring her into his territory and share such intimacies. The last thing he wanted to do was scare her off.

Last night Brady felt it wasn't the time to press for more. He had played it slow and played it her way. Soon enough she'd learn to trust him and understand that he was nothing like the man who had destroyed her belief in "happily-ever-after."

Earlier in the morning, when she'd vowed this was only a one-nighter, he'd seen the emotions churning in her eyes. She was afraid—afraid to get involved again. It was written in her eyes and apparent in her body language. It killed him to think her ex didn't appreciate her the way she deserved to be appreciated.

His thoughts raced to the day ahead. He was looking forward to spending the afternoon with Megan and advancing their relationship to the next logical stage. Last night she'd opened up to him physically, and today, with a little coaxing, he planned on pressing for more.

Brady pulled into the firehouse parking lot. He spotted Dean near the garage doors, basketball in hand. Ever since Dean had fallen for Jenna, he'd been walking around with a goofy grin on his face.

Brady killed the ignition and climbed out of his truck. After stretching his tired limbs, he slipped his keys into his pocket and walked toward Dean.

"What are you doing back here?" Dean asked, going in for a layup.

Brady nodded toward the entrance. Jag stood at the door, tail wagging. "I just drove Megan home and I need to pick up Jag."

Dean stopped dribbling his ball. "You mean Megan actually spent the night? Here? With you?" Dean seemed rather surprised by that bit of information.

Brady nodded and folded his arms across his chest. "Yeah. Why is that so hard to believe?"

Dean ignored his question and asked one of his own. "Have you convinced her yet?"

Brady exhaled slowly and gave a quick shake of his head. He rocked back on his heels and clenched his jaw. "Not yet."

Dean grew serious, the way he always did when he went all Dr. Phil on the guys. He slipped the ball under his arm and rested one hand on Brady's shoulder. "Listen, Brady. Last night, when Jenna and I were talking, she told me that Megan is in it for the sex and the sex only. Megan swore to her that after her messy divorce, she didn't plan on ever falling for anyone again."

Brady paused, absorbing that bit of information. What if Dean was right? What if she really was too scared to try again?

"I know you've been waiting for the right girl to come along, and I know you think it's Megan, but I just don't want to see you hurt, pal."

Brady slapped Dean on the shoulder. "I don't think it's Megan. I know it's Megan. I'm crazy about her, Dean."

"Then I suggest you'd better hurry up and convince her that you're the guy for her."

Brady's mind raced. Dean was right. He had to somehow convince Megan he was the man for her. It was time to play it his way and break down her defenses with his erotic touch before she went back to Trenton and all was lost.

After grabbing Jag, Brady made his way home. As soon as he stepped inside his small bungalow in the suburbs, he crawled in bed.

Five hours later, he awoke to his alarm, feeling alive and refreshed and ready to play. And Lord help Megan, because when he played, he played to win.

FOUR

egan awoke feeling more invigorated than she had in ages. Even though her body felt sore, it was a good sore, one that brought back heated memories from last night.

She glanced at the clock and climbed from her bed. Warm afternoon sunshine spilled in through the window. The sound of children playing on the streets reached her ears and toyed with her emotions. At twenty-nine, she thought she would have had her own family and be living in suburbia by now. She thought she'd be living the fairy tale. A pang of regret tightened her heart.

Pushing those thoughts away, she made her way to the shower. She had one hour before Brady came to pick her up. As her mind returned to Brady, her body trembled. She'd never met a man like him. Completely hot, sexy, and giving. And he knew his way around a woman's body, to boot. Come to think of it, he seemed perfect in every way. But lessons learned long ago taught Megan that when something seemed too good to be true, it usually was.

The house was quiet as she made her way to the shower. The warm spray sluiced over her skin and aroused her body all over again. She took a moment to relive the way Brady fucked her in the shower numerous times the previous night—the way his mouth had touched every speck of her skin, the way his thick fingers brought her to orgasm, and the magnificent way his cock filled her up. She gulped water. Her nipples tightened and her sex quaked with need. After the incredible night they'd had, how the heck would she handle returning to her nonexistent sex life?

After showering, she pulled on a lightweight summer dress. She towel dried her short blond hair, put on a light dusting of makeup, and padded to the kitchen, where she found Brady and Cassie sitting at the kitchen table.

Her insides softened like meringue when his warm hazel eyes met with hers. Her gaze raked over him. Dressed in a pair of jeans and a T-shirt, he looked so goddamn hot.

"Good morning, Megan," he said in a soft tone, a tone she'd only heard him use with her. She suddenly felt feverish.

He had that appealing disheveled look to him again. With his mussed hair, unshaven face, and lazy gaze, he looked all warm and cozy, like he'd just crawled out of bed.

She glanced at the clock and tried not to show how flustered, how aroused, she felt. "Good afternoon, Brady." She turned to Cassie and worked to sound casual and light. "Hey, chicky. Where is everyone?"

Cassie finished her coffee and stood. "Jenna and Sara are out shopping. I'm meeting them for a late lunch, and then we have some last minute wedding errands to run."

"Is there anything I can do to help?"

"You and Brady are doing enough as it is." Cassie hugged Megan and slipped out the kitchen door.

Brady stood up and approached Megan quickly. His scent closed around her while his sexy grin warmed her all over. Her mind raced with indecent thoughts. The urge to haul him upstairs for another quick shower made it impossible to stand.

She cleared her throat, finger-brushed her hair, and sagged against the doorframe. "I didn't realize you were here. Have you been waiting long?"

"No." His fingertips touched her cheek. His soft caress left her insides churning. His hazel eyes darkened as they locked on hers.

She exhaled and gave him a slow perusal. Was there something different about him this morning? She found him even more charming and more charismatic than she had before.

Had he turned up the heat? How was it possible for the chemistry between them to feel even hotter?

He ran his thumb over her lips and leaned toward her without speaking. He brought his mouth close to hers and just hovered there. A melee of emotions and sensations erupted in her. Desire and need moved into her stomach.

She moistened her lips and waited for the kiss, but it never came. Damn him.

Before she melted all over him, she locked her knees and marshaled her lascivious thoughts. "We should take a moment to go over the menu."

His mouth curved enticingly. "Cassie and I already took care of it."

Her eyes lit with excitement. With so much to do, she was

both surprised and delighted that they were one step ahead of the game. "Oh?"

"Yeah," he said, his hand sliding to her arms and, lower, to her hips. He looked like he was about to devour her. "We came up with a menu that we can prepare early in the morning so we will still have plenty of time to get ready for the ceremony."

His spicy, freshly showered scent reached her nostrils and brought on a quiver. Needing a chair, Megan waved her hand toward the table. "Great, let's go over it."

He pitched his voice low. "Better yet, let's do it over breakfast. I know this great place that serves breakfast all day."

Her stomach took that moment to grumble. She forced a chuckle. "Sounds like a plan."

He guided her to his truck with his hand on the small of her back. Once they were driving, she turned to him. Now that her passion had receded, albeit only a modicum, she felt a bit anxious about taking time out for breakfast. They still had so much to do. "We need to look into chafing dishes and renting extra kitchen equipment before we go grocery shopping."

"Already taken care of."

"Really?"

He nodded. "I had to drive by the rent-all place this morning anyway, so I stopped in. Everything will be delivered to the station this afternoon." He met her glance and squeezed her hand. "So relax. With that out of the way, all we need to do is go shopping."

She shook her head in amusement. "Once again you're one step ahead of me."

"And here I'd rather be completely on top of you. Or better yet, underneath you," he added with a wink.

Passion flowed through her at his words. If he kept this up, they'd never complete any of their errands.

Brady gave her a lopsided smile. "We have everything in place, so after our shopping, we'll have plenty of time to prepare the main course." He paused and then added, "And plenty of time for dessert."

Megan's body shook with anticipation. She felt her skin suffuse with color.

Brady veered off at the next exit, and Megan took that moment to gather herself. The last thing she wanted to do was walk into a restaurant looking sexually flustered. She glanced forward and noted Brady had driven into a housing district, not a business district. She crinkled her nose. "There is a restaurant here? Right in the middle of suburbia?"

Brady chuckled and pulled into a long paved driveway. Megan arched an inquisitive brow as she glanced at the small bungalow. "Where are we?"

He waved his hand. "Welcome to Brady's Diner, where the food is good but the company is finer."

Megan threw her head back and laughed. "And where breakfast is served all hours of the day. I should have known."

"Come on." Brady hopped from the car and she quickly followed.

As they approached his door, she heard a dog barking. "Jag?" she asked.

"Yeah, I went back to the station to grab him after I dropped you off."

Since the dog had spent the previous night sleeping, Megan never really had a chance to play with him.

Before Brady pushed open the door, he positioned Megan behind him. At first she didn't understand, until Jag came barreling at them like a bowling ball. If Brady hadn't moved her out of the path, she'd have toppled like a pin.

"Hey, boy," Brady said, bending to calm his hundred-pound chocolate Labrador retriever.

Something inside Megan softened as she watched him nuzzle his rambunctious dog. Warmth stole over her and nearly stopped her heart. Megan dropped to her knees beside him.

"He's so playful, Brady." She scrubbed her hands under his ears. "I just love him." Just then Jag swiped his tongue over her mouth. She scrunched up her nose and Brady laughed out loud.

"I think he loves you, too."

After getting his fill of love, Jag happily followed them into the kitchen, where he snuggled on his blanket and drifted back to sleep. What a life!

Megan glanced around, taking stock of Brady's house. With its sparse furniture, bare walls, and drab colors, it wasn't hard to tell it was a bachelor pad. "Nice place. Very homey."

He chuckled. "Are you mocking me?" he teased.

"Maybe a little," she said, grinning. "I just think it lacks the female touch."

"I work. I play. I don't decorate." He waved his hand toward the kitchen chair.

Megan cataloged her surroundings a second time. It was a great house smack-dab in the middle of suburbia, which made her wonder why a sexy playboy bachelor lived in the burbs.

"I really do like your place." It was the kind of house she had thought she'd be living in by now. She took a moment to imagine how she'd decorate his quaint little home. Suddenly she wondered why he was still single.

She arched a brow at him. Curiosity getting the better of her, she cut right to the chase. "Brady, why doesn't this place have a woman's touch?"

He shrugged and gave her a sexy wink. "I guess I haven't found the right woman to touch it."

For a second she wondered if they were still talking about his house because undoubtedly a skilled lover like Brady would have lots of women *touch it*. Hmm, that thought put a lump in her stomach.

Brady grabbed the eggs from the fridge. "Quiche okay?"

She nodded and stood. "I can't just sit here and watch. I need to put my hands to work. Let me help."

He gestured toward the coffeepot. "Why don't you make the coffee?"

Megan grabbed the carafe and rinsed it. "Where did you learn to cook anyway?"

He gave her a sheepish grin. "My mom." Reaching into the cupboard he found the jar of coffee.

She could hear the love in his voice when he mentioned his mom. What was it that her own mother used to say? Any man who is good to his mom is a man worth having. Megan worked to twist the lid off the coffee jar. Damn thing was too tight. She handed it back to him and he opened it with ease.

"What is it with you and lids anyway?"

She rolled her eyes. "Don't ask." She turned the conversation back to him. "Are you and your mom close?"

"Yeah, it was just the two of us growing up." He paused and said, "It still is just the two of us." He nodded toward his window. "She lives down the street. She's had a few medical problems, so I moved closer in case she needs me."

Which explained why he lived in suburbia.

"When I was growing up, Mom had to work long hours to pay the bills, so I needed to learn to cook if we wanted to eat." He rubbed his stomach and made a face. "And I wanted to eat. A lot. It occurred to me years later just how much I enjoyed it."

Megan met his glance. Something in the way he looked at her and something in his noble expression filled her with the overwhelming urge to learn everything about him. She wanted to ask about his dad but was afraid to pry. "Was it tough, just you and your mom?"

"It wasn't so bad."

"So how come you didn't become a chef instead of a firefighter?"

"When I was four, my father died in a fire. The warehouse where he worked burned to the ground and he got trapped inside. I've wanted to be a firefighter ever since."

Megan reached out and touched Brady's cheek, offering her comfort. "I'm sorry, Brady."

He closed his hand over hers, brought it to his mouth, and kissed it. The warmth in his gaze went right through her. "It's okay. Now I get to save lives and cook for the other guys at the station. Everything worked out the way it was supposed to." He redirected the conversation. "Now tell me, why did you become a chef?"

"I think I just sort of fell into it. My mom and dad ran a small diner, still do as a matter of fact. I worked there for as long as I can remember. I guess my love of cooking just followed along from there."

"And now you want to work for Lucien?"

She opened her eyes wide. "Oh yeah. It would be an amazing opportunity. Someday I want to open my own restaurant, and I know I can learn so much from him."

"Then we need to make sure it happens," he said with conviction. "Together we'll prepare a meal and your fine cuisine will blow his mind."

She looked up from the coffeepot. The tenderness in Brady's expression touched her heart as the softness in his tone played down her spine.

An unexpected wave of emotion caught her off guard. Megan drew a breath and shifted her stance. This guy was just too good to be true. "*Our* fine cuisine will blow his mind," she corrected. Then in a soft voice she added, "Thanks for helping me."

His voice dropped an octave. "My pleasure." He gathered her into his arms. "Cassie and Nick aren't just my friends. They're my family. I'd do anything for them."

Warmth and admiration seeped under her skin. It really was hard to believe this guy was for real. He just never seemed to stop giving. It was also hard to believe how much comfort she found from his touch.

"God, you're so different from—" She stopped herself midsentence, realizing things were getting way more personal than she intended, because this was still just about sex and orgasms, right? Not relationships or marriage.

He dipped his head, the warmth in his eyes bringing them to a deeper level of intimacy. "Different?"

Somehow she knew he wouldn't let that go. The way he looked at her had words spilling like a leaky firefighter hose. "My ex. I'm divorced." She studied him, gauging his reaction. She angled her head and noted his solemn expression. It occurred to her that he knew a lot more about her than she realized. "You already knew."

He shrugged easily. "Nick mentioned it."

"I see."

He ran his hands over her bare arms. "Which explains why you warned me this is a sex-only affair."

She wished he wasn't being so amazing. Then it would be so much easier to keep this about sex. She crinkled her nose. "I just don't want to find myself in that messy situation again."

Brady nodded and dropped a hot passionate kiss on her mouth. "Like I said, Megan, I'm all for that."

She forced a smile. His erotic kiss and touch were penetrating her defenses. As warmth moved into her stomach, she worked to keep her voice level. "Good. As long as you know where I stand."

Except right now, at this moment, she didn't want to stand. She wanted to lie down, in his bed, with him.

His eyes moved over her face. "I know where you stand," he assured her.

Even though her mouth said one thing, the way he looked at her had her aching for something far more intimate. She needed to feel his hands on her, his mouth on her skin, his cock inside her.

Giving in to desire, she said, "Actually, Brady, how about we forget standing." She slid her arm down his. "I want to lie down."

She saw the desire burning in his eyes; then his breath grew shallow, and his voice turned husky. "I always thought standing was overrated," he whispered. His knuckles brushed hers and their fingers linked together.

"Take me to your bedroom, Brady."

Breakfast forgotten, he slipped his arm around her waist and guided her down the short hallway. He pushed open the door and

ushered her inside. His sheets were unkempt and rumpled. His dark
blue comforter lay in a mess at the foot of the bed. Brady shut the
door behind them.

She spun around to face him. Her body collided with his. Strong
hands snaked around her waist and slid down to her ass. "You're always bumping into me, sweetheart." She could hear the heavy desire
in his voice.

She tapped his chest. "You've bumped *into* me a couple of times
too, mister."

He grinned. "I think it's time to take it from a couple to a few."

"I like the way you think." Shivers of warm need traveled all the
way through her.

Brady backed her up until she hit the bed. He dropped to his
knees and slid his hands under her dress, then moved them higher
until he connected with her damp panties. She felt herself lubricate.
Brady groaned when he dipped into her dampness. The sound was
husky with lust to her ears.

Eager and moist for his touch, she widened her legs. Her nipples tightened with arousal. "Looks like I've gone and wet my panties
again, Brady," she murmured breathlessly.

"So you did," he whispered from between her legs. His rich bari-
tone fueled the flames in her stomach, and she knew there was only
one way to smother that fire.

In one swift movement, Brady gripped her panties and tugged
them down to her feet. His hands returned to the apex between her
legs, where magical fingers swirled through her slick heat. She moaned
and arched into his touch. He bent forward, his burning mouth
pressed hungrily against her sex. She writhed and moaned beneath his
invading mouth, needing so much more of him.

As he toyed with her inflamed clit, she reached down and gripped his shoulders so that her hands palmed his muscles. A moment later he stood and positioned his mouth close to hers. His eyes locked on hers, and in that instant, she felt a connection like she'd never felt with another person.

"I want you, sweetheart," he whispered into her mouth. The soft warmth of his voice combined with the potent look in his eyes touched something deep inside her. She drew a ragged breath. An invisible band tightened around her heart.

As his fingers glided over her skin, easing her straps from her shoulders, he kissed her with such passion it left her shaking. He stepped back and watched her lightweight dress slip to the floor. She stood before him naked—all the while craving the feel of his cock inside her.

Without taking his eyes off hers, he touched her shoulder, signaling his intent. Megan understood what he wanted and eased herself onto his bed, her body beckoning his touch. When her head hit his pillow, his rich, familiar scent closed around her. She could spend the rest of her life in that bed, with him, with his enticing scent curling through her bloodstream.

Brady rid himself of his clothes and positioned his body on top of hers. Beginning with her mouth, he kissed a path down her body, his mouth lingering on the hollow of her throat before moving to her breasts, where he greedily pulled one taut nipple into his mouth. The warmth of his mouth seared her skin. Desire reverberated through her blood. He continued his downward path and settled between her thighs.

"Open your legs for me, sweetheart." The pleasure in his voice excited her.

She stretched her legs out wide for him, drew his pillow to her face, and inhaled, pulling his scent into her lungs, savoring the way it warmed her from the inside out.

He spread her sex lips with his tongue and exhaled. The warmth of his mouth caused her cunt to moisten and flutter with need.

"You taste incredible," he whispered to her.

She gripped his head and whimpered. Every square inch of her skin burned. Her breasts felt heavy and achy. Her internal temperature soared and she feared her body would spontaneously combust if he didn't soon release the pressure.

"Brady, please lick me. I need to come."

"Now that would definitely be my pleasure." He tapped her clit with his finger, causing it to swell.

Her body spasmed with pleasure. "Oh my," she murmured in surprise, never having felt anything quite so deliciously intense.

As she concentrated on the tiny points of pleasure, Brady brushed his tongue over her clit. Her body shivered in delight. The rough velvet of his tongue played havoc with her nerve endings. She was burning up from the sensations of his erotic touch.

She whimpered and fisted the bedsheets. Her toes curled in delight. The man sure knew how to work her into a sexual frenzy with the tip of his tongue. A shudder raced through her when he pushed two fingers all the way up inside her. He gave her a minute to get used to the fullness before his warm fingers burrowed deeper.

As she absorbed his heat, her lids drifted shut. Moisture collected on her forehead. Blood flowed hot and heavy in her veins as she floated on some level between reality and fairy tale.

He wiggled his fingertips inside her and brushed her sensitive nub with expertise. Without warning, her senses exploded and her body began trembling. His gentle assault pushed her over the edge.

She threw her head to the side and let herself fall over the precipice. "Oooooh, soooo good," she exclaimed. Her muscles clenched around his fingers as she rode out every delicious pulse and erotic wave. She gripped the sheets tighter when her body splintered into a million pieces.

After lapping her syrup, Brady climbed up her body. She took that opportunity to recapture her breath. He smoothed her hair from her face. "I thought you told me you never came fast," he whispered, teasing her.

She chuckled, enjoying the easy intimacy between them. "Yes, well, it's your fault for turning me into a sexual nymphette," she replied. She moistened her lips and raced her eager hands over the hard contours of his body. A second later she pushed on his shoulders. As he rolled off her, he shot her a perplexed look.

"What is it?"

Her mouth curved into a sultry smile. "What was that you said earlier, something about being underneath me?"

Understanding dawned on Brady; his nostrils flared and his eyes widened in delight.

She flung one leg over his hip and straddled him. Bending forward, she pressed her mouth to his, their tongues joining and tangling in a lover's dance. Her lips moved to his throat, his chest, his stomach. She glanced up at him. "Now it's my turn to kiss you all over."

The corners of his mouth twitched. "Well, if you insist . . ."

She grinned at the playfulness in his tone. "Oh, I insist."

His skin tasted warm and salty and so damn delicious. She eased down lower until she reached his impressive erection. His cock jumped and she gathered it into her hands. With the tip of her finger, she gave him a gentle stroke.

"Damn, that feels good," he bit out.

She flicked her tongue out for a taste. "Mmmm, it tastes good, too."

She heard his throat work as he swallowed.

She cupped his balls and drew his cock into her mouth. With his magnificent size, there was no way she could take in his whole length. But the way he groaned beneath her, he didn't seem to mind. She worked her hands over his cock, while her mouth concentrated on his engorged head.

"Megan—" His words were lost on a moan.

Megan glanced up to see his fingers clutch the sheets and a thin sheen of sweat on his upper lip. She smiled with satisfaction. Warmth raced through her, and she knew she was bringing him so much pleasure.

His hips began rocking, matching the movement of her mouth. He dragged in a huge breath and gripped her head. She worked her tongue over him, smoothly, methodically. His cock pulsed beneath her ministrations.

He began trembling, panting. "Megan, sweetheart, you've got me so hot and hard, I'm going to explode." His voice sounded tortured and rough. His body began shaking, almost violently.

"Explode for me, Brady." Her words clearly indicated her eagerness to taste his creamy sweetness. She increased the tempo. Her hands were sliding up and down with ease while her tongue followed the path. When she felt his first clench, she changed tactics, drawing him in to her mouth again, until his head hit the back of her throat. Her other hand cupped his heavy sack and gently massaged his balls.

His body tightened, his cock throbbed. A sound of pure carnal delight echoed in the room seconds before his seed splashed in the back of her throat.

Megan curled her fingers through his as she drank his tangy cream. After she milked him of his every last drop, she rested her head in his lap, not wanting to break the moment. His hands moved to her hair. He lazily curled a few strands through his fingers, while they both lay there radiating contentment, enjoying the afterglow.

A short while later Brady broke the comfortable silence. "Hey, sweetheart."

"Hey, yourself." She glanced up at him. The second their eyes met, she felt a new intimacy between them. It seeped under her skin and curled around her heart.

"Come here." He pulled her to him and positioned her in the crook of his arms. After Brady dropped a soft kiss on her mouth, his stomach grumbled.

Megan chuckled, put her palms on his chest, and shoved lightly. "Now that we've had dessert, I think we should have some breakfast."

"Well, I guess I did promise you fine dining and even finer company."

"Yeah, but you left out the part about fabulous sex."

He chuckled. "At Brady's Diner, sex is also served twenty-four hours a day." He eased himself from the circle of her arms. "You wait here, sweetheart. It would be my pleasure to serve you breakfast in bed."

Megan's throat tightened. That considerate gesture did the weirdest things to her emotionally.

Looking sexy, warm, and rumpled, Brady climbed from the bed.

He tugged on his jeans and disappeared through the door. Here was one hell of a guy, she thought.

After he left, it suddenly occurred to her just how much she liked him. Did she really think she could keep her emotions under wrap with an amazing guy like him?

A guy who could easily be the poster boy for "too good to be true," she reminded herself, yanking herself back from fairy tale land.

FIVE

Brady's thoughts were preoccupied and he paced restlessly around the firehouse kitchen. The last time he saw Megan was when they'd made love yesterday afternoon and it was making him totally fucking crazy. After they'd gone shopping for supplies, he'd dropped her back at Nick's place. Her hectic schedule left no time for them to get together. And that just wouldn't do, because, with time being of the essence, he needed to talk to her, to touch her, to love her, and to discover if he'd broken through her defenses.

He glanced at the clock and clenched his fingers. He didn't expect to hear from her at all tonight. No doubt Cassie's bachelorette party would run until the wee hours of the morning. His body clenched in frustration. He might be a patient man, but his patience to hold her and kiss her and tell her how he really felt about her was growing thinner by the minute.

"Hey, Brady, want to play a hand?" Dean called from the card table.

"No," Brady bit out with much more anger than was necessary.

Dean climbed from his chair, crossed the room, and put his hand on Brady's shoulder. "How about a game of twenty-one? You look like you need to let off a little steam."

Brady nodded, needing some way to expel his energy. He made his way to his locker to grab his ball. Just as he pulled it open, their special phone rang.

His pulse kicked up a notch. "I got it." With long strides, Brady made his way to the phone. When he glanced at the caller ID and spotted Megan's name, his heart leapt, warmth spread over his skin. The second his fingers closed over the receiver, he felt the tension ease from his body.

"Hello."

"Brady?"

Her sensual voice flowed through his veins and had him aching to lose himself in her again. Need and desire seared his insides. "Yeah, it's me."

"Oh." He detected disappointment in her voice.

He furrowed his brow. "Were you expecting someone else?"

She hesitated for a second and then said, "No, it's not that."

Brady sat on the edge of his bunk and rested his elbows on his knees. His hunger for her was consuming him completely. "What is it then?"

"Nothing. How is your evening going? Any emergencies?"

Brady shifted, aware of her strategy to redirect the conversation. "Things are quiet here. Why aren't you at the Hose?"

"I was, but after the dancer left, Cassie brought all her friends back here. We sure have a houseful." Her voice was low and sultry.

"And I . . . I knew you'd be at the station, so I just wanted to call and say hi."

Everything in him reached out to her. "I'm glad you did. How was the bachelorette party?"

"It was okay, but every time I looked at that stripper, all I could think about was that private dance you promised me." A tinge of amusement laced her voice.

A low chuckle rumbled in his throat. "Yeah, well, I can't stop thinking about that basketball game and how I won you for a whole hour."

"Hey," she said, "we didn't even get to finish the game."

"It doesn't matter. I still won."

"I don't—"

He cut her off. "Megan, I want my hour right now."

He could hear a sound in the background, like she was licking her lips. "Right now?"

"Yeah, right now. Right here."

"What about the party?"

Music and shrieks of laughter came through the phone and reached his ears. "It's only for an hour, and from the sounds of things, no one will even notice you're gone."

"I suppose—"

"I'm on my way."

"No, I can take Cassie's car. She's partying up a storm and isn't going anywhere tonight. I stayed sober in case anyone needed anything."

Brady glanced at the clock. "I'll see you soon." With that, he hung up, his mind sorting through all the wickedly wonderful things they could do for the next hour. As his imagination kicked into high gear, he knew exactly how he wanted the night to play out.

A short while later, with a plan formulating and taking shape in his mind, Brady took a long shower, shaved, then made his way to his locker to grab his basketball. He found Dean and Christian in the kitchen.

"Hey, you two, do you think you can make yourselves scarce for an hour?"

Dean quirked a brow. "What's up?"

"Megan just called and she's on her way over. I want her all to myself."

Christian chuckled and nudged Dean. "An hour?" He shot Brady a look and pulled a face. "That's all you need? One hour? Poor Megan. Maybe we ought to stick around and show him how a real man does it, Dean," he razzed.

Brady grinned at the rookie, noting how well he fit into the brotherhood. "When you do it right the first time, Christian, you only need one hour."

Both Dean and Christian laughed out loud. Brady tossed them the basketball and pointed to the door. "One hour."

As Dean and Christian stepped outside, Megan made her way inside.

Brady's heart nearly failed as he perused her. She looked as sexy as sin dressed in a pair of tight-fitting jeans and a snug T-shirt that showcased her beautiful breasts. Her eyes lit when they met his.

"Where are they going?" she asked, nodding toward Dean and Christian.

His eyes moved over her face. "Outside, so we can be alone." He pulled her in close and felt the quiver that rolled through her. He raced his hands over her curves, unable to get enough of her. "So I can do delicious, scandalous things to your body for one whole hour."

She pushed against him and slid her hands over his bare arms. Her intimate touch nearly dropped him to his knees. "What do you have in mind?" He could hear the lust, the intrigue, in her voice.

He pressed his lips to hers and kissed her. "Well, first, I'm going to turn on some music." Brady reached out and flicked on the radio. Soft tunes from the seventies filled the room.

"Nice," she said, moving to the beat.

He gripped her hips and began rocking them slowly, his body matching her movements. "Tell me, Megan. Did watching that stripper dance tonight turn you on?"

Her eyes brightened. "Are you going to dance for me?" she asked. "A private dance, like you promised."

One hand tugged her T-shirt out of her jeans. "Maybe later. Right now you're all mine for the next hour, and I plan on taking advantage of that."

"I still don't see how—"

"Shhh," he said, hushing her. "I won and I'm calling the shots." He felt her quake with excitement. "And what I want is for *you* to strip for *me*. Nice and slow, so I can savor every minute of it." He positioned her pussy next to his swollen cock and rubbed against her. "Then I want you to dance on the pole for me."

She twisted around and glanced at the slider's pole. When she turned back to face him, he could see the passion building in her eyes. Her voice dropped lower and she said, "Are you serious?"

"Hell, yeah. I'm serious." He slid a hand between her legs and could feel her heat. Leaning in, he filled his lungs with her feminine scent. "I want you to slide that gorgeous, naked body of yours all over that pole." His cock jumped as he thought about it.

Heat flared in her eyes. Her breath grew shallow. "You do?" A lusty moan bubbled up from the depths of her throat. It resonated through his body, creating need and desire.

He dropped his voice an octave. "Uh-huh. I want you so hot, Megan, that I'll be able to smell your desire from across the room."

Her whole body vibrated. "Then what?" Her voice sounded deeper, raspier.

He swiped his tongue over her bottom lip. "Then I'm going to lick every inch of you and drive you mad with desire. I'm going to start with your mouth and work my way all the way down to your sweet pussy." She quivered, desire burning in the depths of her eyes. "And just when you think you're going to explode with need, I'm going to put my cock inside you and fuck you so hard and so thoroughly that in one hour you're not even going to know your own name."

Her gaze shifted to where his hard cock pressed against his jeans. Her eyes smoldered. Her body trembled. "That's one hell of a way to cash in on a bet, Brady." Her hand went to his throbbing dick. He growled and pushed against her palm. Sparks flew between them as the room sizzled with sexual electricity.

Hunger to be inside her rushed through his veins. "One hell of a way, indeed," he said. He turned the radio up and gave her a little nudge, backing her up until she hit the pole.

"Strip."

Heat flaring in her eyes, she quickly obliged. With her movements so goddamn seductive that he thought he'd go mad with need, she peeled off her T-shirt to reveal a peach-colored lace bra. The color looked sexy next to her lightly tanned skin.

"Mmmm, nice," Brady said, licking his lips. "Did you wear that for me?" He could see her nipples grow hard under his inspection.

She nodded. Her mouth curved enticingly. "You like?"

"Yeah, leave it on for now."

Her flesh flushed with color as she wiggled her curvy hips. Deft fingers went to her jeans. With unhurried movements, she unhooked the button and peeled her pants from her long legs to reveal matching lace panties. She kicked her jeans away and hooked one leg around the pole. Her slow seduction pushed him to the edge of sanity.

Megan shimmied against the pole, her palms sliding up and down, mimicking the actions of a hand job, driving Brady wild with the need to fuck her. Saliva pooled in his mouth as he took pleasure in watching her seductive, enticing movements.

With his eyes locked on hers in concentration, he pointed to her panties and said, "Keep going." Impatience to see her pussy wide-open, his for the taking, thrummed through him.

Instead of removing her panties, she began a sensuous dance routine on the pole. Her voluptuous contours curled around the bar, dragging his focus with her. Her body flowed from one movement to the next, beautifully, effortlessly. It was the most erotic thing he'd ever seen.

He swallowed and worked to find his voice. "Why do I get the feeling you've done this before?"

Her smile was slow and sexy. She gave a breathy, intimate laugh. "A few years back my health club offered strength-building exercises just for women. Through a combination of dance and aerobics, we toned our bodies and learned an elegant, slow-moving way to explore our sensuous side."

His muscles bunched. His cock tightened. His heart hammered.

"How fucking lucky for me." Pressure brewed deep in his groin when the scent of her arousal reached his nostrils.

"Take your panties off," he bit out.

She did as he requested and then resumed her sensuous dance. Bracing herself high on the slide pole, she spread her legs wide, giving him a gorgeous view of her drenched pink pussy.

Holy fuck! Lust exploded inside him. His trembling hand dropped to his engorged cock. He rubbed himself as his whole body vibrated with need. The woman took him beyond his wildest fantasies.

When her familiar aroused scent curled through his blood, white-hot desire claimed him. All control abandoned, he moaned in pleasure, tore off his clothes, and closed the distance between them. "You are so fucking hot, Megan." He gripped her hips and pulled her to him.

"Dance with me," she murmured.

Joined hip to hip, they began moving to the music. Brady gripped the bar over her head and rocked against her, slowly, seductively, his cock pressing against her stomach.

Angling his head, he sank into her warm wet mouth as his other hand roamed her body, palming her curves. Her passionate kiss fueled his hunger. Relinquishing her mouth, he moved to her neck, burying his face in the hollow of her throat to savor the warmth of her skin there. Her fingers smoothed his hair from his face, and she began pressing against him, igniting his body to a near boil.

Her whimpers of pleasure urged him on. He pulled her bra down over her full breasts and greedily drew one pebbled nub into his mouth. She shivered under his touch. His mouth moved lower. His fingers dipped into her pussy. He pressed into her heat and found her hotter than a raging inferno.

"Jesus, you're wet, babe."

Dropping to his knees, he probed her opening. When she pushed her cunt against his face, he pinned her hips to the pole with his mouth, his tongue toying with her clit. His growl rumbled in his throat as he lapped harder. "I can never get enough of you, Megan." Emotions thickened his voice.

She writhed and moaned and shook beneath his invading mouth. "I can't seem to get enough of you, either, Brady." He heard the longing in her voice. "I need you inside me. Now," she said.

With that, he climbed to his feet, quickly sheathed himself and drove his cock into her plush softness. She wrapped her legs around him, her thighs hugging his waist as he slammed her against the pole.

Her hands snaked around his neck, her nails raking over his skin before plowing through his hair. She held him close as he ravished her.

"I love the way you fuck me," she whispered into his ear.

"That's good, because I love fucking you," he said, surprised that he could actually speak. As her tight heat surrounded him, he could barely think—he could only feel.

Her breath came quicker, and he could feel pressure building in her body before it came to a peak. "I love the way you come all over my cock." The second the words left his mouth, he felt her hot flow of release. She shuddered, threw her head back, and screamed out his name. Her cunt gripped his cock harder with each rippling pulse of release. Tension grew in his body, his own explosion closing in on him.

"That's it, baby. Let everyone know you're mine." He powered his hips forward, driving impossibly deeper, giving it to her hard, the way she liked, as he doused the flames inside her. A moment later his balls tightened and he shot his come high inside her quivering pussy.

"Mmmm, that feels so good, Brady." Megan tilted her head back and met his eyes. Heart still beating in a mad cadence, he smiled at her. She squeezed her pussy muscles, milking him.

He growled and emptied himself into her. "Damn, you're good at that."

After a long, comfortable moment of silence, he eased out of her and lowered her to her feet. Cradled in his arms, they stood there, holding each other. He exhaled a slow breath and wet his dry lips.

"Megan."

"Who?" she asked, teasing him.

He chuckled. Guess he really did fuck her so hard and so thorough she forgot her own name.

"You're full of surprises, Megan. Tonight I was going to take it slow with you and drive you mad with lust, but you turned the tables on me." When she gave a contented sigh, he said, "I do love the way you dance."

"Hey, you still owe me a private dance."

"Soon, babe, soon. Right now let's grab a soda. I'm parched."

"Okay," she whispered.

After they cleaned up and dressed, he guided her into the kitchen and grabbed two sodas from the fridge. He handed one to Megan and twisted the cap off his. He heard her grunt and whisper something under her breath.

"What are you doing, sweetheart?"

"I'm trying to get this damn cap off my bottle of soda." She handed it to him. "Damn thing's too tight."

"What's with you and screw caps anyway?" He twisted it off and handed it back.

She took a drink and said, "They are not my friends."

"Why?" he asked, amused.

She waved a dismissive hand. "It's silly. You don't want to hear it."

"Sure, I do."

"Fine then." She let out a low breath and got right to the point, the way she normally did. "When I was a teen, I had a dog named Banjo."

His brow knitted together and he couldn't keep the amusement from his voice. "Banjo?"

"Yeah, Banjo." She crinkled that cute little nose of hers. "Listen, do you want to hear this story or not?"

"Okay, okay." He smiled and shook his head. "I'm sorry. Continue."

"Well, Banjo wasn't the cutest dog on the block, and one day, while we were out for a walk, we ran into the neighborhood bully." She drew in air, and under her breath, she murmured, "I hated that guy."

"And?"

"And the jerk kicked Banjo."

Brady winced. "I'm sorry."

"So was he. I slugged him right in the face and broke his nose." She slammed her fist into her palm, mimicking the action.

"You did?"

"Damn right, I did."

He laughed and dropped a kiss on her mouth. "Like I said before Megan, I love how you don't hold back."

"Oh trust me, I didn't hold anything back, but I broke my hand doing it." She held her hand out to examine it.

"Jesus."

Her laugh was silky when she resumed her story. "I know. I was an active teen, and later in the week, I had a track meet that I didn't want to miss. So with the help of my buddy Cody, we cut the cast off. Then I went around pretending my hand was okay. Not my smartest move because it never healed right and now I have no strength in it. My left hand isn't much better."

He took a moment to visualize his feisty Megan slugging some guy. "Remind me never to piss you off."

She shot Jag a glance. He was sound asleep on his blanket. "I don't think you're about to kick any dogs, Brady."

"You're right about that. And if anyone ever hurt Jag, they'd be lucky to walk away with only a broken nose."

"I'd help you, too," she added. Then her voice hitched and she said, "Speaking of help, I want to let you know I've arranged for a van to help us transfer the food from the firehouse to the banquet hall."

He slipped his hands around her waist and cradled her ass in his palms. "Good. I meant to ask you about that. But I had other more important matters on my mind."

"And in your hands," she said, grinning. She glanced at the clock. "I really should be getting back."

He hated that she had to go. He'd like nothing more than to talk with her until the wee hours of the morning. "I guess I'll see you here bright and early Saturday morning, then."

"Yeah, I'll be here at the crack of dawn. We have a lot to do."

"Maybe you should sleep here with me so you're already here bright and early."

She chuckled softly. "Sleep? Brady, I suspect sleep is the last thing we'd be doing. Besides, it will be my last night with Cassie before she gets married and we're all going to have a quiet girls' night in, so I need to be there."

"I understand." He did understand but that didn't mean he had to like it. He walked her to her car and saw her in safely. "I'll see you soon, sweetheart."

"Brady." He heard the turmoil in her voice and knew he was getting to her. In whispered words full of emotion, she said, "I'll see you soon."

SIX

Except "soon" couldn't come fast enough for Megan because everything in her mourned Brady's absence. The soft tenor of his voice had filled her with a bone-deep warmth like she'd never before experienced. She ached to feel his arms around her again, to have him hold her, to feel the connection. Oh God, what had she gone and gotten herself into? Pushing those thoughts to the back of her mind, she made her way back to Cassie's.

A short while later, after the party had died down, Megan gratefully crawled into bed. Although she was exhausted, her mind raced to the sexy, fantasy-worthy firefighter who made her feel things she'd sworn she'd never feel again. When she finally fell asleep, her dreams were filled with images of Brady: talking to him, cooking with him, sharing meals with him, walking Jag with him, and making sweet, passionate, meaningful love with him.

Hours later she awoke to a rush of activities. Friday passed by in a flurry of last-minute wedding preparations, and before she knew it, Saturday, the day of the big wedding, was upon her.

She soon found herself standing in the firehouse with Brady at her side as they put the finishing touches on the chocolate mousse. Completely covered in icing, sugar, and chocolate, Megan brushed her hands together and turned to face Brady.

She said in excitement, "It looks like we did it!"

Brady grabbed her and spun her around. "We sure did."

She glanced at the food. "Everything looks fantastic."

Brady licked his finger and grinned. "It tastes fantastic, too. Cassie and Nick are going to be so pleased, and Lucien is going to love you." Brady glanced at the clock and slapped her on the ass. "Go. You've got two hours to get ready." He gestured toward the door. "You can take off while I get this stuff loaded into the van."

She crinkled her nose. "Don't you want me to help?"

"I can handle it. Besides it's going to take you twice as long to get ready."

She furrowed her brow playfully and planted her hands on her hips. "Meaning?"

He chuckled. "I've been around women long enough to know it takes you all twice as long to get ready."

Megan smiled, but deep inside, her stomach churned. The mental image of Brady *around* other women brought a lump to her throat.

She uncoiled her apron and worked to sound casual. "Okay, I'll see you soon." Before she had a chance to turn, Brady grabbed her and pulled her in close. She melted against him.

He looked deep into her eyes and brushed his chocolate-flavored thumb over her mouth. In his deepest, sexiest voice he said, "That will be up to you, Megan." Then he turned her around and ushered her out the door.

Up to her? Why would it be up to her? She took a moment to analyze his cryptic words and came to the only logical conclusion. After the wedding, if she wanted to see him again, she'd have to call the Hot Line for his services. Because she had, after all, assured him this was a sex-only affair. Obviously Brady was expecting no more, no less.

Ignoring the sinking feeling in her stomach, Megan made her way out to the car and hustled to Cassie's place to get ready. Less than two hours later, dressed in a sexy, body-molding lavender dress, Megan stood at the back of the church with Cassie, Jenna, and Sara. As her gaze panned over her three best friends, her heart swelled. Everyone looked so beautiful and radiant. She wondered if their glow had come from their makeup or if it was because they'd all recently fallen in love.

For a brief moment she wondered if she too had that glow.

She angled her body and stole a glance at the front of the church. Looking utterly handsome in their tuxedos, Brady, Nick, Mitch, and Dean had already taken their positions.

As soon as the music began, a hush fell over the crowd and the three girls all made their way down the aisle. Heart fluttering in her chest, Megan took her position across from Brady. He stood there looking like sex personified with his hair combed and his face freshly shaven. Gone was the mussed, tumbled-out-of-bed look. But that certainly hadn't detracted from his sexy surfer-boy looks at all. When her glance met his, he mouthed the words, *You look beautiful.*

Megan felt her body flush with desire and heat flooded her cheeks. Her body caught fire, and flames lapped at her thighs just from one of his sexy glances her way.

She worked to reminisce about all the wonderful, everyday things they'd done together over the last few days. From shopping and making love in his quaint little home in suburbia, to pole dancing and cooking, she loved the give and take between them and the normalcy in their relationship.

When she realized she was staring at him, she pulled her gaze away.

The wedding march started and drew her complete attention. She turned her focus to Cassie, who looked absolutely exquisite in her bridal gown. Warmth seeped into her soul as she watched Cassie saunter down the aisle and take her place beside Nick. God, she'd never seen a more beautiful couple. They were so perfect for each other. It was like a fairy tale come true.

After the nuptial exchange, they all headed off to the banquet to celebrate with fine champagne and even finer cuisine, according to Megan. Sitting at the head table, centered between Cassie and Jenna, she could barely eat. Just knowing Lucien was dining on her cuisine had her stomach in an uproar and her pulse racing.

Once the meal had been served and the dishes cleared, the stage was set for dancing. Megan soon found herself alone, standing at the edge of the dance floor watching Nick and Cassie make their way to the center. She spotted Jenna and Dean and Sara and Mitch move in beside them.

Her glance flittered around the room in search of Brady. When she felt him step up behind her, a shiver traveled all the way through her.

His voice was low, sounding deeply seductive. He pressed his strong chest against her back and whispered into her ear, "Megan, I'm taking off."

She angled her head to see him, aware of the disappointment settling in the pit of her stomach. "Really? Already?"

"Yeah, there is something I need to do." The warmth and intimacy in his hazel eyes made her breath catch.

"Oh, okay. See you soon," she managed around the lump forming
in her throat.

He winked at her. "Like I said earlier, that will be up to you." A
moment later he disappeared into the crowd.

Feeling like something was constricting her heart, she turned her
attention back to her friends as they danced to a love song. The way
all three couples looked at one another played havoc on her emotions.
Loneliness enveloped her. She wanted fairy tale love like that. She
deserved fairy tale love like that.

The lights dimmed as all three couples swayed on the dance floor
looking too good to be true.

But they *were* true.

Megan could see it with her own eyes. Could feel it deep in her
soul. This was the real deal.

Her thoughts raced to Brady. She'd never met a man like him. So
honest, so caring, so giving, and so damn noble. She knew all of that
beyond a shadow of a doubt. Brady Wade was the real deal, too.

As she watched her friends a moment longer, Cassie's words
rushed through her mind: *Brady is one of the good guys.* Deep in her gut
Megan knew it was true. She also knew it was time to push back old
fears and tell him exactly how she felt.

Honestly, she saw things in Brady that she'd never seen in her
ex. Before her own wedding she'd always considered her ex to be
attentive and giving, but never to this degree. She mulled that over
a bit longer. Maybe there were signs that her ex was going to turn

into a house hippo and she'd missed them or chosen to ignore them.

Deep in her soul she knew Brady was the kind of guy who'd never stop giving. Too bad she'd told him this was about sex only. And too bad he'd readily agreed to her terms.

Oh shit, she needed to find him.

As she weaved her way through the crowd, hoping to find Brady before he left, Master Chef Lucien Beaufort stopped her.

He touched her shoulder. "Megan Wagner?"

She nodded and wrung her fingers together. "Yes," she answered, only half focusing as she scanned the dance floor.

"I understand you are responsible for this lovely meal."

She swallowed. "Yes, with the help of Brady Wade." Oh God, just saying his name filled her with love.

"I'm always on the lookout for new talent, Megan, and Cassie told me with a little persuasion I might be able to convince you to come and work for me."

A little persuasion? She almost laughed out loud at her friend's antics. "Are you serious?"

He returned her smile, his blue eyes glistening. "Of course. Now what would it take for me to persuade you to come work for me?"

"It would be my honor to work for you, Lucien." Megan grabbed his hand and shook it. "All I'll need is two weeks to tie up other matters." And maybe even another two weeks to tie up Brady and keep him captive until she convinced him to give up the Hot Line. Because she, and only she, was the girl for him.

Lucien grinned. "That was easy. Very well then. I'll see you in two weeks, Megan."

She nodded. "Two weeks it is."

Needing to find Brady, she turned and bumped into Sara and Jenna as they made their way to the ladies' room.

"Whoa. Where are you off to in such a hurry?" Jenna asked her.

Megan's gaze brushed over the crowd. "I need to find Brady."

"Why?"

"Lucien just offered me a job at Chez Frontenac."

Both girls squealed in delight. "And you were going to tell Brady before you told your best friends," Sara admonished.

Planting her hands on her curvaceous hips, Jenna arched a knowing brow and took a moment to study Megan. "I wonder if the girl who swore she'd never fall for a firefighter has gone and done just that."

Megan threw her arms up in the air. "How could I not?" she said. "But I told him this was a sexual affair only. And he agreed."

Jenna gripped her shoulders and turned her toward the crowd. "Go find him, Megan, and do what you always do: Tell it like it is and don't hold back."

Megan rushed through the crowd and made her way into the kitchen, but Brady was nowhere to be found. He must have already left. Distraught, she made her way back into the banquet hall. She bumped into Cassie and Nick.

"I just talked to Lucien," Cassie said. "Congratulations."

"Thanks," Megan rushed out, but she had more important matters on her mind. "Have you seen Brady?"

"I was talking to him a few minutes ago," Nick said. "He mentioned that he had to run out for a bit." Nick nodded toward the side doors.

"Is he at the firehouse?" Megan asked.

Nick shook his head. "No, he's not on the schedule today. I think he had to run home."

Megan was barely able to comprehend Nick's words; her gaze flew to the side doors. "Nick, I need your keys."

Without question, Nick fished them from his coat pocket and handed them to her.

Twenty minutes later she pulled into Brady's driveway and took note of his truck. A light flickered inside the bay window and caught her attention. Megan climbed from the car, hiked her dress up, and rushed up the walkway to knock on his door. She pulled her hand back when she noticed the door was ajar.

He'd better not be in there with a date from the Hot Line. Jealousy surged inside her. She didn't care that she had no claim on him after making it perfectly clear that this relationship was just about sex. She clenched her hands into fists. Brady was hers alone, and so help him if he was entertaining some chick who'd called for his services.

She moved deeper into his house while calling out his name.

As she passed the living room, she noticed candles burning and fresh scents coming from the kitchen. The room was warm and alluring and set for seduction.

Brady stepped into the hallway looking . . . adorable. He'd changed out of his tux and into a pair of low-slung jeans and a T-shirt. His expression was unreadable. "Hi, Megan."

She looked past his shoulders, the green-eyed monster getting the better of her. "What are you doing?" she blurted out without censor.

Warmth and desire registered in his eyes. "I'm making dessert."

She planted her hands on her hips. "For who?"

He grinned. "Is that jealousy I detect, Megan?"

Maybe it was but she wasn't about to admit that to him. "Yes." Dammit.

His lazy gaze moved over her in appreciation. He walked toward her. His advance was slow, predatory.

"Why are you here?"

She drew a breath, ready to lay it on the line. No holds barred, she announced, "Because I'm crazy about you, Brady. I know I told you this was all about sex, but I recently realized how perfect we are for each other."

After they exchanged a long, lingering look, she held her ground and challenged him with an unwavering stare. "I'm here to prove I'm the woman for you and to convince you to give up the Hot Line."

He flashed a grin and pitched his voice low. "Done."

She stared at him in fascinated excitement. Her heart skipped a beat. Her knees wobbled slightly. Quickly regaining her composure, she gave a defiant tilt of her chin and toyed with the ribbon in her hair. Trying for casual, she said, "Good, that saves me from having to tie you up and use extreme measures."

He stepped closer and tugged her to him. His hazel eyes darkened and locked on hers. His chuckle was low and sexy. "Extreme measures, huh? Hmmm . . . I never knew you were so kinky."

Heart filled with joy, she twisted her lips and said, "I still have a few tricks you don't know about."

Brady laughed out loud and brushed her cheeks with his thumb. His hand felt warm and smooth on her flesh. "Just so you know, I haven't participated in the Hot Line for a very long time. I leave that to the rookies."

"You answered last night," she said.

"Megan, sweetheart, I answered the phone last night because caller ID told me it was you."

She took a moment to process the words. Tightness settled in her chest. "Yeah?"

Brady chuckled, his eyes soft with desire. He tucked a loose strand of hair behind her ear. "You see, Megan, I've just been biding my time waiting for the right girl to come along."

"Oh," she said, her stomach fluttering with joy. "Continue."

He grinned. "Sweetheart, you're that girl. I've wanted you since the first time I set eyes on you."

She angled her head and saw the play of emotions crossing his face. "Then why didn't you tell me?"

"You weren't ready."

Heart racing, she took a moment to mull that over. He was right. After her divorce she'd closed her heart off, never believing she'd find fairy tale love and "happily ever after" again. She touched his cheek, realizing that he'd left the ball in her court, letting her come to him when she was ready to advance their relationship to the next stage.

"You're right. I probably would have run the other way."

He brought her hand to his mouth and kissed it. Her whole body came alive. She melted into him, reveling in the sensations he aroused in her.

"So this dessert you're making—it's for me," she said. It was a statement, not a question. She drew a shuddering breath, her heart soaring, everything in her reaching out to him.

"That's right. For when you were ready to come to me."

"I am ready, Brady." Truthfully, she'd never been more ready in her life.

Brady palmed her cheek and she soaked in his warmth, his love. Need flickered across his face. "The wait nearly killed me, sweetheart.

But now that you're here, get used to it because I'm never letting you go. I plan on keeping you here with me and catering to your every whim, your every desire, day and night."

"Brady." Her lips parted, welcoming him into her body and her heart.

"Yes, sweetheart," he whispered in a voice full of emotion.

When she caught the inflection in his tone, she glanced into his soulful hazel eyes. Her body quaked as heat rushed through her. Every nerve ending in her body came alive and screamed for attention. Fire rushed through her bloodstream and gained her full attention. She moaned deep in her throat, needing Brady to douse the flames inside her.

His eyes darkened with desire when he recognized the passion rising in her.

"Can we start now? In the bedroom? I need to feel you inside me."

"My pleasure." His hand moved to the small of her back. "Come with me."

When she noticed he was guiding her into the kitchen and not his bedroom—or his shower—she asked, "Where are we going?"

"First, I have a present for you."

"You do?"

"Cassie and Nick called to tell me you were on your way. They also told me about Lucien's offer." His sexy grin broadened as he hugged her. "Congratulations, Megan. I knew you could do this." Then he stepped back and handed her an automatic jar opener. "No great chef should be without the ability to open screw caps."

She threw her head back and laughed out loud. "Brady, this is the nicest present anyone has ever given me."

As her heart filled with love, she eyed the whipped cream on the kitchen table. "About that dessert." She moved past Brady, dipped her finger into it, and let it spill on her dress. "Oops, I'm all messy again."

As Brady's warm chuckle wrapped around her, so did his arms. "Maybe we should get showered."

She smiled. "I think you might need to soap me all over."

He pulled her in tighter and whispered, "My pleasure."

She jabbed his chest. "Oh, and don't think I've forgotten about the private dance you owe me."

He laughed. "I'll dance for you every day if that's what you want."

"Oh, I want."

With that, Brady closed his mouth over hers. As Megan kissed him with all the love inside her, she realized that she'd finally found her "happily ever after" with her very own fairy tale prince—or rather her very own fairy tale firefighter.

EPILOGUE

ith the Caribbean sun beating down on her bikini-clad body, Cassie shaded her eyes and turned in her lounge chair to face her husband. Although they were now three days into their honeymoon, this was the first time they'd left the cabana and ventured onto the beach. Cassie gave a long, satisfied sigh. "It sure is hot out here," she said.

Nick's hand snaked out and grasped hers. He caressed her palm with the pad of his thumb. "You're scalding, babe. Want to take a swim?"

She shrugged easily, in no hurry to do anything. "Maybe in a minute. I'm too lazy to move." As Cassie lay there radiating contentment, she took a moment to reminisce about all the prewedding activities and how wonderful it was to have had her best friends around. She was so pleased to know that in the near future they'd all be taking up permanent residence in Chicago, close to her. "So what do you think, Nick? Should we go into the business?"

Nick scoffed and shook his head. "No, thanks. I've done enough matchmaking to last a lifetime."

Cassie chuckled. "You really were fantastic. Telling Mitch to keep his distance from Sara was brilliant, especially knowing it would only entice him all the more."

"You liked that, did you?"

"Yeah, I especially liked how you acted all surprised and distraught when you caught Sara and Mitch kissing back at the house. You could have won an Oscar for that performance."

"And here I thought all those high school drama classes were a waste of time." He squeezed her hand tighter and said, "I must say, it was also brilliant on your part to tell Dean he couldn't come back for Jenna's fashion show."

She furrowed her brow. "You know, even though he's an intuitive guy completing his psychology thesis, it sure was easy to pull a little reverse psychology on him."

Nick laughed. "Yeah, Dean and Jenna were made for each other, but in Dean's case, love really was blind. He needed someone to open his eyes."

Cassie moistened her dry lips. "Once he saw her in the lingerie, I knew he was in it for the long haul. Fortunately we had Megan conspiring with us. Tying Jenna's bustier too tight was the perfect setup for her to call the Hot Line."

"You know, I'm sorry Kate Saunders came down with food poisoning but it couldn't have worked out better for Dean and Jenna." Nick took a long pull from his water bottle and handed it to Cassie.

She took a sip and said, "Speaking of food poisoning, we really were in a bind there for a moment with the wedding banquet. But talk about sheer luck that Megan and Brady were there to bail us out. And honestly, things really couldn't have worked out better career-wise and relationship-wise for Megan."

Nick shook his head in agreement. "After I told Brady about Megan's ex, like you wanted me to, he was determined to convince her he was nothing like him. So helping Megan with the banquet preparations gave him the opportunity to prove himself to her."

"And Megan the opportunity to see all men aren't assholes wanting to be catered to like her ex," Cassie added.

After a long moment of silence, Cassie said, "Honestly, I think we should go into the business in our spare time."

Nick pulled a face. "Babe, you know I love you like mad and would do anything for you, but please don't ever ask me to play Cupid again." When Nick's eyes locked on hers, he gave her a wicked grin full of sensual promises. "Besides, I have better uses for my spare time."

Cassie wiped the moisture from her brow and let her gaze rake over the amazing man who completed her in every way possible. Her body caught fire and she knew it had nothing to do with the hot Caribbean sun.

"Nick, I'm burning up."

He arched a brow and gestured toward the water. "Ready for that swim?"

She nodded toward the cabana behind her and gave him a sultry smile. "Actually, the cool water won't help with these kinds of flames."

His eyes darkened and his voice deepened. "You're insatiable, babe. Just the way I like you." He stood and pulled her to her feet.

She bumped into him and felt his erection. She bit back a moan. "You make me this way."

His hands raced over her body, burning her to her core. "Good, because every night for the rest of our lives, I plan on extinguishing your every little fire."

Cassie stepped away from his arms and gave an enticing shake to her backside as she made her way toward the cabana. She could hear a low growl catch in Nick's throat.

In her most sultry voice she said, "Nick."

"Yeah." She could hear the hungry desire in his tone.

"Are you coming?" She tossed a glance back over her shoulder in time to see him adjust his bathing suit.

He gave her his signature smart-ass grin. "I believe I just might be."